THE HIGHLANDER'S STOLEN BRIDE

Book Two: The Sutherland Legacy

ELIZA KNIGHT

KNIGHT
MEDIA

About the Book

THE HIGHLANDER'S STOLEN BRIDE

After a harsh betrayal, Magnus "Strath" Sutherland, Laird of Dornoch, accepts a commission from the king to squelch an English lord's siege at the Scottish border. What better way to torment his new English enemy than to defeat his army and steal his beautiful bride? At first, Strath plans to toss the *Sassenach* lass into a dark cell and forget about her, but there is something about the way she defies him that he finds alluring, not to mention how very much he'd like to kiss her.

Eva de Clare, youngest daughter of the Earl of Northwyck, is pledged in matrimony to a cruel lord blackmailing her family. Her salvation comes in the form of a terrifying Highlander who interrupts the ceremony. But salvation turns to horror when she's plucked from where she stands and whisked across the Scottish border. Eva isn't about to be made a prisoner of war, and once she sees the kindness beneath her captor's hard exterior she decides she won't be sent back to England to be wed either. In fact, she just might be the woman to warm the Highland warrior's hardened heart.

Published by:

KNIGHT
MEDIA

More Books by Eliza Knight

The Sutherland Legacy

The Highlander's Gift
The Highlander's Quest — in the Ladies of the Stone anthology
The Highlander's Stolen Bride
The Highlander's Hellion — Fall 2018

Pirates of Britannia: Devils of the Deep

Savage of the Sea
The Sea Devil
A Pirate's Bounty

The Stolen Bride Series

The Highlander's Temptation
The Highlander's Reward

The Highlander's Conquest
The Highlander's Lady
The Highlander's Warrior Bride
The Highlander's Triumph
The Highlander's Sin
Wild Highland Mistletoe (a Stolen Bride winter novella)
The Highlander's Charm (a Stolen Bride novella)
A Kilted Christmas Wish – a contemporary Holiday spin-off

The Conquered Bride Series

Conquered by the Highlander
Seduced by the Laird
Taken by the Highlander (a Conquered bride novella)
Claimed by the Warrior
Stolen by the Laird
Protected by the Laird (a Conquered bride novella)
Guarded by the Warrior

The MacDougall Legacy Series

Laird of Shadows
Laird of Twilight
Laird of Darkness

The Thistles and Roses Series

Promise of a Knight
Eternally Bound
Breath from the Sea

The Highland Bound Series (Erotic time-travel)

Behind the Plaid
Bared to the Laird
Dark Side of the Laird
Highlander's Touch
Highlander Undone
Highlander Unraveled

Wicked Women

Her Desperate Gamble
Seducing the Sheriff
Kiss Me, Cowboy

Under the name E. Knight

Tales From the Tudor Court

My Lady Viper
Prisoner of the Queen

Ancient Historical Fiction

A Day of Fire: a novel of Pompeii
A Year of Ravens: a novel of Boudica's Rebellion

For every woman striving to forge a path... You've got this!

Chapter One

Spring, 1322
Northern England

E va de Clare had been told that every English lady looked forward to her wedding day. But she was pretty certain that was a lie. In her case, her wedding day was fast winning out over her worst nightmare.

Standing in her father's study was her betrothed—a man who'd been blackmailing her family for at least two years that she knew of. Somehow, he'd managed to wheedle his way down to this—her hand in marriage.

Lord Belfinch stared down his nose first at her, and then her father. His thick brown hair was cropped close to his head and his face was as cleanly shaven as a sheep shorn too close to the skin, revealing pockmarks along his jaw line. Thin purple veins were visible at the plump parts of his cheeks, creating a map to his bulbous nose. Sharp, black eyes bore into her as he assessed her with a sneer of his yellowed teeth.

This man who made her physically ill was to be her husband. Her father might as well have sentenced her to death, for she wasn't only ill from looking at him, although he was extremely unpleasant, but rather because there was no blood pumping through his veins. Nay, a man that evil had to be filled with tar.

Eva tried to hold in her shudder. She wished her sister, Jacqueline, was here to talk sense into their father. More than anything, she wished her mother was here to hide her in the woods on one of their wilderness adventures. A gust of wind banged against the closed shutters, as though her mother spoke to her from beyond the grave, or maybe tried to scare away the vile beast about to force her into marriage.

Not a day went by that Eva didn't mourn the loss of her mother, her dearest friend and champion. Lady Northwyck had allegedly passed away from a sweating sickness some years ago—after being abducted by the father of the man who stood in front of her.

From what Eva had gathered, the *illness* had come about swiftly and ravaged her mother's once-strong body. No matter how many times Eva tried to escape to go to her mother's side, even if that meant she would be abducted as well, her father stopped her. She'd not even been able to say goodbye. Mother had never been sick in all the days Eva could remember. Imagining her wasting away and being helpless to do anything had only made Eva more aware of the fragileness of life.

Eva had always wondered if her death was real or not, because just last year she'd received a letter in her mother's hand saying that soon she would work out a plan to rescue Eva. But nothing had come of it. Her father had raged about falsehoods and trickery when he'd seen the letter. After that, any correspondence that came to her was opened and read by her father first.

And now, it was painfully evident how much she missed her mother's level-headedness.

Belfinch's blackmailing had started shortly after her mother's death.

With her sister married off to a lord nearer to London, and her mother gone, the only one she could argue her case with, and the only one who *should* protect her, was her father. But apparently, Lord Belfinch had a tight hold over her father.

She'd discovered her father was being blackmailed by accident. She'd seen Belfinch leaving her father's study two summers prior with a large jingling sack. Shortly thereafter, her father had levied an additional tax on their tenant farmers. Many were already struggling to make ends meet, and the tax nearly broke them. Eva had taken up the cause with her father, and when he'd stubbornly refused to back down, she'd asked about the coin he'd paid Belfinch. The look on her father's face had been all the confirmation she'd needed. When he then admitted he didn't have a choice, and he would not give her the reason as to why Belfinch was blackmailing him, Eva guessed it must have something to do with her mother's disappearance. But instead, her mother's disappearance had only been the beginning.

Despite her pleading, her father had continued to make exorbitant payments to Belfinch without explanation. As a result, their farmers were defeated in mind and spirit, and even in body. And so was Eva. Where was her mother? Was she truly gone?

Eva did all she could to help her people. She even wrote to her mother's family in Scotland, but when she never heard back she assumed either her father was taking the letters or they'd not written her back. Jacqueline, too, tried to write to their family in Scotland, but when her husband found out, he burned the letter.

After pilfering a few coins from the coin purse her father was supposed to give to Belfinch, she'd finally been able to convince a traveling bard to take a letter and send it out. Still, she'd not heard back.

Too keep herself from going mad, Eva continued her wilderness excursions, teaching women to forage for food in the forest, since they often went without even their own portions of farmed produce. Jacqueline sent money that Eva snuck to the farmers so their children wouldn't starve. But this couldn't go on forever. Belfinch had to be stopped.

But how? Was this it? Would spending the rest of her life with the lout be payment enough? And how would her people get on without her?

There would be a revolt. The people of Northwyck would be in danger and once again, she felt completely helpless.

Over the last few weeks while the negotiations were taking place, her father's hair had grayed completely and lost the luster it had once held. New deep grooves had etched themselves in his face, and the whites of his eyes had gone yellow. Was it the stress of Belfinch's noose closing around her father's neck, or the guilt for the wrongs he'd done himself?

"Papa," Eva pleaded. She grasped her fingers tightly in front of her waist, wanting desperately to tell her father all the reasons this was a bad idea, but the man standing two feet away held a power over her that made her tongue dry and brittle.

Even with the short distance between them, she felt like he was on top of her, suffocating her.

Lord Belfinch was twice her age, and where her father had gone completely gray, this man looked to be getting younger. Not a wrinkle marred his eyes despite his years, and not a single gray strand colored his hair. There was a gleam of malice in his dark eyes that frightened her, and the way her father's shoulders stooped as though the devil himself had given him a whipping was extremely disheartening.

It would seem the only one who could stand up for her in this situation wasn't her father, but herself.

Turning from her father, she faced Lord Belfinch head on. Shoulders squared, spine straight, her stance belied the fluttering in her belly.

"Lord Belfinch," she started, fixing him with a steady gaze. "While I confess I do not understand the arrangement you've had with my father—"

"You are correct," he cut her off, sounding strangled, as though it took all of his willpower to keep himself from shouting.

Eva pretended as though he'd not just interrupted. She was certain any reaction would give him the satisfaction he was looking for. "I am not chattel up for bidding. I must beseech you—"

The man held up his hand, interjecting once more. "That is where you are wrong, young lady."

Eva bristled at his tone and his use of young lady, as though a lass of twenty-two summers were a mere babe. Well, in his case, she practically was. Even still, her chest tightened with anger. She stood so erect her spine might snap. It was hard for her to hold her tongue. Her mother had believed that children or women should be seen and not heard, and she'd grown up voicing her opinions, much to the irritation of her father. Lord Northwyck had indulged his wife, but could not tolerate the behavior in his children. But with Belfinch... Her throat was tight, and she lost her senses and the ability to speak.

He rolled his eyes, disgust wrinkling his nose as he spoke low and nasally. "You see, you are chattel. Every daughter is."

Her belly threatened to upend its contents. Daughters were currency to him. Zounds, but if she were to actually marry him—which she swore right then and there she'd never do—Lord save her from having any daughters.

She *had* to get away from him.

"He's right, Daughter. You must do your duty."

Another gust of wind rattled the shutters. Even her father, who stared hard at her as though he were mentally willing her to be quiet, jerked up as though the rattle had been just for him.

"And this you must also understand," Belfinch said. "I am not *bidding* on you, quite the contrary. Your father *wants* me to marry you so badly he is willing to part with a small fortune in order to see it done. I am getting paid to take you off his hands."

Eva opened her mouth to respond, but no sound came out. Her tongue and throat were so dry, she was certain if she were to breathe, her insides would turn to dust. How had he done it? How could he make her feel like less than nothing with a few disdainful looks and hurtful words?

But perhaps it was not so much the power he had over her, but instead the lack of objection from her father. The fact he was allowing all of this to happen. Deep down, Eva questioned whether her father could truly want to get rid of her. In her heart of hearts, she just couldn't believe that he would pay anyone to take her. He was being forced. That had to be it. Her father was forceful, harsh sometimes, but he couldn't be completely without feeling, could he?

What hold did Belfinch have over him? If he'd only trusted her enough to tell her when she'd asked those two summers ago, she might have been able to stop it.

Feeling the telltale sign of tears prickling the backs of her eyes, Eva shifted her gaze to her father, who wouldn't look at her.

"Please, Papa..." She hoped her plea and the hurt she knew must be showing on her face would jar her father out of his decision.

Before her father could answer, Lord Belfinch was once more interrupting.

"The deed is done, my lady. The contract is signed. And I'll teach you a lesson in contradicting me."

"Contracts can be broken." The words escaped her before she had a chance to pull them back.

Before she even knew what was happening, there was a loud crack, and her face exploded with pain.

Eva stumbled backward, her mind a mushy jumble. Tears blinded her as the truth of what had just happened dawned on her. She caught herself, righting to her full height once more, the pound of pain in her face, the taste of blood on her tongue.

Lord Belfinch had *hit* her.

In front of her father. And her father had done nothing to stop it.

Eva brought her hand to her face, feeling the heat of where his fist or palm had connected. She shot her father a look of pure exasperation. He was no longer looking at the floor. His gaze held hers, and he shook his head. Was she imagining it, or was it sorrow making the grooves in his face even deeper?

"That is only a *taste* of what you can expect should you raise your voice to me again." Belfinch stood before her, puffing his chest, his yellowed teeth bared.

She hadn't raised her voice, merely contradicted him. Done only what she'd done all her life, which was to express her point of view.

But with a man like Lord Belfinch, any sign of disagreement would be seen as hostile. From this day forward, if the priest should give his blessing, if she was not able to escape, she would be his property, and all opinions she might have would be forfeit.

Eva would rather die.

And she'd just had a taste, as he said, of his temper—which was probably child's play compared to whatever his true rage must be.

She might actually die.

The way he was looking at her now, she wasn't so certain he wouldn't kill her on their wedding night. Or was he more sadistic than that, excited about the prospect of tormenting her for the rest of her life?

A fiery heat fluttered in Eva's chest. She couldn't decide whether to escape or to fall to the ground in a trembling heap. She'd never felt it before, this fervent, contradicting itch in her heart. Her hands started to tremble, and she had the intense urge to run. But where could she go?

When had her life turned to this? How had she not seen it coming?

Curses were on the tip of her tongue, demands that he never touch her again. But if he were willing to hit her with her father present, and now knew her father would not call the guards or tear up the contract, what worse thing would he do next?

Her mind raced as she waited to see.

She calculated the number of steps it would take to get to the door. How many seconds it would take for her to reach the stairs, the bailey, and what she could say to convince the stable master to give her a horse then demand the gates be opened without argument. How long would it take to ride to her sister's? Two weeks, at least.

But the odds were not in her favor. As soon as she reached the door, Belfinch's vile hands would no doubt grasp her and tug her back. Then he'd likely beat her within an inch of her life and her father would just watch.

Mayhap the priest would see the red on her face, the slowly manifesting bruise, the swelling of the corner of her lip, and call off the wedding. Or maybe he would look the other way. She had to figure out how to get out of this. To escape. To help her father, else he be dragged to an early grave by the greedy bastard. Or by his rebelling peasants.

"Let's go." Belfinch didn't even wait for her. He turned his back and headed to the door, so confident that she would follow.

When her feet made no move to step forward, her father manifested beside her and took her by the elbow, tugging.

"Forgive me," he murmured, true anguish in his voice, but how could she take him seriously?

Anger now boiled inside her. Whatever hold Belfinch had, it couldn't be worse than giving away his own daughter.

How could she truly believe his anguish when he was for all intents and purposes leading her like a lamb to slaughter?

"Save me, Papa."

"It is done." His response lacked emotion, as though he'd already long ago resigned himself to this.

"Nothing is ever only one way. Please," she pleaded, her voice cracking. She dug her heels into the floorboards, refusing to move.

Belfinch returned suddenly, perhaps having taken note of their whispered words, and gripped her other elbow, his fingers pinching into her soft skin.

Instantly, her father let go.

A startled cry sounded from somewhere, like a wounded animal, and at the growl of her betrothed, Eva realized the noise had come from her.

All the saints above, someone rescue me.

But there was no one.

Her sister was far away and unaware of what was happening. For certes, if Jacqueline had a clue, she would have raised an army on her own to come and save Eva.

Belfinch dragged her down the stairs, his steps long as he skipped them two at a time. Without the use of one arm, Eva fumbled with her skirts to keep them out from under her feet, afraid if she told him she was having trouble, he would simply toss her the rest of the way down.

At the bottom of the steps, a priest in long black robes waited, as though he'd been summoned even before she had. But it wasn't their usual priest. Belfinch must have brought this man with him.

Which meant the priest would not help her. He wouldn't care about the ache in her cheek or whether she consented to this marriage at all. The man would do as he was told, likely fearing for his life.

A shudder took hold of her, and she hugged her middle, trying to tug free of Belfinch's grasp.

Eva looked around the great hall desperately, taking in the stunned expressions of the servants and the warriors that stood on the perimeter. Would one of them step forward? Would one of them question this farce? At some point in her short life, she'd helped every one of them. Given them food, coin, sewed their shirts, made a tincture for an illness, or comforted a wife when her husband went to battle. She had given them the very best of her.

But no one stepped forward.

One by one, they looked away.

Eva's heart broke then, shattering into a million tiny pieces. This was really happening; they would simply let her go, and there was no way for her to be saved. Holding back tears, she stared each of them in the eye as she passed, silently lancing them with her pain.

I have to save myself. Somehow.

"Take us to the chapel," Belfinch ordered her father.

With stooped shoulders and a slow, shaky gait, her father led them out of the great hall and into the bailey of their castle, the distant mountains looming up in the afternoon gloominess.

Overhead, the clouds covered the sun, making what should have been a bright day very dull indeed. Gloomy. As though Mother Nature knew exactly what was happening and somehow wished to warn the world of the impending doom.

"Wait," Eva said, stalling. "I am not dressed for a wedding. At least let me put on my best gown."

"What you wear doesn't matter," Belfinch said dismissively, yanking her along. "It is the deed itself."

If they were talking about anything other than a wedding she didn't want to happen, Eva might have thought his words wise.

"But every woman dreams of wearing a beautiful gown on her wedding day."

"Not my wife."

Eva bit her lip against the retort, still feeling the sting in her cheek. *His* wife wouldn't have an opinion or dreams.

"At least allow me to get my mother's necklace."

At this, Belfinch paused, and she could see the gleam of greed in his eyes. "Necklace?"

"Aye, she gave it to me before she... passed away. It is made of pearls and gemstones in the most brilliant colors." She was exaggerating, but it didn't matter, she just wanted to get away from him, lock herself in her room if she could, anything to put this wedding off.

"All right. I shall allow it."

He turned them back around, steering them toward the castle again. Once inside, he started to lead her up the stairs.

"I can go myself."

Belfinch let out a short, sharp laugh. "I don't trust you'll come back."

He wasn't a stupid man, that was for sure.

"I swear I will," she lied, her voice not even shaking, even though she was one giant wave inside.

Belfinch narrowed his eyes. "If you're not back in five minutes, I *will* kill your father."

Eva gaped at him but nodded anyway, because he was allowing her a few moments alone. As she climbed the stairs, she let the tears stream down her face. Because she wasn't going to lock herself in her room. Even if her father had betrayed her, she couldn't let him be killed.

Once in her room, she hurried to her wardrobe and unlocked the special chest her parents had given her as a young child to hide her most sacred treasures. Inside was her mother's necklace, the only thing she'd brought with her from her clan. It was indeed made of pearls, fine iridescent pearls that took on pink and purple hues in the right light. The clasp was gold, and there was a large sapphire in the center of the necklace. Scattered throughout the pearl strand were several other light-blue beryl stones. Not as glamorous as she'd made it out to the greedy monster, but it meant the world to her. Clutching the necklace, Eva raced from the room. She'd need help with the clasp to put it on, and there was not enough time to struggle with it herself. Taking the stairs with her skirts clutched up, and without someone dragging her, was a lot easier this time around.

But once she made it to the bailey, tension filled the air, and the men looked to be on edge. Eva stopped short, the pearls digging into her palm she gripped them so tightly.

"What is it?" she asked, looking toward her father, whose pallor had turned gray.

She'd only been gone a few minutes, what could have possibly happened?

"Get in the chapel," Belfinch ordered.

But he made no attempt to go with her. Instead, the priest took her arm and hurried her inside with several servants. Once inside, they barred the door.

Eva yanked free of the priest's hold. "What is happening?"

The priest stared gloomily toward a stained glass window of the Virgin Mary. "Riders were seen. They fear an attack."

Chapter Two

What is the bastard up to?

What is the bastard up to?

Magnus "Strath" Sutherland, the Laird of Dornoch and Earl of Strathnavor, sat on his horse in the woods just beyond the perimeter of Northwyck Castle. He'd been sent south on a mission by his King, Robert the Bruce. One, to determine if the daughter of Lord Northwyck was dead as had been claimed, and also to stop a certain vile *Sassenach* lord from his continued raids at the border, who may or may not be holding her captive. That man was in the castle before him.

A plan to ambush Belfinch and his men on the road had been thwarted when the whoreson disappeared. Unfamiliar with the land this far past the English border, Strath and his men had found their quarry on the moors riding at a clipped pace toward this castle. This turnabout would work in their favor it seemed, since he could now take care of both of his king's requests at once.

The keep was only about four stories high, if he had to guess, and the wall was about half that. There was a thin moat around the perimeter, and a village to the west. Smoke filtered out of a few chimneys in the village, but it was only late afternoon, so most of the peasants would likely be in the fields working. Smoke came from several chimneys in the castle keep.

From the intelligence Strath had been able to gather, this was the home of another man, the Earl of Northwyck. None of Belfinch's men had waited outside, which meant the Earl of Northwyck was used to the men coming here, or he'd been forced. But Strath was betting on him being an ally. If that were the case, which seemed likely, it would behoove him and his men to remove all the threats.

This was war, after all. And if he let them go, they'd only continue the border raids he'd been sent to stop. Strath wasn't about to disappoint his king. As to why the king cared about a lass, that was a question he'd have to leave unanswered, for his liege had not offered the information.

"What did ye find?" he asked when Tomaidh, his finest scout and best mate, returned.

"Two entrances that I could make out. The main gate has a wide drawbridge over the moat, still lowered from when Belfinch's men went inside, and a postern gate that looks to be accessible only by a narrow drawbridge, but it was not lowered. The walls are guarded by a dozen men, more concentrated on the front gate with only a few at the postern. And I think one spotted me."

"Damn." Strath, as any warlord about to lay siege, much preferred the element of surprise.

"I was careful, but when I mounted my horse by the woods, I think my sword hilt caught the sun just when there was a break in the clouds. I heard a horn blown in the distance, which I'm guessing was the warning. I didn't come straight here. I rode in the opposite direction and circled back through the woods in case they sent anyone out to follow me."

"Ye did good."

"I'm sorry, laird."

"Dinna fash over it, Tomaidh. We'll wait then. If they spotted ye, they'll likely be preparing for an unwanted guest. With enough time, they will think spotting ye was nothing more than someone riding through. They will let their guard down." Probably not all the way, but enough so he could still attack with success.

And he would succeed.

There was only one thing he hated more than a butchering bastard, and that was a *Sassenach* butchering bastard.

Lord Belfinch's nasty deeds were known well across the Scottish borders.

Just this morning, prior to Strath's arrival, they'd passed an annihilated Scottish town. Strath and his men had stopped to see if they could help anyone, but they'd arrived too late. The bastard had killed everyone and burned it to the ground, leaving his signature as a way to scare the Scots—a finch with a bell tied around its neck and its foot tethered to a stake.

A tremor of rage shuddered through Strath. He wanted to stake the bastard himself.

Belfinch was attacking Scottish towns for no other reason than he didn't like that the Scots were fighting back. Prior to Robert the Bruce sending Strath on this mission, one of the towns Belfinch had attacked was ready for him. They'd fought back—and fiercely. In return, he'd burned their supplies and executed their livestock. There'd been no point to it other than to torment the surrounding people. After that, his attacks on border towns had picked up, though he'd not had the ballocks to attack Berwick-upon-Tweed, the border holding the Scots had just so recently regained.

Nay, Belfinch preferred to fight those he deemed inferior, like the true villain he was.

If only Strath had gotten here a day or two earlier, he might have been able to save those who were killed so recently. But he couldn't blame himself. He'd left as soon as he'd received the command. If there was one thing he could make certain of, it was that Belfinch would not lay a hand on anyone else.

"Have the men rest," Strath said. "I'll keep watch for now."

"Aye, laird. I will, too."

Tomaidh issued the orders to their warriors. The men dismounted, ate dried venison and bannocks, and rested in silence for the signal from their laird.

Strath's men were good at being silent. He'd taken them into the wild for weeks of training in the past. They were the Bruce's silent brigade, and they'd earned themselves quite a reputation for being so in the Highlands. Strath took pride in his men and their skills, because he'd taught them himself. His father, the Earl of Sutherland, and for whom he was named—was one of the most well-respected warriors in all of Scotland. Magnus senior had taught his son everything he knew, and then some.

Tomaidh handed him an apple, and Strath nodded his thanks, dismounting to take watch on his feet and give his warhorse, Beast, a rest.

Strath should be the proudest man in all of Scotland, but after what had happened so recently in Sutherland, the weight of disappointment hung like iron shackles around his neck.

Regret had left a bitter sting in his gut that didn't seem to dissipate with time. If only he'd seen what was coming, he might not have essentially led an enemy right to his father's doorstep. The blow had been significant to Strath's ego, and he wasn't certain if he was more upset with the idea that his father would not look at him the same way again, or that he'd been completely betrayed by someone he'd trusted.

The woman he'd been handfasted to had tried to pass off the child in her womb as his. As a result, Strath had broken the handfast, delivering her to her father, Laird Guinn, along with the man she'd sinned with. Humiliated, her father had attacked—but instead of striking Strath's castle at Dornoch, Laird Guinn had attacked Strath's father in Sutherland. Luckily, the Guinn attack had not been successful, and the official marriage between Strath and Jean Guinn had never taken place. But that didn't mean the damage to his ego and reputation had not taken a hit.

Och, but his da had tried to comfort him, had not openly claimed to be disappointed, but Strath couldn't believe his father wasn't. Sutherland lands and the clan had been in danger because Strath had been blind to the truth.

Trust was not something to be considered overrated.

To a warrior, trust was the difference between life and death. Trust between a man and a woman was the difference between knowing if her heart was his or not. Trust between clans was the comfort of your borders being safe, or having danger lurk right next door. Trust between father and son was the entirety of a man's honor.

For Strath, his trust had been obliterated, and he'd not even seen it coming.

Soon after the incident, he'd helped one of his sisters, Bella, and her husband, Niall, in thwarting an enemy attack, but that did not prove to assuage his own guilt at being the cause for his father's holding being attacked.

So when the king had approached him about taking on this task, Strath had jumped at the chance to redeem himself in his father's eyes, and his own.

As the sun settled around them, the lights from the castle and village twinkled in the distance. No one had either arrived or left the castle, which led Strath to believe they were letting their guard down after all, though they had raised their drawbridge with the setting sun.

Perhaps Belfinch and Northwyck were settling down for a mug of ale as they sat before the hearth and chatted about the heinous things they would do together.

Northwyck's name had only been mentioned briefly by the Bruce, and though he'd not associated any of the raids with the man, he hadn't said he wasn't part of them. Northwyck could simply be the supplier for Belfinch's army. Funds, weapons, food, horses. It all had to come from somewhere, because the Belfinch estate was impoverished, or at least that was what intelligence had uncovered.

And still, Strath wondered what that had to do with the lass? Her name was Lady Eva. What role did she play in all of this?

"Will we wait until midnight?" Tomaidh asked.

"Nay. I think now. That way we can ride back to Scotland under the cover of darkness."

"Good."

"Ready yourselves," Strath said quietly to his men. "'Tis time."

Without hesitation, they rose from their positions and mounted their horses. The men knew who they were looking for and what needed to be done.

When they were all ready, Strath gave the signal for them to move. They spread out, leaving spaces between them so as to not appear as an obscure cluster moving over the darkened moors. It was a trick of the eye he'd learned on many a raid. They moved slowly, so anyone who spotted them would wonder if their sight was playing tricks on them.

A gentle breeze blew across the heath, ruffling Strath's shirt, plaid, and Beast's mane. Crickets chirped, and in the distance, an owl hooted. The sky was ominous. Clouds covered the moon and stars, blanketing them in darkness.

Be afraid, Belfinch, be verra afraid.

The closer they got to the castle, the hotter Strath's blood ran. He loved a good battle, especially when he had the chance to defeat an enemy who thrived on tormenting others.

They were nearly halfway there, and still no calls of warning had gone up over the walls. A grin spread over Strath's face. He loved surprising nasty bastards.

Three quarters of the way there...

Closer...

Closer still...

He sent out a hawk call to the man at the outer flanks of his brigade, and they peeled off. They would meet at the postern gate and be ready. A second call sent the second regiment to the sides of the outer wall, where they would toss up their grappling hooks and start climbing.

As for himself, Tomaidh, and the half dozen other warriors he had left, they stopped just out of range of the torchlight.

The men up on the wall suddenly came to life, straightening and peering into the darkness as if having sensed their presence, although their horses had made not a sound.

"Who's out there?"

Strath grinned. "Just a few men on the way to Berwick looking for shelter." Strath used his best English accent, one he'd practiced often with his uncle Blane. Blane had been a spy, and had often been sent to the border and to England for his king. Though of late, he'd retired from the ruse, moving into more of a leadership position.

"Our village has a tavern. Go there," was the answering call.

Strath was prepared for that. "We've no need for food. But we wouldn't mind sleeping in your stables. Please, good sir, we promise no ill will."

From what he could see, the guards on the wall were all moving toward Strath to see who was out there, exactly what he wanted, leaving much of the wall unmanned. Good. They were all idiots.

"Go on to the village. We'll not be opening the gate for you."

Strath inched closer, giving them a shadow, but nothing more. "'Tis far and we are weary. We've got coin. We can pay ye for the night."

"We're not a bloody inn. Get out of here afore I have one of my men shoot you."

Strath grinned into the night, knowing that while he argued with these foolish bastards, his men were likely nearly over the wall on the east and west sides of the fortress.

"Oh, come on then, there's no need to be hostile," Strath said in his perfect English accent. "We heard the Earl of Northwyck is known for his charity."

The men on the wall scoffed, confirming what Strath had already surmised. Northwyck was anything but generous. In fact, he'd been taxing his peasants to the point of starvation.

"Don't know who you've been getting your information from," the man called down, "but I warned you." An arrowed whizzed down, splashing into the moat. Either the man had terrible aim, or he thought a move like that would scare someone. He was wrong. "Next one goes through your heart."

Strath held up his hands in surrender, though he was certain the man couldn't see him fully.

"All right, we get the message."

Just then, a rumbling sounded from the men on the wall, and they all jerked around toward the noise of weapons being engaged. And just as quickly, Strath's men appeared, and the *Sassenach* imbeciles dropped like flies. The *clink-clink* of metal hadn't lasted more than a few moments.

A few seconds later, the drawbridge was lowered, but the gates weren't opened. The shouts from inside warned Strath that more enemy warriors were about to engage. Lucky for his men, they had the advantage of being on the wall, and they made use of the arrows left behind to shoot anyone climbing the stairs to the ramparts.

But Strath didn't want to be a bystander, and his men needed the seven of them out here to be in there helping. The quicker they got this done, the better.

"Get your hooks ready." They would climb the wall and join the fray since the gates had yet to be opened.

But seconds later, just as their hooks attached to the top of the wall, the gates were thrown open by one of his men, and Strath and his six wasted no time in riding over the gate to engage the enemy. On horseback, he was at an advantage against those in the bailey.

If he had to guess, there were about twenty warriors left.

As they fought knights with both Northwyck and Belfinch livery, one thing became evident—the two bastard lords were missing.

"Belfinch!" Strath bellowed. "Northwyck! Show yourselves, ye cowards." Gone was his pretense of an English accent; he wanted the bastards to know exactly who'd come for them. "Attack the Scots, and we'll come back to haunt ye."

Several of the English knights crossed themselves as though Strath was serious. It could be they were a suspicious bunch, but more likely, they were guilty of heinous acts and feared for their souls.

The *Sassenach* knights started to line up in front of the chapel, as though to defend it from Strath and his men.

Strath grinned. "Ye gave them away ye slimy bastards." Didn't they know they'd show him exactly where to look for Belfinch and North-wyck with that simple act?

Strath urged Beast forward, and his men followed. If they thought he was going to politely wait for them to move or beg them to step aside, they were denser than he'd originally thought. Strath did not wait, just barreled over the knights, trampling those that didn't leap out of the way beneath his warhorse. And those that did leap took the brunt of his men's swords.

Strath raised Beast up on his hind legs in a move they'd practiced countless times, allowing his warhorse to pummel the chapel door until it splintered. Whatever bar they'd used to block his entrance shattered under the weight of the horse, and the door burst open to reveal the inside of the dimly lit chapel.

Without dismounting, Strath rode his horse right inside, passed the worn wooden pews, and took in the sight before him.

Standing before the altar with a priest were two men, one older than Strath's father, the other a decade or so older than Strath, and a terrified looking lass. Was it the one he was looking for? The younger of the two men held her elbow tightly enough that the knuckles of his fingers stood out white. She trembled, her eyes wide as she glanced from him back to the men. They could be none other than Belfinch and Northwyck. By the way they were standing, it was obvious this man was attempting to wed the wench. Perhaps she *was* Northwyck's presumed dead daughter after all.

She was beautiful even in her terror. Wide blue eyes, a shocked red mouth, and pale high-arched cheeks—except for a slowly growing bruise marring her cheek and scab on the corner of her lip. Had someone hit her?

Golden hair in disarray looked as if it had been braided but that frightened it had come loose from its confines. Had he come upon a struggle? Instinct knotted his gut. If he were to hazard a guess, she'd fought this wedding. But then again, she was an English wench. Mayhap she was simply clumsy and had tripped as she ran to the altar to be wed to the jackanapes. What did he care?

The older man rushed to stand before his daughter, though the only weapon he grabbed was an altar candlestick. The lass, rather than looking ready to faint as he would have expected, seemed to straighten.

The middle-aged one—Belfinch—withdrew his sword and took two steps forward. "How dare you interrupt my wedding ceremony? How dare you attack this castle!"

Strath raised a brow and suppressed the urge to chuckle. "Och, but that's where ye are wrong, ye limp goat, I dare *a lot*. And I'll dare to fight ye, too. Though it willna be as much of a challenge as I typically prefer."

Belfinch sputtered, and in the background, the lass now looked to be trying to convince the older man of something. She took up a candlestick of her own, as though she were prepared to go into battle, too. From the look of it, she might even use it on the old man.

What the devil?

Belfinch waved his sword, making a circle in the air, his face full of a rage that was actually comical.

This time, Strath did laugh, and he exaggeratingly looked toward the Englishwoman. "What were ye thinking, lass? Ye'd have done much better with a real man than this pathetic slop heap."

The lass's gaze darted back to him, and she looked confused before a spark of spirit soared into her eyes. But there was no time for him to admire her spunk, because Belfinch rushed at him haphazardly with his sword drawn.

With an arc of his claymore, Strath blocked the blow and sent the man stumbling backward. His foot caught on a pew, and he fell over, his arms flailing madly before he lost all balance and hit his head against the stone floor with a resounding thud that echoed in the small enclosure. He didn't move after that.

For the love of all things holy... Strath dismounted and sheathed his claymore, not at all worried about being attacked by the three standing before the altar. By the time he reached Belfinch, a pool of blood flowed beneath his head.

"That was entirely too easy," Strath muttered. He held the back of his hand against the man's mouth. Slow but steady breaths came from him.

Strath glanced back toward the lass, who did not seem in the least horrified as she regarded the felled man. When her gaze met his, there was a bit of terror that flickered. At least she wasn't completely daft.

Turning his attention back to Belfinch, he rolled the man's head to the side to get a look at the wound. On closer inspection, he could see that the blood spilling from the gash on Belfinch's head only looked terrible. He would probably wake with a tremendous headache and need a few stitches, but the wound had not crushed his skull. The bastard would live.

He'd live for Strath to kill him.

He pulled his *sgian dubh* from his boot, pressed it to the man's neck. A simple flick, and the bastard would bleed out. No more attacks on his people. But his king had demanded he bring Belfinch back to him in one piece.

As Strath looked toward the lass, an idea sparked in his mind. If he were to finish off the man while he lay unconscious, that would go against his own sense of pride. He liked men to fight him back.

Their journey back to the Highlands would be long and treacherous if they had to bring along an injured English lord. And Strath wasn't going to sit here and wait for the man to heal. Not with his own small band of warriors. They'd come prepared for a sneak attack, not a massive battle should reinforcements arrive.

Strath touched the *sgian dubh* to Belfinch's neck. Mayhap, he should just slit the bastard's throat and be done with it.

The lass let out a whimper, stilling Strath's hand. Had she guessed what he planned to do? When he looked at her, he saw that the old man had collapsed to the floor and was holding his heart. Poor bastard was having a fit of apoplexy. Served him right for having taken up with bloody Belfinch. The man hadn't even tried to fight Strath. The way he had weakly cowered with the lass had Strath pausing over whether or not he could have been a willing participant in the destruction of the border towns. Then again, the man had an army at his disposal and could have put a stop to it.

Tomaidh stood at the entrance to the chapel, his expression not giving away his thoughts, and no help at all for Strath.

"Ballocks," Strath muttered. There was only one thing he could do that would satisfy both him and the king.

He needed Belfinch to come to him. And there was only one way he could think of to make that happen. He had to leave the bastard alive.

Without hesitation, he took a large coin purse from Belfinch's belt, the rings from his fingers, the heavily jeweled collar from around his neck, and a large iron key he found strapped to a girdle at his waist. Then he marched toward the altar.

The lass leapt to her feet from where she'd knelt beside the old man, brandishing the candlestick as though it were the mightiest of swords. In her other hand, she clutched a pretty necklace, reminding him of the bobbles his sisters coveted.

"Take the necklace."

"Adorable," Strath muttered sarcastically. "But I fear it is not to my taste."

He tossed the other items he'd filched to Tomaidh and closed the distance between himself and the lass. As predicted, she swung the candlestick at his head, but he caught it mid-air, and with a flick of his wrist pried it from her hands. It landed several feet away with a dull ping.

"I won't let you kill him," she said.

"Kill who?"

"My father." The long-lost lass...

"Are ye Lady Eva?"

A flicker of question flashed on her face. "Aye."

"I'm not going to kill him, my lady."

"I won't let you take him either." Her arms were outstretched, blocking the man from Strath's view. "Take me instead."

He'd already decided to do just that. What better way to show his king that he'd found the alleged dead lass than to drop her at his feet?

"If you insist." Without hesitating, he lifted the lass up off her feet and tossed her over his shoulder. She beat at his back, shouting nonsense. When he reached his horse, he tossed her over it, face-first, placing his hand on the small of her back to keep her there.

At the altar, her father sat up, still clutching his heart and staring at them in stunned silence.

Strath caught the old man's gaze. "When Belfinch wakes, tell him to come find me in the Highlands, and should he harm anyone along the way, I'll kill her. And ye'd best accompany him, old man."

"Nay!" the lass shouted, struggling to shimmy off his mount. "Belfinch won't care! He won't come!"

Strath mounted behind her, holding her belly first over his lap. "Oh, he'll care. Trust me, lass. A man doesna like when his enemy takes his possessions, and I've taken his coin and his woman."

She let out a bellow that sounded like a wildcat shot with a bow. Angry, in pain, and hell-bent on destruction.

"Scream like that again, and I'll have ye gagged. Besides, ye asked me to take ye."

With that, he turned Beast and rode out of the chapel. In the bailey, his warriors were tying up the men who'd surrendered. A hell of a lot less than those who'd given their lives. A shame. If they had simply let him in and laid down their weapons, he would have only disposed of Belfinch.

Strath whistled for his men to mount up, and they left the castle without anything other than the lass and a large coin purse.

His men had sustained only minor injuries, thank the saints.

The woman no longer made a peep, though she did struggle every once in a while. Apparently, his threat of a gag had worked, or else she'd remembered that she'd offered herself. Luscious curves rubbed against his thighs, and he could feel the indentation of her narrow waist and the swell of her hips beneath his arm. Against his better judgment, his body reacted with primal desire, blood rushing to his groin.

Strath ground his teeth together. This was going to be a long ride. If he was a man like Belfinch, he would slake his need on her body and then continue on without the distraction. But honor won out. He was not a ravager of innocents. Even if he was abducting one.

Mayhap they should have taken a horse for her. Then again, that would have only made it easier for her to escape him. Ruminating on maybes and should haves would not help the situation, and he wasn't turning around to get her a mount.

After they crossed the heath and entered the forest, they slowed their neck-breaking speed to a trot. "What were ye going to marry that bastard for anyway?" Strath asked.

"None of your business," she ground out, punching his thigh for added insult.

"Well, I've made it my business." And the king needed to know that the lass he'd been looking for was possibly an enemy of Scotland.

She didn't reply, but he didn't find it annoying. Instead, he was amused by her spirit and surprised. Weren't all English lasses supposed to be limp rags? Besides his mother, of course, who was well and above all women in the world.

"Suit yourself." He chuckled and tapped her on the rear, biting the tip of his tongue to keep from making a comment about how it bounced seductively against his palm.

That sparked a whole new round of bucking and hitting. "Let me off, you savage oaf," she demanded, her words stilted as her belly bounced against his lap with each of the horse's trotted steps.

"Not going to happen, Princess." Strath tightened his hold around her hips.

"At least let me sit up." The lass flailed again, and he was in serious danger of tossing her off just to teach her a lesson. Then again, having grown up with three meddling sisters, he was well aware of how to negotiate with a woman. Perhaps such a tactic would work on this one.

"If I let ye sit up, will ye quit flailing?"

She stilled and contemplated that for several moments. "Aye."

"Good." Strath lifted her up around her ribs, the undersides of her breasts brushing his fingertips. He gritted his teeth as he plopped her bottom on his thighs where her belly had been. And promptly groaned. So lush...

Perhaps tossing her off the horse would have been a better idea.

Chapter Three

Eva sat rigid, unsure of what to do with her hands other than hold the front of the saddle for dear life, which was very difficult given the necklace in her hand, but what else could she do? If she let go of the necklace, her only piece of her mother would be gone forever. If she let go of the saddle, the warrior behind her might just let her fall off.

The warrior behind her... Drawing breath was difficult. Every suck of wind left her lungs burning and her heart pounding. She was frightened, angry, surprised, horrified, and also intensely speculative. Her mind whirled in a thousand different directions, none of them connecting or making any sense.

She'd just been abducted.

Ripped from everything she knew.

By a Scottish warrior who was unfairly handsome and bold in his heathen woolen plaid and bare legs. And he'd known her name. Had the bard been successful in getting her letter to her relatives in Scotland? Was that why he'd been sent?

Or was there another more nefarious reason? She wanted to ask, but she didn't dare.

Was he going to kill her? Bury her in a shallow grave where no one would ever find her? Ravage her first and then pass her amongst his friends?

She chanced a glance at the warrior who rode beside them. He was just as tall, just as dark, and just as scary looking. What had she called him? Tomaidh? What a heathen name it was... And what was her captor's name? She didn't even know. Everyone simply called him *laird*, a savage sounding *lord*.

Eva shuddered.

Everything she'd heard about Highlanders from her father—for that was most assuredly what this warrior was—had been true. They were savage, brutish killing machines that took what they wanted, including women, without thought.

Her mother had been a Lowlander, and when she'd run away from her betrothed at the tender age of sixteen, she'd found Lord Northwyck at the border, where he'd fallen in love with her. They'd married almost immediately. Her mother rarely talked about her family in Scotland, only saying she came from the Lindsay Clan, and that they'd disowned her.

A flash of the chapel door splintering to reveal this massive devil of a horse and his master assaulted her memory. It had taken every ounce of her willpower not to faint right then and there. How easy it would have been to simply let her consciousness slip away as the ensuing scenes took place. But then she would have missed the blood pooling beneath Belfinch's head. Most of all, she would have missed the satisfying and uncharitable happiness when he did fall.

Zounds, but when her father fell and clutched his chest, Eva had been certain he was going to die, but he'd kept on breathing, his eyes wider with terror than even her own. With so many of their men decimated by the heathen Scots, she doubted very much that anyone was coming after her.

But this man had promised that Belfinch would. That he wouldn't be pleased with her being taken. He would more likely be angry that his coin had gone missing. She had no idea of how much was in that purse, but it probably amounted to a great fortune.

The warrior who'd picked her up off the floor of the chapel had barely slowed down since he'd kicked his horse into a gallop, and he showed no signs of doing so. When they'd entered the woods, there had been a slight change of pace, but they still whipped past trees, and she'd had to duck to avoid being struck by a low-hanging branch more than once.

The danger of being knocked in the head was a good reason to pay attention, if only she weren't being distracted by the hard thighs beneath her bottom. At her back, his hard chest. Around her middle, hard arms.

Everything about him, including his demeanor, was *hard*. The line of his square jaw. The breadth of his shoulders. Even the color of his tempestuous gray eyes. They matched the storm clouds that threatened to explode at any moment into a thunderous downpour.

And yet, he seemed a better alternative to the man she'd been about to wed. At least so far. He could prove to be entirely worse. She wasn't certain what frightened her more—the idea of marrying a man she knew was evil, or being abducted by a man who could be evil. Either way, she was his hostage. And either way, she had no say.

But that didn't mean Eva didn't have a lot *to* say.

Why, if she could leap off this horse and give the bloody savage a piece of her mind, she'd do it. Well, after she put a good amount of distance between them. Because despite his massive size, he moved incredibly fast. And she had no intention of being tossed over his shoulder, or over his knees again...

Tears threatened between bouts of panic and moments of sheer hysteria. Her dear mare, Mimsy, whom she'd had since she was a girl of twelve, and her cat, Monkey, who curled up in the spot between her shoulder and neck every night when she slept. The people who'd served her house for all her life. The villagers and peasants she'd cared for. Dearest Jacqueline, her older sister and best friend, didn't even know she was gone. Her favorite pillow. Her best shoes. Her cloak.

Eva glanced down at the string of pearls and jewels she clutched for dear life. At least she still had her mother's necklace. She gripped it so tightly it had to be leaving precious indents on her palm. It wouldn't be long until she dropped it. And that wouldn't do. With this being the only tie to her mother's family, perhaps she could use it at some point to prove who she was. Or gain their help. She had to put it somewhere... Without a satchel for safekeeping and not being able to settle the clasp around her neck, she did the next best thing and shoved it down her bodice. The necklace was warm against her skin from having clutched it for so long. She'd expected the warrior to make a comment on what she'd done, but he remained oddly quiet.

Eva's mind raced with what she wanted to say, what she wanted to do, and all the while, she kept her tongue in check, because she was fairly certain he'd make good on his promise of a gag. And *that* she could not abide. Just the idea of having a dirty rag shoved into her mouth made her want to retch. Besides that, she had a fear of not being able to breathe. As it was, she had struggled most of her life with breathing out of her nose, especially in the spring when everything was blooming.

A massive sneeze at that moment shuddered her against him, and then launched her backward with the force of it.

"What in blazes?" he mumbled.

"A sneeze, pardon me."

"G'bless ye."

Eva mumbled her thanks, a little surprised he had the manners to issue her such a sentiment. Perhaps she'd been right in her assessment of a softness beneath all that hardness.

"Dinna do it again."

And just like that, he proved her wrong once more.

"I cannot help it if I sneeze," she countered with a roll of her eyes.

"Hold it in."

She jerked her head to the side, trying to eye him up, which didn't matter considering it was still very dark out. "How am I supposed to do that?"

He pinched her nose. "Like that."

She batted away his hand, exaggeratingly drawing a deep breath. "Preposterous."

"Try it."

"I will not."

There was a rumbling in his chest that vibrated against her back. Was he growling? Or laughing?

The gall of the man. But to his credit, he did not answer her, nor did he threaten to gag her to keep her from sneezing. And when the next one came—as they inevitably came in threes—she did try pinching her nose, but that only caused her ears to pop, and she let out a shriek.

He shushed her, as the men around her grumbled their irritation. "What the devil is wrong with ye?"

"That was the worst idea. I would not subject anyone to such a tactic, sir."

"Holding your nose when ye sneeze?"

"Aye."

"Huh. I will remember that *Sassenach* wenches are delicate, except when it comes to sneezing. For I've never seen one so violent as yours."

She gritted her teeth, not wanting to satisfy him with a response. Instead, she concentrated on the softness of the horse's mane flicking over her hand. Even in the darkness, she could see the sleek black tresses as they trailed over her hand. The coloring reminded her of her captor's hair, too. It was just as wild and was probably flying with the wind as they rode, but she didn't want to look. Not that she would see. And why should she care anyway? She should ignore him and everything about him.

But then again, that would be very stupid.

She should get to know her captor, shouldn't she?

She shuddered.

Dear God, she didn't *want* to know him. She *wanted* to find out the truth about her mother. She wanted to go home.

Nay, she didn't want to go home. Because going home meant marrying Lord Belfinch. Going home meant having to face the weakened man her father had become, and wondering why she'd become so worthless to him that he would rather toss her out than protect her.

She could go to Jacqueline, not that she knew the way. She'd likely only get lost. And there was also the chance that her sister's husband would send her back.

Somehow, she had to contact her king. Then again, King Edward II was not known for his kindness. In fact, many said he was crueler than his father Longshanks had been. Knowing she was half Scots would likely not help her case. Eva had never met the king. He was busy with the civil war and rising tensions with France, which was largely why she thought Belfinch had been so easily able to abuse her father.

She had to find someone who would fight for her. Or at the very least help her father get rid of Belfinch's greedy hands. And of course, save her from this heathen.

Though the savage had knocked the man out with one blow, she was certain that Belfinch would come out of it thriving. He was a wicked fiend, and one little knock on the head wasn't going to stop him from the plans he had. Though she still wasn't entirely certain what they were, and at this rate, she might never know.

The smell of smoke hung on the air, startling her from her thoughts. Eva breathed in deeply, taking note of the strong scent.

"There is a fire," she said, suddenly fearful for those who might be involved.

"There *was* a fire." As he spoke, the laird stiffened, his hold on her waist tightening.

"Was? You know of it." Eva wriggled in his grasp, hoping he'd take the subtle hint to ease his grip.

"Aye." There was a bite to his tone that hadn't been there in any of their previous conversations.

He didn't say more. But the fact he'd known about it was telling enough. The barbarian behind her had to have been the cause of a massive fire. By the scent of it, an entire village had burned. It would seem attacking her castle hadn't been all he'd done on this voyage. Did he have to destroy everything in his path? Eva imagined she could hear people still crying out in anguish with every blow of the wind. How could he be so brutal?

Why was she even asking?

He'd had no reservations about hacking the guards to death or taking her. If there was one thing she should remember, it was that this man was very dangerous.

And any kindness he'd shown her since was simply a show to force her into letting her guard down.

Suddenly, he veered the horse off the road, his men scrabbling to follow. With every stride of the horse, the scent of smoke grew. They broke through the trees to find the burned village. Only the stone foundations remained of what had to be at least twenty or thirty huts. Black shadowy angles of wood jabbed at the ground and sky.

Tears trekked down her cheeks at the destruction. Thankfully, she did not see any bodies, though she knew they had to have been there. Death hung in the air. What if this were the Lindsay lands? Her mother's people? She wouldn't know. And she couldn't ask. That bit of information she had to hold close for now.

"Why did you bring me here?" she asked quietly through her tears.

"So ye could see the devastation men left unchecked can cause."

Was that a confession? A way to bring her terror, to let her know he would burn her if she didn't comply? The warrior was thoroughly confusing. He acted in violence but had not attempted to harm her. Had not tried to kill her father or Belfinch.

What was she supposed to make of that? Of him? Of his words?

Eva didn't give him the satisfaction of a response. Tomaidh glanced at her, his expression unreadable in the darkness. Why did she get the feeling she was being blamed for this?

Moments later, without a word, the laird turned his horse back toward the wood and the road beyond.

As the minutes turned to hours, Eva's spine started to hurt from holding it so rigidly away from her captor. She didn't want to touch him any more than she had to. The murderer, this destroyer of lives. But her eyelids dipped closed, her back slumping before she bolted upright. More than once, she knocked her head against his solid chin. After half a dozen times of knocking against him, he grunted.

"Is that how ye intend to escape, Princess? Knocking me into oblivion with that hard head of yours?" There was a note of humor in his tone that belied everything she knew about him, so she forced herself to ignore the teasing note and focus on that scent of smoke, the suffering of the people, both of which still lingered in her memory.

"When I make my escape, you will not see it coming." It was a risk for her to say something like that, but she didn't care. She needed him to know that despite his threats and the danger, she did intend to stand up for herself.

Even if it scared the wits out of her.

But rather than issuing a rebuke, gagging her, or smacking her as

Belfinch had done, the brute laughed so uproariously loud that several of his mates shifted in their saddles to watch. The vibrations from his chest went straight to her toes. Confusion warred inside her, and she forced herself not to think about him, about his reactions, or anything. For there were no answers that made sense.

Most confusing of all was her reaction to him. The fact she didn't feel as terrified by him as she certainly should be. Body aching, exhaustion causing every limb to shake, Eva forced herself to relax a little bit, to sleep. If he'd not killed her yet, he wouldn't decide to do so simply because she fell asleep.

A short time later, she woke and started to squirm with an urgency in her bladder that refused to be ignored. The sun was starting to rise, giving everything along the side of the road a faintly orange glow. Dew glistened on the grasses, bushes, and tree leaves, reminding her of her thirst as well. When was the last time she'd had anything to eat or drink?

"Stop moving," he growled behind her.

"I cannot." She wriggled again, trying to find a position that didn't pinch her bladder to the point of pain. But with every jostle of the horse's stride, she was renewed with vigor at her body's insistence on relief. Her hands cramped as she clutched the saddle to situate herself better. Probably from having gripped it so tightly throughout the night.

"Aye, ye can. Just stop."

She squirmed, feeling her insides warning she needed a chamber pot, or garderobe, or bush, else the warrior was getting the brunt of it.

"I need to... I have to..."

"Och, for the love of," he grumbled and then blew out a whistle to his men.

They veered off the road into the woods, and when they came to a stop, Eva realized this would be her first chance to make an escape. With her gaze darting around, she took in the various trees, bushes, the sound of trickling water, how many men there were, and the sheer daunting amount of weapons.

The laird, whose name she'd yet to learn, set her on the ground, and she almost buckled under her own weight. At some point during their long ride, her body seemed to have forgotten how to function. Her feet were tingly and numb, her legs wobbly. She stretched and shook out her limbs, forcing blood to flow back into them.

The men dismounted, walking past her without looking in her direction, thank goodness. Because she'd not been able to get a good look at them last night, and now that she could see them all in the daylight, she fairly gaped with horror. They were all as tall as trees and built like mountains. As fierce and forbidding as their leader.

Every one of them looked just as brutal as their laird, too. Hard lines, jagged edges. They made a terrifying bunch.

Eva forced herself to look down toward the ground as they passed by so as not to show them exactly how she felt, for she was certain it was written all over her face. When she could feel every wiggle of her toes, she started heading in the opposite direction of where the men had taken up refuge to meet their own needs.

"Where are ye going?" The savage wrapped his strong grip around her arm, stilling her forward momentum.

"I need privacy." She looked up at him like he had lost his head and was struck silent.

In the light of the rising sun, his features were dangerous but also incredibly...beautiful. If he'd not just abducted her out of a house of worship—which he'd insolently ridden his horse into—she might have thought he was a woodland fairy or a god sent to tempt her. But she was all too aware of how very human he was—and that if he were from another realm, it would be filled with hellfire.

He gave a subtle shake of his head, indicating where the men had gone. "Over here."

Eva yanked against his hold, surprised when he let go. "That is where your men are. I'm a lady, and I will not be subjected to such barbarism."

A wickedly arched brow rose on his forehead. "Ye may be a lady, but ye're also my captive."

"And what does that distinction matter?" Her hands flew to her hips before she could stop them, so she forced them to drop at her sides. "If you intend for me to be ravaged by your men, by all means, let us get it over with."

"What?" He actually looked surprised.

Was he really going to make her spell it out for him? "They are... doing what they needed to do, the same as I need to do. And should I be exposed to their...parts, or they exposed to mine..." Oh dear heaven, her face was blazing hot, and she kept tripping over her words, not able to put a single thought through to him.

He looked behind him at the men and then raised his eyebrows with dawning understanding as he turned his gaze back to hers.

"Ah, I see. Well, go ahead then." He waved her in the opposite direction now. "But I'm coming with ye."

"What? Nay!" She almost stomped her foot.

"Och, Princess, ye mentioned afore ye planned to escape. Ye dinna think I'll actually let that happen, do ye?"

Eva gritted her teeth. Of course he would want to make certain she didn't escape, she knew that much. Foolish of her to have thought it would be so easy. Even still, she dug in her heels. If she didn't at least try, she'd regret it.

"Just stand here. I will be right around those bushes."

Straight-faced, he shook his head.

Eva crossed her arms over her chest. "You plan to watch me then, ye wicked rogue?"

A slight, mischievous grin curled his lips, once more unsettling her from the hard vision of him she wanted to keep in place, but the grin vanished just as quickly as it had come.

"Go on then, lass, but know I'm watching, and if ye should run, I'll be right behind ye."

The idea was in itself unnerving, as she was certain he could run faster than her by the sheer fact that his legs were so much longer. For a moment, she envisioned running through the woods, only to have him tackle her from behind, his hard body pinning hers to the ground. But rather than a fearful shudder racing through her, it was one of desire.

In disgust, she whirled around and marched toward the bushes she'd indicated to before he could change his mind and come after her. What was wrong with her? This man was a killer. Not a beau. Apparently, her baser side couldn't tell the difference.

With a harrumph, she rounded the bushes.

Once there, she lifted her skirts and took care of business efficiently. In her ducked position, she realized he couldn't possibly see the top of her head. And the gown she wore was a dulled enough shade of blue that it wouldn't be a beacon of color through the bushes. Which meant this moment might be her chance to escape. But as she tried walking forward two steps, she understood how very awkward it was. If she continued, her legs would give out on her in protest.

Lowering herself to all fours, Eva crawled forward one step, then two. This was a lot easier. Biting the inside of her cheek, she forced herself not to breathe so she could hear if her captor was coming after her. So far, nothing. She made it perhaps fifteen feet forward when her skirt snagged on an uprooted tree root. She tugged it lightly, but it wouldn't budge, and so she tugged harder and the sound of the fabric ripping rent the night air.

"What was that?" the warrior called over the bushes.

Eva sucked in air, cursing herself for not paying more attention. "I tore my skirt."

"Careful. Come on now. Ye've wasted enough time back there."

This wasn't how it was supposed to go. She was supposed to crawl away, then get up and run. All the way back to England. All the way to Jacqueline. How she'd get there was not entirely certain, but she would, by God.

His boots crunched on the opposite side of the bush. He was coming closer. If she was going to make good with her escape plan, there was no time to think. She had to just go.

With that thought in mind, she went back to crawling but stopped short when something furry ran over her hand and took a good nibble on her pointer finger.

Eva let out a shout, jerked her hand up, and shot back on her heels, scrambling toward the bush. A squirrel scurried around and then headed toward her, arms outstretched as though possessed by a demon, making her scream all the more.

Next thing she knew, the warrior had her up in his arms, and the animal had completely disappeared.

"What the devil?"

"Something...bit me."

"What?"

Eva held up her finger with the tiny drop of blood on the tip. "An animal bit me."

"How in blazes did it get to your finger?"

"I was crawling," she admitted before realizing it.

"Crawling?"

"I...dropped something."

He narrowed his eyes at her. Eva's heart thumped against her ribs hard enough to crack them, and she felt dizzy from the rush of nerves and exhaustion.

"That'll teach ye to try and escape." He swept her up into his arms, carrying her like a lover—or a child.

"I wasn't trying to escape," she said petulantly.

He grunted. "Whatever ye say, Princess."

Chapter Four

Though she was light as a feather in his arms, the woman weighed heavily on his mind.

Her soft curves pressed to his were in contrast to her biting tongue. He could hold on to her for days. If they weren't in flight back to the Highlands, he might have laid her down in the meadow, teased her skin with his fingertips, finding a way to calm the intensity in her that seemed ready to fight at every second.

What had she been through before he'd arrived?

And why the bloody hell did he care? He shouldn't. It wasn't his place. The lass was his prisoner and needed to remain just that. When they arrived in Dornoch, he would toss her in a cell and walk away, only to see her again when the king arrived.

Even as he thought it, he gritted his teeth against the idea. It wasn't her fault she'd been in the wrong place at the wrong time. Or was it? She had been about to marry the bastard. Whatever the king had wanted to know about her, he had to know that she'd been in league with their enemies. Then again, what choice did a woman have in who she married?

Enough to say *aye* or *nay*.

His mind was immediately brought back to the woman he'd been supposed to marry months before, and an indignant sense of hurt gripped him again. Women, unless blood related to him, couldn't be trusted.

And Lady Eva was a woman.

A woman who was clinging to his shirt and likely staining the fabric with the drop of blood from her finger. But he didn't care at all about the shirt, and that made him want to put her down, to not feel the warmth of her body curled into his.

Not for the first time since he'd impulsively grabbed her up in the chapel, Strath regretted his choice. She was quickly becoming more trouble than she was worth. And what in the world *had* happened in the woods? Attacked by a small animal?

He doubted it. More likely, she'd been pricked on something as she tried to crawl away. He'd been watching the entire time, seen her go from a crouched position to all fours. And he knew no one, not even a strange woman, pissed like that. Besides, who got bloody attacked by a small rodent in the middle of the forest?

He'd never heard of such a thing. Larger animals, aye. But rodents? They weren't predatory animals.

As they reached his horse, she started to shove against him, seeming to have finally woken up and realized she was clinging to him. "Put me down, *heathen*." Her tiny hands pushed against his chest. He could tell by the veins straining in her neck she was putting a lot of effort into it, and it made him smile. Adorable.

Rolling his eyes, he said, "I have a name, wench."

"I don't care! Let me go, *heathen*."

Strath did as she bid and let go, mayhap a little too gleefully.

The lass screeched as she promptly fell into a soft patch of grass he wished were a tub of mud.

With his arms crossed over his chest, he stared down at her with an arrogant raise of his brow. "Ye can call me Laird Dornoch or Laird."

Teeth bared, she growled up at him, "That is not a name, but a title." She glared up at him, yanking on the grass in a show of temper.

He shrugged, finding it a challenge not to laugh at her exasperation and ire. "Doesna matter, that is what ye'll call me. Not heathen, or beast, or whatever other nasty name ye come up with.

"I won't. I swear I won't."

Again, he shrugged. "Suit yourself, my lady." He added that last part to show that even he had better manners than she did.

Surprising, really, because he'd always been under the impression that *Sassenach* lassies were uppity wenches concerned overly with propriety and rules. This lass was giving his impression quite a run for his coin. She was bossy, and mouthy, and had quite a temper.

"Up now," he demanded. "We ride."

The look she tossed him would have set a lesser man on fire, but he refused to be unnerved. The lass could show her temper all she liked. He'd grown up with three sisters, and whatever she tossed at him, he'd likely had before threefold.

When she didn't make a move to budge, he took a step toward her. "I've no qualms about lifting ye back onto the horse, lass, but I think ye'd much rather be in charge of your own faculties."

"I would," she grumbled as she shoved herself to standing, and he realized perhaps for the first time, just how tiny she was. She was perhaps only slightly taller than his youngest sister, but shorter than the elder two by far. Standing before him, he measured her to come up to about the middle of his chest. A wee thing comparatively.

But despite her wee stature, the lass was full of curves. Breasts pushed the limit of her worn and now torn gown. He was certain his hands could span her waist, and her hips flared in a way suggestive of how he could hold them when he—

Ballocks! Nay! This was exactly the opposite string of thoughts he should be having. *Prisoner. English. Involved with evil bastards.*

"Can ye climb up?" he asked when she stood where she was, her gaze on Beast and her expression contemplative.

"You think I've never mounted a horse before?" She rolled her eyes toward him and marched toward his warhorse with a huff.

Hands on the pommel, she lifted her foot, not getting anywhere near the stirrup. She swiped her skirts out of the way, revealing a delicate, curvy calf partially hidden by woolen hose.

Mo chreach... Was she trying to mount the horse or drive Strath to distraction?

Again, she lifted her foot and wiggled it up and around, trying to get it in the stirrup that was swaying with his horse's good effort to thwart her. Strath stood stock still, admiring the sight of her flesh and thinking how he'd like to run his hand up the length of that curvy leg.

But then she let out an annoyed sound, drawing him away from his wicked thoughts. The lass let go of one hand on the pommel to steady the stirrup for her foot. Firmly in place, she then hoisted herself up onto the horse, giving him a healthy flash of her tempting thigh as she did so, before settling in the saddle and straightening her skirts.

Strath could have dropped to his knees and begged her to lift that skirt back up just so he could memorize every inch. He raked his gaze over her, stilling when he caught sight of her haughty stare.

"Where is *your* mount?" she asked with a smirk.

"Funny." He gave a half smile, stroked his hand over his horse's mane, and then gripped the saddle and swung up behind her.

He groaned as his already awakening groin slid against her plump bottom. This was going to be another long ride. A torturous one where all he could think of was roaming his hands all over her lush body, kissing her neck, and enticing her into a private clearing where he could show her all the ways in which a man could pleasure a woman.

Strath shifted in his seat, attempting to ease the strain. But it didn't work. So he suggested the one way he thought might entice him *less*.

"Would ye rather sit behind me, lass?"

"Whatever for?"

He should have guessed she would argue. "Might be more comfortable for us both. We've got a few hours left before we stop for the night."

She thought about it for a few torturous moments. "All right."

"Good."

"How should I get back there? Climb over you?"

Strath bit down hard on his tongue as he imagined her climbing over him, and him gripping her hips and bringing her down exactly where he wanted her with her legs wrapped around him.

"Nay. I will help ye down and lift ye back up." He nearly breathed a sigh of relief when she agreed. The task was easy.

But once she was behind him with her thighs pressed to his... His arse right between her legs. Her arms wrapped around his middle, breasts crushed to his back... Strath did groan then. Perhaps it would have been safer to have her still in front of him where at least she sat rigid enough he could almost pretend her sweet bottom wasn't teasing his cock.

"Are you all right?" she asked.

Strath cleared his throat, forcing himself to recall exactly why she was with him, and that it had nothing to do with sweaty, sated bodies. "Aye," he said a little too sharply.

He signaled for his men to move out, and they continued on their journey. Within a couple hours, the sun was starting to rise on the edge of the landscape, and the lass's arms were starting to become less tight around his middle. She was growing just as exhausted as the rest of them. They all needed to rest, and they needed to rest the horses for a good stint before they continued on their hard journey north through the mountains.

If he were not in a hurry, they would take a much less grueling pace. At this rate, his horse would need a week of rest to recover.

They'd reached the Scottish border some hours before but still were not within the range of any of the holdings he was familiar with. They'd have to make camp in the woods. Not something he and his men were unused to. The only difference between the woods and a roof over their heads was added protection. At least they were back on Scots land, where the threat was a little less.

With that in mind, he steered his men off the road and into the lush foliage until he found a spot near a small burn for the horses to drink their fill and for them to replenish their waterskins. The grass was plush enough for sleeping, and the surrounding trees would provide enough coverage for anyone just passing by to perhaps not notice them.

"We'll take shifts," he informed his men, who readily agreed.

Strath dismounted and turned to assist the lady when he saw her falling backward, eyes closed. How long had she been asleep? Reflexes sharp, he caught her as she fell off the horse and startled herself awake. Bleary, reddened eyes stared up at him from where he cradled her against his chest.

"Did I fall?" She rubbed her eyes.

"Aye. But I caught ye. We've stopped to camp," he told her, and she nodded. Strath set her on her feet, holding her elbow as she steadied her wobbly legs. "Have ye a need to crawl through the woods?"

She narrowed her eyes and let out a soft laugh when she grasped that he was teasing her about her earlier exploit.

"Aye, I do."

"Come down by the water. Ye can get a drink as well."

He took her hand in his, realizing after the fact what he'd just done, and then let go as he led her to the water's edge. It wouldn't do to hold her hand. That would only lead to him doing the other things he'd been fantasizing about...

At the water's edge, she knelt down to splash water on her face. Rivulets ran down her long slender neck, and droplets caught in her light hair. She took a long sip, and all Strath could do was stare, wishing he were the water sliding over her tongue and dripping in long, teasing lines down her neck.

Clearing his throat once more, he said, "There's a crop of bushes just there, go ahead and make use of them."

"Are you catching something?" she asked. "You've been doing a lot of throat clearing."

Strath frowned and didn't answer. The lady shrugged, and without a word, she went toward the bushes he'd indicated. He turned away from her to take care of his own business. When he finished, he watched her head duck down and then rise back up shortly thereafter. For a split second, he was certain she was going to try to crawl away again, but she reemerged, holding a cluster of wildflowers.

"Aren't they pretty?" To be able to appreciate something as simple as a flower in the midst of what had to be a terrifying situation for her spoke of a kind heart.

"Beautiful," he answered, but he wasn't talking about the flowers. He meant *her*, not just her face or her body, but the essence of her. He hadn't known her that long, and he realized she didn't even know his name, but there was an aura of goodness about her that made him question everything he'd thought up until this point.

"How old are ye?" he asked as he led her back toward the makeshift camp.

She glanced up at him, her blue eyes having taken on some of the purple of the flowers. "Twenty-two summers."

"And not yet wed? Or a widow?"

"Not yet wed."

"Your name, Eva, 'tis pretty." Why was he complimenting her? Those eyes were making him muddle-headed.

She blushed and looked back toward the flowers, a small smile on her face. "Thank you, my laird."

Strath tried not to react to her using his title after she'd sworn not to. The men had already split up shifts when they reached them. Tomaidh nodded and then disappeared into the wood where he'd scout to make sure they were the only ones in the vicinity.

"We'll sleep for a little while. Allow the horses to rest. Are ye hungry?" Strath asked.

Lady Eva shook her head, looking ready to collapse. "Just tired."

"All right, but ye should eat when ye wake to keep up your strength."

"All right."

Strath untied the blanket on the back of his horse and laid it out for her, surprised she hadn't argued with him.

"Thank you," she murmured, kneeling on the blanket and then rolling onto her side, the flowers still clutched in her hands.

Strath watched her for a moment and then sat beside her, his back to a tree while she curled up on the ground beside him. In a trice, she was asleep, her even breaths causing her ribs to rise and fall. She slept sweetly, all the consternation gone from her face, her hands pressed beneath her cheek, knees tucked up toward her middle.

Not being on first shift and his appetite gone, he closed his eyes. But instead of drifting into sleep, his mind wandered and contemplated all the reasons why he *should* imprison her and stop...courting her. For that was what he was doing by admiring her beauty, by telling her that her name was pretty, and lusting after her.

She was English. Her father and her betrothed were enemies of Scotland. The man she was supposed to marry had just murdered and set fire to an entire Scottish town, not for the first time. And she'd tried to pretend as though she didn't know.

Her lies were another reason he should imprison her. The flowers could have been a tactic to deceive him. Hadn't his last betrothed deceived him, using her feminine wiles to blind him?

Lady Eva was good. Very good.

Maybe he should take what rightfully belonged to her husband, get her with child, and when the men eventually came to pay the price to get her back, Strath would send her back to England with his Scottish blood in her womb.

But that notion made his stomach churn with distaste, reminding him only of Jean and her treachery. He frowned. He would never do that. For one thing, he wasn't a rapist, and for another, he'd never willingly send his own child into enemy territory where it would only be tortured. Lastly, Eva had yet to prove she had a dark soul. Quite the opposite. Although he was inclined to believe she was pretending at being good, there were the flashes of temper and her opinionated mouth mixed in with appreciation of nature and genuine smiles.

Bloody hell. Why is she so confusing?

Nay. Taking advantage of her innocence wouldn't work. But imprisoning her until the king came to collect her...that would work. And it would protect him from whatever confusion he felt toward her.

Lady Eva rolled over and snuggled closer, her bottom scooting nearer until it was pressed firmly to his thigh. Strath held in the groan he wanted to let out as he almost went to wrap an arm around her before he stopped himself. Even in sleep, she was tormenting him.

He opened his eyes, drifting his gaze over the soft waves of her golden hair, the swell of her hips, the tiny feet tucked beside his knee. A sudden and strong desire to protect her ran through him—which absolutely wouldn't do. Hadn't he just spent the last hour or so reflecting on how he needed to stop that?

She was his prisoner, for bloody hell's sake. Protecting her was not his job. He was the one who'd put her in danger—or had he?

There was no point in pondering the fact. What was he going to do, take her back to England?

Like hell.

With one hand pressed to her back and the other to her shapely bum, he shoved her away. They needed some distance between them. He couldn't think straight with her touching him.

It was for her own good.

And his.

Chapter Five

Eva awoke with a gasp. A low muttered *oof* quickly followed her flailing arm as she connected with hard muscle. The sun beamed through the trees, momentarily blinding her. She prodded where her hand had connected. Wool scratched her fingertips, and beneath that, solid muscle strained with power.

What is that?

A sense of dread enveloped her in a suppressing cloud.

She bolted upright and jerked to the side, yanking her hand back as she took in the sight of the Laird of Dornoch beside her. She'd been molesting his thigh. Even sitting he was larger than life and broad. So broad. Muscles strained against the linen of his shirt. How did a man get so big? What did his mother feed him? Did the cows in the Highlands produce magical milk?

As her gaze roved from his long legs, the breadth of his torso, thick neck and face, she realized his stormy eyes were open and locked on her. He stared intently at her, and in that dark-gray gaze, the memories of all that had happened came flooding back to her, and with it a hard knot in the back of her throat.

She was his prisoner. And now she'd just openly groped the man.

Good heavens, what if her hand had landed somewhere else when she'd jolted awake?

Swallowing, she said, "I'm sorry." What in blazes? Her voice had come out throaty. She'd never heard it that way before.

His penetrating eyes darkened, and the muscle at the corner of his jaw flexed. "Do ye often wake like that, lass?"

Eva cleared her throat. "Only when I'm startled."

He winged a brow. "What could have possibly done that? We're in the middle of the most tranquil woods surrounded by people sleeping."

"Aye," she muttered, glancing around at the lumps of sleeping warriors. The gentle breeze blew through the trees, and the horses munched grass nearby. It was tranquil. Beautiful even. "'Tis true, but even the most tranquil settings and quiet people cannot quell the torment in my head or quiet the fear in my heart."

Dear all the saints in heaven, why did I just admit to that?

Eva rubbed at her eyes and threaded a hand through her hair, which was wild and unkempt. The wind from their desperate ride over the border had not done her hair any favors. And it had clearly also rattled her brain.

"Have ye ever slept outdoors before?"

Taken aback by the question, Eva returned her gaze to his. Memories of her childhood assaulted her. Had she ever slept outdoors? Was the sky blue?

Eva shook her head and moved to stand. She wasn't certain why she'd lied, only that for some reason it seemed like she needed to protect herself and what she might know. If he knew she was comfortable sleeping outdoors, he'd ask why, and then she'd have to reveal parts of her past she'd rather keep close to her heart. Sweet, tender memories of her youth with her mother that she rarely brought out because the pain of loss was too much.

"I need some water. And I can go by myself."

The laird nodded. She was surprised he readily accepted her answer, perhaps because she knew she wasn't telling the truth and had expected him to call her out on it. She stared at him a moment longer as he studied her, wishing she could see the thoughts going on behind those intense eyes, but he kept them well hidden.

At last, he did speak. "Do ye know how to swim?"

"What?" Eva cocked her head, completely taken aback by his question and wondering if she'd heard him correctly.

"I but wonder if ye'll be trying to swim away?" There was a teasing glint to his eyes that almost made her smile back, but her mind was whirling, and the cobwebs of sleep made her unable to trust her own instincts.

She should hate her captor. Fear him even. But time after time again, he was proving himself to be of higher morals than the man her father had intended for her to marry. Under different circumstances, he was a man she might have admired. His men respected him, even if they distrusted her. He'd not tried to ravage her; in fact, he'd protected her and kept her safe, caught her when she almost fell off the back of a horse. When she argued, he argued back but didn't gag her as he'd warned he might, which she now realized had been an empty threat. He teased and flirted, and she didn't feel in danger with him, which was at odds with everything.

Aye, he'd then dropped her on her arse, which had stung her ego, but turnabout was fair game wasn't it? Why did that thought make her smile?

How was she turning an abduction into a flirtation?

Ugh, why was she even contemplating all this nonsense? Why was she trying to make light of her situation?

He was a conundrum. Rough, yet caring. Rude, yet sweet.

But she must remember he was also a murderer—wasn't he? A heartless warrior who killed people and burned down their village. That thought had her immediately chilling. Part of her mind rebelled against it. How could he have done such a thing? Besides riding his horse into a church and raising his sword to Belfinch, she'd not seen a violent streak in him at all.

And yet it would appear that he had one.

Aye, it wouldn't do for her to forget just who the man was.

"I know how to swim, but I'll not be swimming away, as my gown would only end up drowning me, and I've no intention of swimming unclothed."

At the mention of being unclothed, his gaze boldly raked over her, slowly skimming her form and lingering on her hips, her breasts, and then her mouth. A shiver of heat washed over her with the intensity of his stare. She was both shocked and appalled that her body would react so viscerally to a look from a man. And not just any man. This man, who should scare the wits out of her.

Eva let out a resigned sigh. It didn't matter how much she told herself he was dangerous, she just couldn't believe it. With a roll of her eyes, partly at him and partly at herself, she said, "Oh, do get your mind out of the chamber pot."

"Och, I assure ye, my lady, my mind is nowhere near a chamber pot."

Fisting her hands at her sides, she let out a frustrated groan, whirled around, and marched toward the water.

On the way, she nodded and smiled at the men on watch, but they only returned her acknowledgment with blank stares bordering on hostile. Like men made of stone. Cold and unmoving.

With a shiver running down her spine, Eva hurried the last few steps to the water's edge, jumpy at their obvious distaste for her. Their laird might be treating her with more kindness than any prisoner in the history of prisoners, but it was clear that if it were their choice, they would not do so. And how could she blame them?

She could see the deep respect the men had for their laird. And she was almost entirely certain that none of them would go rogue and seek to do her harm. *Almost.*

She'd expected him to follow her, perhaps assuming she was tricking him about not swimming away or trying to escape some other way, but he didn't, which was surprising and frustrating.

He didn't think she would try to make an escape because she'd failed so miserably at it before. Truthfully, escaping would put her in more danger than she was already in.

Eva knelt before the water, cupping her hands and pulling sips of water up to her lips. She sat a moment at the trickling burn, watching a squirrel on the opposite bank running up a tree. He might have thought her story about the squirrel was crazy, but she knew she'd been bitten by one.

Eva shuddered, sat back on her heels, and pulled her mother's necklace from between her breasts. Clutching it to her heart, she sent up a prayer for her own safety, and that soon she'd have some answers. She tucked the necklace back into her gown and rose, reluctantly making her way back to camp.

The men on first watch had been relieved, and Laird Dornoch now stood on the perimeter of camp. He spotted her and began to approach.

"Eat," he ordered, handing her a strip of dried venison and a bannock cake.

She wondered if he felt the gazes of his men on him too, hence his shortness with her.

Eva took the food gratefully, her belly rumbling. She sat on the plaid he'd laid out for her, eating slowly as she observed all the men in the camp. Those who'd stood watch quickly fell asleep. Most of them slumbered quietly, but there was one man in the group whose snores carried on the wind, rivaling a thunderstorm. The man nearest to him reached out a long leg to nudge him with his foot, but to no avail.

She tried not to laugh at the noise. More than once, Strath met her gaze and raised a questioning brow, as though this was normal and not funny at all. Each time, she ducked her head, not wanting him to think she was laughing deliberately at his men. But honestly, the sound of the snoring was so incredibly loud. If they were trying to hide out from their enemies, this man should never be allowed to sleep. That thought made her laugh all the more, perhaps a bit manically, because all she could imagine were enemy warriors pausing mid-step to listen for the sounds of troops and the snores confusing them.

Eva curled up again after eating, pulling the blanket around her and tucking her hands under her chin. The plaid smelled like Laird Dornoch. Earthy, spicy. She breathed in deeply, feeling a level of comfort she shouldn't.

Go to sleep, she told herself. Because when they set out again, she'd not get much sleep on his horse, and who knew when he would stop again.

A short time later, she was woken by his gentle shake on her shoulder. The largeness and warmth of his hand was a welcome way to wake, and she did not startle. She blinked and found him kneeling beside her.

"Time to go, Princess."

Princess. His nickname for her. He knew her name now and was still using it. Eva gave him a sleepy smile and then rose, rolled up the blanket, and followed him to the horse. The rest of the men were also getting ready to head out. She excused herself for a moment of privacy, certain he'd not want to stop shortly after they got going. The brightness of the sun had dimmed, leaving a purple-gray haze everywhere. When she returned, the men were moving silently toward their mounts.

The wind rustled in the trees, and she watched as Laird Dornoch stopped to listen, his head cocked to the side, as though he spoke the language of the wind. Then he continued forward. He moved to lift her, but then paused, and instead held the stirrup steady.

"My lady," he said, a sweep of his hand toward the held stirrup.

"You do not prefer me to ride behind?"

He shook his head. "Not this time."

She didn't argue. It was less work for her to ride in front and hold on to the pommel rather than his muscular middle. The movement of his rear as they'd ridden had sent shivers she didn't want to think about surging through her insides. So, aye, she would much rather sit before him and not have all the distractions.

Then he mounted behind her, put his arm around her waist, and hauled her backward. Her spine aligned against his sinew sent a shiver coursing through her. When she tried to sit straight, to put distance between them, he hauled her back against his firmness, and this time, she didn't fight it.

Why? Because he was warm, and it was starting to chill with the sun setting, and she didn't have a cloak. Aye, that was a good enough excuse. It might be the height of spring, but that meant nothing the more north they traveled.

From what she'd learned as a lass from her father, the Highlands were always covered in snow and icicles. Much like the lairds who ruled the land, it was stark and cold. She'd better take all the warmth she could get in preparation for the deep chill that would likely settle in her bones once they reached their destination—especially if the laird tossed her in a dank, frozen prison. And how long would it take for Belfinch to come after her? Would he?

Aye. But not because he wanted her.

Nay, he would be coming after her because Laird Dornoch had messed with his pride. Just as he'd said, Belfinch would bristle at both his coin and woman being taken. Not to mention that his being bested by Laird Dornoch had been humiliating. He'd want to make up for being shown as a lesser man. He'd want to retaliate, to hurt the man who'd mortified him in front of his men, in front of her father, even. Because her father had now seen he wasn't the biggest and baddest out there, and Belfinch would be compelled to prove his strength.

A shudder wracked her.

"Are ye cold?" The warrior's words were softly spoken by her ear and sent another shudder racing through her.

His voice, so low and sensual and...expectant, caused her to lean farther into him.

"Nay. I was just...thinking?" Oh, but why did her words have to come out a question?

A soft chuckle sent another shiver over her skin.

"About what, Princess?"

Eva shook her head, knocking against his chin. "I'm sorry."

He laughed. "I'm used to it by now. In fact, ye knocked me so much last night, I've lost all feeling in my face."

Eva smiled and let out a quiet giggle.

"Now, tell me, what are ye thinking about that sends shivers down your spine?" The way he said this against the shell of her ear had her thinking about something entirely different—like his breath on her skin, the hardness of his body that surrounded her...

Clearing her throat, she told him the truth of what had originally made her shiver. "I was thinking about...Lord Belfinch."

At that admission, he tensed behind her, obviously taking her meaning for something different. Of what, she had no clue. She wasn't as adept to the workings of men's minds as he seemed to be with women. But she could tell that her confession bothered him. And not in a good way.

From then on, they no longer spoke as they rode. Stopping every few hours to relieve themselves, stretch their legs and water the horses, he continued to keep his distance from her. As much distance as could be had when two people rode the same animal.

Perhaps that was for the best. It was easier to remember just who had taken her and why she was here when she wasn't distracted by his heated breath on her skin or the sound of his gravelly voice sending tingles to places she shouldn't even be considering as a lady, let alone a maiden.

Still, he was wicked, and so she wasn't surprised he made her think wicked thoughts.

"Are ye all right, lass?" His words jolted her from her thoughts once more.

"Aye."

"Ye're breathing hard."

She glanced down to where his arm was wrapped around her middle. Of course he would be able to feel the way she was breathing.

"I'm fine."

He grunted but didn't ask her to expound on her answer.

An hour or two later, they stopped once more for a longer rest as the sun rose. Laird Dornoch found a similar looking spot as the one they'd slept in the day before. This time, he took first watch, and she was forced to fall asleep wrapped in the plaid on her own. She should have been relieved; instead, she was cold and she lurched awake at every sound, including the crunch of boots as the men switched shifts.

The laird settled against a tree behind her, close enough that she could sense him there, but not close enough to touch.

She should have been glad for that. So why did she miss his closeness?

Because she was a fool. And foolhardy.

Gone were the notions of escape. Now, she only wanted to figure out a way to convince the man not to accept any terms when Belfinch approached him concerning her release.

Aye, very foolhardy indeed.

Chapter Six

The next several days were passed in much the same way as the first two. They slept by day, rode by night. After more slices of dried meat than she could count, and hungering for something other than a strip of what was essentially dried leather, Eva was determined to make a semi-decent meal for these men. Perhaps she could even show them she wasn't someone to be feared or loathed.

Not only had she often helped out in the kitchens at Northwyck, but on the outdoor adventures her mother had taken her on, they'd often cooked together. Her mother used to say the woods were a veritable marketplace, filled to the brim with nourishment if you only looked closely enough.

The men would appreciate her efforts, wouldn't they? They couldn't possibly be enjoy eating leather meal after meal.

With her decision settled, Eva approached the laird. "I would like to make a stew for your men."

"A stew, my lady?" He eyed her skeptically, as though she'd just told him she wanted to eat grass.

"I saw that one of your men carries a large pot." She nodded toward the horse where a pot was very obviously tied to the saddlebag. "And he's not making use of it. I could. I saw some wild herbs and greens just over there. Some mushrooms, too. If someone would be good enough to catch a rabbit or the like, I can make a stew for supper, instead of dried meat."

One seductively arched brow rose. "What's wrong with dried venison?"

Eva had not been expecting a question like that. At all. "There is nothing wrong with it..." she drawled, trying to decipher if he was teasing her or not. "Only that perhaps they might enjoy a tasty repast instead? A heartier meal? Besides, I want to do something nice to show that I appreciate they've not eaten me yet." She said this last part with a little laugh.

The laird's nostrils flared, and his eyes blazed with a heat she felt all the way to her toes. *Zounds...* What had she said to make him look at her with such...hunger? Images of his lips nibbling over her neck had her eyes widening as she took in what he might have imagined—or was it all in her head? Why did the idea of him doing just that entice her so much?

"All right," he said tightly. "But ye might have better luck catching something crawling around as ye did the other night."

Eva's cheeks heated all the more, and she blew out a breath. "Very funny."

A crooked grin curled his lips. "Aye. Verra funny."

She tapped her toe and resisted the urge to cross her arms over her chest. "Well, what will it be?"

"Aye. I'll catch ye a rabbit or two."

"Thank you." Excited that he'd agreed to her plan, she headed back in the direction of where she'd seen the herbs and mushrooms. When she'd been a lass, her mother had taught her, Jacqueline, and the other village girls how to find things that were edible in the forest. It had become a game throughout the years. Even now, when she visited with her sister or the women in town, it was customary to bring something they'd found in the forest along the way.

Emotion filled her chest, and sat back on her heels and stared up at the sky. The pain of losing her mother never dulled. It was an ever-present ache in the center of her heart. God, how she prayed her mother was truly still alive. Tears threatened, but she couldn't let them fall. She had good memories. Many of them. And she thrived on those. Drawing in several steady breaths, she forced herself to focus on the task. Herbs. Mushrooms. Any edible roots.

She gathered the items in a makeshift basket she made with the outer layer of her gown. Part of her chemise was exposed as she headed back toward camp, but given she'd seen several of the men without their shirts, and she'd been riding in a rather unladylike position for days, them seeing a few inches of her chemise was nothing.

She spotted the lad who had the pot, and smiled without pretense. "May I borrow your pot, sir?"

"What for?" he asked none too happily, eyes raking over her in much the same manner the other warriors did.

"I'm going to make a stew." *And you're going to like it.*

"Nay, ye arena." He dismissed her with a wave of his hand.

That took her aback. His laird had given her permission to do so, so why was he suddenly denying her? Mistrust clouded his eyes, and his face was wrinkled in distaste.

"Please, sir. Laird Dornoch has given me permission and has even gone to fetch a rabbit."

Unable to deny that, he begrudgingly went to his horse to untie the pot. She was certain he was going to toss the heavy iron vessel at her head by the look of him, but instead, he held it out and waited for her to load her items into its center and take it from him. A good sign she might be able to slowly etch away at the stony resolves of the men.

"Thank you." Eva smiled, but he did not return the gesture. Instead, he just grunted and backed away from her, obviously not giving her his back as though he expected she would stab him.

Well, she'd known it wasn't going to be easy. Progress would come in small measures, and she'd accept the giving of the pot as a small victory.

"Wench is making a damn witch's brew. Going to poison us all." The murmured words put a damper on her spirits. How dare he insinuate such a thing? And with her not even out of earshot? *Barbarian.* Accusations like that held strong in the minds of the superstitious, and even the not so superstitious. An accusation like that could get a person killed. Eva quickly surveyed the men, and though they all looked at her much the way they had before, none of them seemed to have a spark of fear or sudden bloodlust.

Eva pursed her lips, preparing to defend herself, but he walked away, and she'd not the energy to go after him and make a fight out of it. While his behavior did make her angry, she wasn't about to commit murder by poisoning them all, even if they were dangerous.

Besides, she could empathize with the warriors' feelings, even if she didn't agree. If she had been in their place, she might have behaved the same way. To these men, she was an enemy. Even if she knew that to be the furthest thing from the truth, they didn't know any better.

And she'd given them no reason to trust her. This stew, while it might seem like a minor thing, was a big step in the direction of peace. Not simply because she couldn't deal with their glowers and barely contained hatred, but because who knew how long she was going to be among them. For her own sanity, she couldn't imagine spending months facing hostility. Perhaps if they saw this gesture for what it was, they would start to warm to her.

And if they warmed to her, their laird may not toss her in a dark, cold cell, and instead allow her some free rein.

Or was that too much hopeful thinking?

ONLY STEPS AWAY FROM CAMP, Tomaidh approached Strath with purposeful steps. "My laird."

"Aye?" Strath slowed enough to allow his friend to reach his side then increased his pace through the forest, wanting to get a safe distance from camp before he started firing arrows.

Tomaidh had that march about him that he got when he was questioning his laird's logic. Strath was fairly certain what he wanted to talk about and was fairly certain he didn't want to hear it.

At last, Tomaidh spoke. "Do ye think it is wise, my laird?"

"What? Hunting?"

"Allowing the lass to make a stew for our entire caravan."

Strath shrugged. "I'm tired of dried venison."

Tomaidh shook his head. "We all are, my laird. But the lass... She was to wed the enemy. Her father is a powerful lord in the north of England, certainly at fault for many of the calamities we were sent to fight against."

"I dinna need a lecture from ye, Tomaidh. Ye tell me things I'm already aware of. Or do ye think me so addled I wouldna recall where we took her from? The king wanted to know if she was alive. Delivering her will answer his question."

Tomaidh held up his hands and took a step back. "I trust ye, my laird. I didna mean to make it seem otherwise."

Strath continued forward. "The lass will not cause us harm."

"How can ye be sure?"

Strath paused, seeing a rabbit in the distance who'd stilled from munching on greens. He lifted his arrow, lined up his mark, and took the shot. "I feel it in my gut." As he retrieved his arrow, he eyed Tomaidh. "Ye said ye trust me."

"Aye."

"Then ye and the men will follow my lead when it comes to our prisoner."

"We always do. I trust ye."

"Good. Just as I trust ye." Strath clapped his friend on the shoulder. "I appreciate ye coming to me."

Tomaidh nodded. "She is verra beautiful."

Strath grinned. "Is this going to be another lecture?"

"Nay, nay. But I have to ask..."

"Ask then."

"Is she truly a prisoner?"

Strath lightly shoved his friend away and continued marching through the forest to find another rabbit for the stew. "She belongs with us."

"Belonging is different than being a prisoner."

"I know." He cleared his throat. "To be clearer, she is mine, under my protection."

"Yours."

"Aye." Strath wasn't even completely sure what he meant when he said it, only that it felt right.

Lady Eva was under his protection. And if circumstances were different, he might actually make her his in truth. Binding. But for now, telling his men she was under his wing of protection ought to be enough to have them warming toward her, for he'd seen the wary expressions that passed between them when she approached.

Suddenly, a realization came to him. He trusted her.

Ballocks.

❦

EVA TOOK the pot down to the water, ignoring the murmurs from the men. She rinsed the herbs and vegetables, filled the pot with water, and brought it back to camp. There was no fire, not as they had the other days, and she could only think they'd refrained on purpose. No matter, she knew how to build a fire, and she would not allow their reticence for her or her darn stew to take her down.

She set the pot in the perfect spot to build a fire and then moved off toward the edge of camp to gather twigs and larger pieces of fallen branches. With the heel of her boot, she broke the larger branches into smaller, more manageable pieces. After gathering the wood, she took the pile back to camp and stacked them in place, clearing debris from around the edges until it was perfect. Then she realized she didn't have a flint to light the blasted thing.

Every man in the camp seemed suddenly busy, their backs to her after. They must have realized what she needed and did not want to give it to her. But Eva was determined.

Biting her lip, she knelt next to the pile, recalling the trick her mother had showed her on one of their excursions. She picked up a sturdy yet thin piece of kindling and placed its tip on one of the larger pieces of wood. Clasping the kindling piece between her palms, she started to quickly rub her palms back and forth, twirling the kindling against the larger piece of wood. Heat built up in her palms at the same time the wood started to give off just the tiniest amount of smoke.

Eva couldn't help but smile. It might have been a few years since her mother had taken all the ladies out for a wilderness excursion, but the skills she'd learned hadn't faded.

Just as her mother had showed her, Eva blew lightly on the smoking wood and kept on twirling. Men in the camp had started to inch forward, but she ignored them. No doubt, they were surprised she knew how to do this. She was sure every Scottish lass was born with skills to survive outdoors—especially since she'd heard it was rare to have a hearth in a Scottish house or castle—but she knew how even more rare it was for an Englishwoman to build a fire from nothing but wood.

From the surprised murmurs of the warriors, it was obvious the idea of Eva starting a fire had never crossed their minds. While she'd heard rumors about the Scots, she'd also heard what they thought about the English. That the women were like babes who couldn't survive without the help of men or servants. That left to her own devices, an English lady would perish for lack of skill at feeding one's self. And what was it the man had murmured earlier, that she was going to make a witch's brew? Englishwomen were witches—*bah*. Mayhap they would even think the fire she was slowly growing now was some feat of magic rather than skill.

With her churlish thoughts, Eva had slowed her rubbing, and the smoke started to dissipate. *Nay!* She wasn't going to lose, not with all these curmudgeons betting against her. With renewed determination, she picked up the pace, blew gently, and watched the smoke increase. Shortly thereafter, a small amount of tinder sparked from the shavings of the wood created by her ministrations. Eva blew gently on a spark and held the tip of her kindling stick to the glowing ember. Within a moment, it also started to smoke and glow, until a flame leapt up from its tip.

She'd done it.

A secret smile curled her lip, and she kept her gaze toward the ground, not wanting to see the faces of the men who surrounded her, certain their disappointment at her succeeding would put a damper on this moment of triumph.

Warmth flooded her chest, and at that moment, she was fairly certain her mother was right there with her, holding her, hugging her. A ray of hope. With the end of a stick, she poked the pieces of wood in her makeshift campfire until the flames leapt from various pieces, and then she placed her pot of water on top to boil. If there was a moment to be proud of herself, this was it.

And she knew her mother would have been proud.

All she needed to do now was add the ingredients. Tearing the herbs and plopping them in the pot was easy, but she needed a knife to cut the mushrooms and root vegetables.

This time, Eva did look up, but as soon as she raised her head, the men all avoided her gaze, pretending to be busy.

At that moment, Laird Dornoch returned with two rabbits and a few squirrels. He nodded at her fire and the slowly warming water.

"Smells delicious."

"You exaggerate," she said with a roll of her eye. "'Tis only wood burning that you smell."

He laughed. "Soon it will be meat." He held up his catches.

"Nicely done," Eva said with a smile.

He nodded and settled down near her to prepare the meat for cooking. Eva watched him for a moment, not surprised to find the way he worked to be precise and accurate. Then she recalled her need to cut up the vegetables.

"Can I borrow a dagger, my laird?"

"What for?" He glanced up at her and winked. "To kill me and cook me up?"

Eva blushed at his teasing and pointed at her pile. "Nay, I want to chop these."

He scanned the vegetables and then pulled a small dagger from his boot and wiped it on his plaid. "Will this do?"

"Aye. Thank you very much." The handle was warm from where it had been pressed to his skin.

"Who started the fire for ye?" he asked while he continued his ministrations.

"I did it myself." Eva chanced a look at him through her lashes.

He shook his head and chuckled as though she'd just told a joke.

"I'm serious." She chopped some of the mushrooms a bit too ener-getically in irritation. Was it so impossible to imagine a woman could do such a feat? Or just her?

"Did ye really?" He stopped what he was doing to once more look at her, awe in his regard.

"Aye. And without a flint." She couldn't help bragging a little and thrust her chin out.

The laird's eyes returned to her fire, a newfound respect etched on his face. "Skill with a fire is rare in a woman. While I've an affinity for sparking flames, I'm not certain my sisters would know. Where'd ye learn to do that?"

Eva's mind snapped to what she'd seen of the burned out village, and she couldn't help but mutter, "You of all people know exactly how one starts a fire."

Once she'd spoken the words she wished she could pull them back. She waited for the explosion. For him to knock over the pot and perhaps toss her into the flames, but a flicker of confusion flashed over his face.

"My lady? I dinna take your meaning."

Eva licked her lips. "'Tis nothing." She tried to wave it away, but he pressed.

"Ye're referring to something. I'm not an idiot." And then it must have dawned on him. "I see. All roads dinna lead to the same place, lass. 'Haps I should have known *ye* had the skill all along. 'Twould seem ye and your kind are fond of fires."

Everything about his statement gave her pause. What could he possibly mean by that? Why did it feel like he was turning the tables on her?

"My kind?"

"English bastards."

Such venom filled his voice that she sat back with the knife paused in the middle of a root vegetable. Just another reminder she was this man's prisoner, that he had no cause to be kind to her. A drop of English blood and she was lumped in with everyone he hated. Despite his flirtations, the teasing, and smiles, this was a stark reminder of exactly what they were to each other. She'd been a fool to read anything more into it.

Eva stood and brushed her hands against her skirts, leaving the food where it was. Everything that had happened in her life over the past two years culminated in a rush of anger.

"Well, at least I'm not a murderer. A destroyer of lives," she said.

"Are ye nay?" He looked up at her slowly, accusation in his gaze.

"I am not." She spoke each word loudly, clearly. "But I've witnessed firsthand the violence you have in you."

The laird leapt to his feet then, his eyes glaring accusations. "And ye hide the harm ye cause others behind your skirts and refinery."

"You know nothing about me."

"And ye know nothing about me." His voice was quiet, cold, an exacting declaration of just how stupid she'd been.

"I know enough." Eva straightened her shoulders and waited for the punishment that had to be coming.

"What? That I attacked your castle and knocked your lover on his pompous, vile head?"

Eva bristled, and for the briefest of moments, she wished she had picked the wrong mushrooms for the stew so she could watch him writhe in pain. She was immediately contrite for her mean thoughts.

"You attacked my castle unprovoked and murdered my father's men. Then you wrenched me from everything I know and love."

"What could a woman like ye know of love?"

His words cut her. She knew a lot about the love of a mother, the love of a sister, the love of friends. But his words only served to remind her she was naïve in the ways of loving a man. Still, she couldn't let him know that his words hurt. "More than you, I imagine."

He grunted in response, a cloud filling his features and then swiftly disappearing. "Maybe so."

What demon from his past had just attacked him?

Oh, why should she care? She should be throwing the dagger clutched in her hand at his heart.

"I'll tell ye one thing, Princess," he said as he sat down to finish skinning the animals and preparing the meat for her to put in the stew, all the fight apparently gone from him. "I dinna kill innocents. I protect my people, my countrymen and women."

She wasn't certain how to take his words. Was he saying she was not innocent, nor a Scot, and could therefore not expect protection? Well, she wasn't surprised.

"I've never killed anyone. My soul is clean," she said confidently.

"Not with your own blade."

"Nor with anyone else's."

"What of the fire?"

At his question, she stepped back in surprise, all of what he'd said now making complete sense. "The fire."

"The one ye so cleverly pretended not to know about."

All the color drained from her face. "You think I had something to do with that village being burned down?"

"Aye."

"Why on earth would you think that?"

"Do ye not know, Princess?"

Eva swallowed hard, not sure she wanted to know. Nay, certain she didn't want to know. And at the same time, she had to find out what he was talking about. Because it was slowly becoming clear the relationship she'd built in her head with him was not the only thing she'd been foolish about.

She shook her head, gripping the sides of her skirts to keep her hands from trembling.

"Your betrothed set that fire. Ye might as well have done it yourself."

Chapter Seven

The devastation that flashed across Lady Eva's face was real. Strath had experienced anguish, disbelief, and shock enough times in battle and when he'd informed the wives of his men about the loss of their husbands to recognize the emotions.

Eva sank to her knees and pressed her hands to her throat, tears brimming in her soulful blue eyes. The expression on her face tore at his heart, unsettling him. It took every ounce of willpower he had not to get up and pull her into his arms. To offer her comfort.

More disconcerting was that she did not dispute the accusation.

"Ye knew?" he asked her.

She shook her head, her lips forming the word *nay* but no sound coming out.

"Did ye suspect?"

Again, she shook her head. "I thought... I thought 'twas you."

Strath narrowed his gaze. "I had an idea that was what ye meant earlier."

"You. I thought..." Her voice trailed off on a sob, and she pressed her fingers to her eyes, whether to hide her tears or ebb their flow, he couldn't be certain.

"Ye thought I would kill my own people and burn down their

village. That I was a monster. I might be a Highlander, lass, but that doesna mean the lives of Lowlanders are any less precious. The English have done enough devastation in my country, I'll not be adding to it."

She was shaking her head now and swiping tears from her eyes. "I don't understand."

"What is there not to understand?" Strath leaned back, jabbing the tip of his dagger into the ground. "Belfinch, your father, Englishmen who worship your devil king...they do not hesitate to kill my people."

"Not *all* people of English blood."

Strath pressed his lips together, acknowledging she had a point. "There are very few that wouldna, and I happen to be related to one who would never."

"You have English relations?"

"Aye. My mother is English."

Why had he told her that? It was none of her business.

"You see? You must know not all English are evil. I am not evil."

"Aye. My mother is a saint. And her relations are right there with her. But ye...why would ye be marrying that bastard Belfinch?"

Lady Eva frowned. "I'd not pegged you for an imbecile."

He paused, regarding her. "Explain."

"What woman has the right to choose a husband? My sister didn't. I didn't. What woman has a right to refuse the man she's been told to marry?"

He thought about his sister Bella. She'd chosen her husband, Niall. In fact, many of the women in his family had done much the same. But he understood what she meant, for it was not the norm. And the knowledge she'd not chosen Belfinch and had not wanted to marry him lifted his mood.

When he didn't answer, she continued. "Are you married?"

Strath didn't like the path this was taking. There was no way he was going to reveal that his betrothed had betrayed him. "Nay."

"Do you expect the woman you choose to marry to do as she's bid or to choose you freely for her husband?"

He thought about the woman he'd been betrothed to. She'd not been a part of the dealings. In fact, neither had he. His father had approached him about it, and Strath had been obligated to agree to grow their lands. But it didn't matter, that had nothing to do with this current situation. And she should know that. Was this a way of distracting him?

He shrugged. "Ye might have refused. My da would never force my sisters to marry an evil bastard."

"I tried." She shifted her gaze away. "We are not all blessed with situations that are black and white. Some of us live in the gray."

She picked up a stick and stirred the stew, leaving Strath at a loss for words.

"No one wanted to hear my pleas." She touched her cheek, where the faint yellow outline of a bruise marred her skin.

The vague outline looked almost like fingertips. He'd not known what to think of it before now, but seeing the pain in her eyes, rage filled his chest.

"Your father hit ye?"

"Nay." Her tone was so soft he could barely hear her.

"Belfinch?"

She barely nodded, but even that slight tilt of her chin toward her chest was a stab in his gut.

"And your father let him?" He couldn't help the exasperation in his tone. His father would never stand for it. Hell, Strath wouldn't stand for it. Any bastard who laid a hand on a woman he cared about could count on retribution.

Again, she nodded. "He...he had no choice either."

Strath narrowed his eyes. "That's a load of ballocks, lass. As your father, he's got an obligation to protect ye. No matter the cause for his ire, Belfinch shouldna have raised a hand to ye. Dinna tell me ye think ye deserved it."

"I did not." She looked up at him then, tears in those light-blue eyes that again had his protective urges surging.

What is it about her?

It wasn't as if she was the first beaten woman he'd come across. In fact, just a few weeks prior, he'd had a stern talking to with a crofter after his wife brought a basket of eggs to the castle with her eye blackened. Strath had nearly choked the life out of the man, only letting up when he'd sworn never to do such a thing again on pain of death.

Strath's da had taught him to respect women. They were precious. And if growing up with three sisters who could try the patience of a saint wasn't enough to prove that violence was never the answer, he didn't know what was.

"I am sorry for ye, lass."

She frowned, anger brightening her eyes. "I don't want your pity."

"'Tis not pity. I promise." He held his hand over his heart. "Know that as long as ye're under my protection, I'll not lay a hand in violence upon ye."

Lady Eva cocked her head, staring at him a long moment. He wished he could see what was going on in that pretty head of hers. At last, she asked, "Why would you be so kind to me?"

"'Tis not just ye, but every woman." Strath brought a small flask out of his sporran, took a swig of whisky, and passed it her way.

At first, she hesitated. Then she took a tentative sip and wrinkled her nose before taking a bigger gulp. "That has a bite to it, but it is good."

He grinned. "Comes from my da's land."

"A well of spirits? I've never heard of such a thing, but I suppose you Scots would have discovered it long ago."

"A well?" Strath couldn't help bursting out into laughter at that. "I didna mean it literally comes from the land, sweetling, but that it is made on Sutherland land."

"Oh." Her cheeks turned crimson, and she busied herself with stirring the soup.

Strath took the time to clean up the cooking preparation mess and then sat back down before the hearth.

"Laird, why did you take me?"

"I made that clear when I did." He picked up a stick and chewed on it.

"To draw Belfinch north."

"Aye." He hated lying. He should tell her about the king's request for information about her, but something held him back.

"But why? Was it because of the fire?"

"And the like." She was fishing for an answer.

"There's been more than one fire?"

Strath let out a sigh and pulled the stick from between his teeth. Her naivety appeared genuine. Was she really so sheltered from what was happening in her own castle?

"Aye. He's a bad man, lass, and I hate to tell ye, but so is your da."

She leaned over the pot of soup, breathed in the scent, and shook her head. By her action, he thought the succulent scent of the stew cooking was unpleasant, but then she spoke, "My father is not a bad man. You don't understand."

"Och, lass, I understand perfectly."

"Nay," she said sadly, "you don't. Because I don't either." That last part was filled with such despair, it could be nothing but the truth.

"Why do ye not try to explain it then?"

"I can't."

"Ye could try," he prodded.

"But I don't know. How can I explain something I don't know?"

"Try me."

She just shook her head though, not willing to part with whatever secrets she had stored. Strath waited, not wanting to push too hard.

"The stew should be done soon."

All right, perhaps she needed a little more time to mull things over. "Smells good."

"Thank you."

"Where did ye learn to cook?"

"My mother."

"Ah, my mother loves to cook."

She glanced up at him, a teasing smile on her face. "Was she tired of dried venison, too?"

Strath let out a hearty laugh. "Maybe so. What else did your mother teach ye?"

"Many things. Fires for one."

"She sounds like a good woman."

"Aye...she was."

Was. He couldn't imagine the loss of his own mother, who was so very dear to him.

"I'm sorry for your loss."

"Thank you." She bit her lip as though she wanted to say more, but didn't.

"Was it recently?"

"Two years ago. But the ache is still fresh."

Strath passed her the whisky, and she took it and smiled wryly as she sipped. "To numb the pain?"

"Aye, something like that." Strath rose, went to his horse, and pulled out two small metal cups and two spoons. "Ready to eat?"

She wiped a drip of whisky from her lip. Oh what he wouldn't have given to be the one to do it.

"You're going to have some?" She seemed surprised.

"I'm starving. And ye were right about the dried venison."

"But are you not afraid I've poisoned the stew?"

"What? Why would ye do that?"

"I wouldn't."

"Then why would ye suggest it?" But the truth dawned on him quickly as he studied the men he traveled with. His warriors. Most of whom he'd known since they were barely out of swaddling clothes. They shook their heads at the pot.

The men didn't trust her, and he supposed he should have known that they wouldn't. She was English and had been about to wed the man they'd traveled all the way from the Highlands to attack.

"Ah, I see. Well, I dinna think ye'd poison me, lass. Because that would only leave ye alone in these woods with no way of getting back to England. Besides, from what ye revealed to me, I think Northwyck is the last place ye want to be right now. Not to mention an English lass in the Scottish wilderness, all alone, would not fare well."

"I might. I do know how to start a fire, and to forage for food."

"That is true. I suppose I'll just have to take my chances then."

He reached his cup into the pot and scooped up a healthy portion for her before scooping another cupful for himself.

"Smells like heaven, and definitely worthy of a painful death." He grinned and lifted the cup.

"Make her taste it first," one of his men called out. It was Wee Duff, called such on account of his feet being incredibly small for his stature.

Strath frowned, took a long sip of the tasty broth, and then shoveled a spoonful of meat and vegetables into his mouth.

"Delicious," he said around the mouthful.

And he wasn't lying. The stew was divine. And not because they hadn't had a decent meal in weeks. The lass truly had a talent.

Eva smiled and took a dainty spoonful of stew. "Thank you."

The men watched for a few minutes, perhaps waiting for Strath to fall over dead.

"Come get your fill, else I eat the rest of the pot myself," Strath called out.

One by one, the men gathered their cups and spoons from their satchels and filled up on the stew. Though they'd turned around enough to eat the food Lady Eva had made them, they still did not join the two of them around the campfire.

The blatant distancing had Strath bristling, but there was naught he could do about it besides demand his men sit. And he wasn't going to do that. Trust was earned, not forced. When they didn't die from eating her stew, their trust would grow. By the end of this journey, when they reached Dornoch, his men would be sitting beside her.

Why was he doing this? Allowing her to cook, and then eating it and asking his men to do the same? Over the days since they'd taken Northwyck Castle and stolen Eva along for their journey back north, he'd noticed how his men shied away from her. He'd also had taken note of the goodness in her. His own desire to be around her. To make her laugh. To have her jut out her chin and argue with him. There was a strength about her that he found inspiring.

Several hours later, when the sun fell, the men appeared more rested than they had in days. Likely because they'd slept better with full bellies.

Strath mounted his warhorse and pulled Eva up to sit on his lap. As they rode out of the camp, she said, "I hope no one gets sick."

"Why would they get sick?"

"I didn't poison the stew," she hurried. "But if anyone gets sick from anything else, they will blame me."

"They willna." That wasn't exactly the truth. If anyone were to start something, it would be Wee Duff, and Strath would be forced to put the man in his place. But that was something he'd seen coming for quite some time.

The man had been causing rifts between the other warriors for years. If there was ever a rumor to dispute, or a brawl to break up, nine times out of ten, Wee Duff was at the heart of it. The more he thought on it, the more certain he was that before this journey was over, Duff would indeed be at the core of some sort of commotion. Whether that be blaming the lass for something, or just slowly wearing away at Strath's patience, he wasn't certain.

"You sound very confident," she mused. "I wish I was."

Strath grunted. "I am their laird. They will follow my lead."

The lass nodded, and he narrowly avoided the bobbing of her head against his chin once more. The woman wielded her skull like a weapon.

"That is nice that they trust you enough to follow you, and that you trust them."

"Aye. Trust is necessary for warriors."

"Trust is necessary for families, too, but it is not always freely given."

"Aye. Trust is earned."

She was quiet for a moment. "Do your parents trust you?"

"Aye. With their lives. Just as I'm certain your father does."

"I'm not convinced he does."

That admission piqued his curiosity. "Why?" he asked softly, hoping not to scare her off the topic.

"Never mind," she said, her head angling down, dejected.

Strath wanted to push, but if he knew anything about women, and he'd learned a lot from his sisters, pushing would only make her clam up. Without thinking, he said what he always did to his sisters, "I'm here if ye ever want to talk."

That had her head shooting up again, and this time, he didn't see it coming. The sharp pain of her skull cracking against his chin caused him to bite the tip of his tongue.

"Ballocks," he cursed, tasting metallic.

Eva tried to turn around in her seat, her beautiful face pointed up toward his. "I'm sorry. Are you all right?"

"Aye. I've had many worse injuries than a bruised chin."

"That is not truly a consolation."

The lass looked so concerned, and Strath realized in that moment that her soul would have been completely crushed married to a man like Belfinch. A woman like Eva deserved so much more. She deserved to flourish.

Involuntarily, he stiffened and tightened his hold on her.

"Laird," she said pushing against his hand. "I truly am sorry."

"Och, nay, lass, I'm sorry. I was but thinking of that bastard hitting ye."

"How did you know, before when you asked?"

"Ye touched the fading bruise on your cheek when we were talking earlier."

"Oh."

"And, lass, ye need only call me Laird in front of my men. When it is just the two of us, I'd like ye to call me Strath."

"Strath? I've not heard that before. The name suits you."

"'Tis short for my title."

"Your title?" She shot her head around to look at up him accusingly, and with perhaps a little mockery. "So, what you're telling me is that you've given me permission to call you by another title?"

He grinned, and then let out a chuckle. "I'd not thought of it that way. My friends and family call me Strath. I share a name with my father, we are both called Magnus. I was given the title Earl of Strathnavor when I was a lad, and it stuck."

"Ah. Well, then I suppose I will not be as offended as I was planning."

"Aye, I didna mean offense."

"*Strath*. Hmm." She played with his name, rolling it off her tongue a few more times.

And he liked it. Perhaps too much.

Chapter Eight

Eva let out a sigh, sinking against him. Why did he have to feel so wonderful?

She closed her eyes, imagining that instead of riding away from England toward his home in the Highlands, they were courting, and were out for an evening ride near her father's home. Her mother was still alive, and Belfinch had never come to collect on some unspoken debt.

Strath would bow to her father, kiss the back of her hand, and lead her gallantly to his mighty steed. When he lifted her up, his hands would wrap possessively around her waist, and he'd look deep into her eyes.

"Are ye all right, lass?" Strath asked from behind.

Eva's eyes shot open, and she blinked into the darkness, letting the cover of the night hide what she was certain was the cherry-red of her cheeks. "Just fine, aye."

"Ye were breathing hard."

She bit the inside of her cheek to keep from laughing. If he only knew.

"What were ye thinking about?"

"A lady doesn't divulge her fantasies."

"Aha, a fantasy. Let me guess...was it about a handsome prince or delicious cherry tart?" Every word was laced with mirth, but not taunting.

"Well, if you must know, it was the cherry tart."

"I dinna blame ye. I often dream of cherry tarts."

"Do you really?"

"Aye. The sweeter the better."

"And does your cook gift you with sweet cherry tarts?"

He snorted behind her, and she couldn't help but feel she'd missed out on some sort of joke. "Oh, nay, lass, not my cook."

"Then who?"

"I only accept cherry tarts from lassies who intrigue me."

"Hmm. Do you often find lassies lining up to gift you with their cherry tarts?"

This time his bark of laughter caught the attention of Tomaidh who said, "Only on days that end with Y."

"What?"

Now Strath was laughing almost uncontrollably, and Eva narrowed her eyes, certain there was a jest she was not privy to.

"Tomaidh," she said, "Have you seen the lassies giving Strath their cherry tarts?"

The warrior beside her snorted so loudly his horse mimicked the sound. "How many lassies have given Strath their cherry tarts?" he called out to the other warriors. "Lady Eva would like to know."

The line of warriors laughed so hard some of them were doubled over their horses and looked in danger of falling.

Eva tucked her forehead beneath Strath's chin. "What is the jest?"

He grinned down at her, mischievousness in his eyes. "A warrior doesna divulge his fantasies."

Eva pursed her lips. "I suppose that is fair. If I share mine, will you share yours?"

"Alas, I am not in possession of a cherry tart to share."

"I see you want to make this a game. A guessing game. Fine, I'll play."

He chuckled behind her, his chest rumbling against her back and sending shivers racing over her skin.

"If I'm right, say aye, and if I'm wrong, say nay," she continued.

"How about if ye're right, I say aye, and if ye're wrong, ye have to kiss me."

"Kiss you?" Her belly flipped at the thought.

"Ye're right, that was entirely too forward of me."

"Aye, it was."

"But I could tell ye liked the idea from the hitch in your breath," he whispered against her ear.

Her breath hitched again, but she quickly got a hold of herself. "You're a rogue."

"I'll never deny it. But ye wanted to play a game, and this is how rogues play."

"Well, if you get a kiss if I'm wrong, I need something if I'm right."

"What do ye wish for?"

"My lower back is sore from all this riding and sleeping on the ground. If I'm right, you have to rub my back."

"Och, my lady, how verra forward of ye."

"Desperate times." This time it was her turn to laugh.

"Why do I get the impression that ye're a bit of a saucy wench?"

"You don't know the half of it." Oh, dear heavens, what had gotten into her? She was being incredibly brazen in her flirtations. Never before had she acted in such a way, and she found...she rather liked it. There was no way she would have ever flirted with Belfinch in this way, and in the past two years, her father had not let any other men near her. Perhaps because he'd known all along Belfinch would require her for a bride.

But thinking of such things put a damper on the good mood she was in, and she wanted to continue being happy with the man who helped her achieve it. How ironic that with Strath, fun was easy?

"I accept your terms," he said.

"All right. Then let us begin this guessing game. I am going to guess that when you say cherry tart, you don't actually mean an actual cherry tart."

"Aye."

"One point for me." She bent forward. "And a rub please."

He pressed a large palm to the small of her back and began to massage with the heel of his hand. At once, the tension started to ease, and she had to bite the tip of her tongue to keep from moaning.

"Now, lass, ye must guess what it means." He ceased rubbing.

Eva sat back up and focused on the dark line of warriors in front of them. The gently waving trees they passed looked as though they were inviting the group into their midst.

"Hmm," she said. Each man had laughed without question about the gifting of cherry tarts. Not having grown up with brothers, she wasn't particularly knowledgeable to what jests might pass between lads, but given she wasn't aware of one with tarts among ladies and the uproar of laughter, she had to guess it was likely a vulgar sort of jest.

And then, all of the sudden, she knew exactly what it was. She gasped, her hands flying to her cheeks.

Behind her, Strath barked a laugh. "Bend over for the rest of your back rub."

"But I didn't say it," she said.

"Aye, but I can tell from your reaction that ye've guessed just what the roguish jest was."

"Oh my," was all she could say. "I can't believe I asked Tomaidh..."

Strath laughed all the more, so hard she was certain he probably had tears running down his face. But bend over she did, delighting in the massage.

"You really are a rogue."

"Ye dinna know the half of it," he teased, giving her back her own words.

She sighed into the massage, already feeling so much better from his ministrations. "You are much better at this than my maid."

"Do ye often have need of a back rub?"

"Nay, not often." She sneezed, her entire body bouncing. And then she sneezed again.

"One more to come?" he asked, humor in his tone.

"Aye—*choo!*"

"Bless ye, lass." His hand ran up her spine, and she sighed with pleasure.

"Nay, bless you and your talented hands."

Beside them, Tomaidh snorted once more, and she realized too late just what she'd said and how it could be implied.

FOR THE NEXT TWO NIGHTS, Strath and Tomaidh procured meats for stew while Eva foraged for different vegetables and herbs. One of the warriors even gave up a stash of dried herbs and salt his wife had packed in his satchel. Each time Eva came back from the water's edge with the vegetables washed and the pot full of water, someone had built the fire for her. Nobody admitted to it, and so she gave her thanks to the air surrounding the men since no one wanted to be acknowledged.

This new change was proof that either the men were starting to trust her, or they were just as tired of eating what tasted like strips of leather as she was. But she preferred to think it was the former. It had been so long since she'd felt a sense of camaraderie with anyone. Ever since the cherry tart incident, the men had been more apt to smile at her. No more statues. Even her own worries were starting to ease.

Secretly, she wanted to thank Strath for having laid siege to North-wyck. For if he'd not done so, where would she be now?

Broken. Bruised. At the mercy of a monster.

Instead, here she was on an adventure in the woods, laughing with the men, and even sharing secret smiles with Strath. The way he looked at her was different, changing every day, and she felt herself wanting to preen a little more, to find something funny to tell him so she could hear his laughter.

But not only that, being on this journey had brought her closer to her mother than she'd been since her disappearance. Though Eva, her sister, and the village girls had continued the ritual of presenting gifts to each other they found in the wild, they had not resumed the wilder-ness excursions. Being outside the castle walls, touching the grass with her hands, and lying beneath the stars were ways to relive all over again the things she now missed.

What she did not miss was the looming and menacing presence of Lord Belfinch, nor did she miss the shifting eyes of the people who'd once loved her. Even the friends she'd grown to love so much, the girls she'd grown up with, had started to distance themselves from her at their parents' request. Come to think of it, the last wildflower or batch of herbs left for her had been months ago, even though she'd continued the tradition.

Slowly, Lord Belfinch's hold on her father, the demand for coin that her father had then turned on his people, had affected her, and she'd hardly seen it coming until it was too late.

Despite that, she couldn't help but wonder how they were all faring now. Because no matter how much they'd distanced themselves from her, she still cared. That made her wonder if Strath was a good leader. Was he good to his people? The men of the camp appeared to respect him a great deal, which made her think he must be good to them. Good to their families.

The fact that he'd taken her prisoner and then treated her as anything but was enough to convince her he had a kind heart beneath his hardened exterior. And he'd not been the one to set those fires. A tear slipped over her cheek. She swiped it away and curled into the plaid he'd given her to sleep in on the wooded floor.

Oh, Father, what have you done?

As she drifted into a fitful sleep, she thought how the happiest she'd been in a long time was lying beneath the stars surrounded by men she should hate.

There'd been no sign of Belfinch following as yet, but Strath had told her the man would need a few days convalescence from the gash on his head. There was also the fact that Belfinch had no idea where to look for her. That notion gave her comfort. While she worried over her father's safety—the last tie she had to her mother—she hoped Lord Belfinch had been gobbled up by the devil himself. Maybe her father had found the strength to stand up to Belfinch after she'd been taken. Then it wouldn't be that blackguard coming after her, but her father, intent on apologizing for all the wrongs of the past two years.

Strath woke her with a gentle shake of her shoulder just before the sun set to continue on their journey. She jolted upright, almost crashing her head against his. When had she fallen asleep?

"Whoa, lassie, 'tis all right."

She laughed. "I'm sorry. I must have been in a deep sleep."

"Ye were mumbling."

"What did I say?" She stretched the kinks from her body, feeling the ache of so many hours on horseback and sleeping on the ground.

"Nothing that I could make out, but ye did seem quite concerned."

Eva wiped at her eyes and blew out a breath. "I'm worried about... everything. Even my father."

Strath frowned, and even though she tried to read the expression, she came up empty.

"I know he is your enemy, but he is still my sire. Despite all he's done, I can't forget that. I owe him loyalty." She hoped to appeal to his own relationship with his father, and it seemed to work, because his frown ebbed a little.

"I understand, my lady."

"I hope you know he is not as bad as Belfinch."

Strath gave a curt nod. "I believe ye."

"You do?" She was a bit surprised to hear it.

"Aye. I wish ye could tell me more about their connection."

Eva moved to her knees, inching closer and pressing her hands over her heart. "If I knew more, I would."

Strath regarded her with warrior's eyes, but she wasn't afraid; rather, she tried to open herself up and let him see she was indeed telling the truth. He nodded, though the frown didn't quite leave his face, and then he changed the subject. "Tonight, we ride to Glasgow Castle."

"Glasgow?" Her heart skipped a beat. "Will they let us in?" What she really meant was would they let *her* in?

"Aye." He winked. "Laird Montgomery is my uncle."

"Ah, then you would know." She smiled, though questions still whirled in her mind. "He is your father's brother?"

"Nay, he is married to my father's sister, Lorna."

A Scottish lady... Oh, how she hoped the woman wouldn't judge her based on her English blood alone.

They finished packing up the camp, and she waited for Strath to mount the warhorse and pull her up onto his lap. She'd gotten very used to riding this way, to the warmth of his body behind her, the strength of him, and how safe she felt.

"Will your uncle give me a horse?" she asked, not because she desperately wanted one; quite the opposite, in fact.

"Aye." Was it just her, or did he sound just as disappointed as she was?

"You're not afraid I will ride away?"

"With the way ye sleep while riding?" He chuckled. "I'm thinking ye'll not get far afore ye fall off."

Eva laughed and playfully pinched at his forearm where he held her around the middle. "You're only saying that because you want me on your lap." She bit her lip when she realized just what she'd said. Who was this brazen woman she'd become?

Over the past couple of days, they'd grown a lot more comfortable with each other. While the sense of prisoner versus captor had never been very strong between them beyond that first night, it had now all but disappeared. One day, she hoped to repay the kindness he'd given her by taking her away. If only she could figure out just how to do that.

Strath urged his horse out onto the road, his lips brushing the shell of her ear. "What's wrong with that?"

A shiver of excitement raced through her, a tightening in her breasts and a warming in her core. Never before had a man elicited that kind of a response from her. And she found she liked it. With it, an intense desire to kiss him assaulted her. Longing warred inside her with propriety, causing her to question her own morals. Was there a question on morals when it came to attraction? Desire between a man and woman wasn't a sin in itself. Only if acted upon in a way that brought shame to one's self.

Well, Eva wasn't ashamed. So what was wrong with these feelings? What was wrong with him wanting her on his lap?

"Everything." She hadn't meant to say it out loud, but it came out in a breathy whoosh all the same.

Fortunately, he seemed to think that was funny, and he laughed and tucked her closer against him.

The sun set as they rode, and even though she'd napped throughout the day, Eva found herself drifting comfortably off to sleep once more.

She slept hard but fitfully, dreaming of home, fearing for her father's safety. If only there was a way to find out if he was all right. What might Belfinch do to him? Drag him to Scotland? Lock him away? Worse?

A gentle stroke along her jawline and a pinch on her nose woke her fully. Eva sneezed violently. Not once, nor twice, but three times.

"Always in threes," Strath murmured, then laughed and handed her a strip of linen.

She nodded, using the linen. "Aye. Why did you wake me?"

"See there?" The shadow of his arm lifted as he pointed toward twinkling lights in the distance that broke through the darkness of night. "Glasgow."

"We're nearly there." The vast spread of lights showed the city was large in comparison to any she'd seen before.

"Aye. Before this night is through, ye'll be able to sleep in a real bed."

"That will be divine. It is a grand city."

"Mhmm. One of the reasons the English have come to take it over the years. Stirling Castle, just a day's ride north of here, has seen many battles. My father was at the battle for Stirling Bridge. In fact, 'tis where he met my mother."

Eva perked up, interested to learn about his past. "What was she doing there?"

"She'd come to marry the English lord who'd taken it over. That day, my father and his men took the castle, and he stole my mother away."

Eva couldn't help but see how their two stories paralleled.

"And what happened?"

"He married my mother to keep her safe, but theirs has always been a marriage of love."

"From the beginning?"

"I think partly. She teases him about how terrifying he was, but my father has never been anything less than sweet to her."

Eva smiled, loving a good romance. "I'm glad they found one another."

"As am I," he chuckled, "else I wouldna be here."

"And neither would I." She bit her lip.

"I'm sorry, lass, for having taken ye away from your home. Your family."

An apology from him was the last thing she'd expected. "Thank you for that." She chewed her lip, recalling what she'd been thinking about the day before. "And thank you for interrupting the wedding. I know you didn't come for me or to put a stop to it, but I must express my gratitude all the same."

He was silent a long time, and Eva could hear her heart pounding; even the sound of her breath seemed loud.

"I would not wish that bastard on anyone, my lady. And especially not ye."

His words, spoken with such depth, touched her. They were not meaningless. And that was the part that really got her. To truly mean the words was different.

"Why not me?" she couldn't help but ask.

"Ye're special, Lady Eva. Anyone can see that. And ye were raised with a spirit that inspires. Not like some of the lassies I've met, and certainly none of the statue-like English wenches I've come across. A man like Belfinch would have broken ye."

Heavens, how well he knew her. And yet, he didn't know she was part Scots. The fact that he'd come to those conclusions believing her to be full English warmed her heart. How she admired him all the more. "You are right, he would have."

"And not that I've a right to say it, but I will besides, your father should nae have aligned himself with the man."

"He had no choice." She left it at that.

Perhaps sensing she no longer wanted to speak on the topic, Strath asked, "Have ye never seen a village larger than Northwyck?"

Eva shook her head. "My sister lives near London, but I've never visited her."

"Is she happy there?"

Eva cocked her head, thinking it an odd question. Men did not often ask if a woman was happy. "She wasn't at first, but she and her husband have...found a pattern."

They rode on a few more moments in silence, and then he asked, "Have they any children?"

"Not yet. There was one, but she lost him mid-way." Eva's heart broke for her sister and what she'd had to go through. There were plenty of parents who lost children, and plenty of them who expected it, but it was still a heavy blow to one's soul.

"Ah. I'm sorry for that." He tightened his arm around her as though he would protect her from the pain.

"So was I. My sister came home to grieve. I think the stress of being so far away from everything she knew had something to do with it."

"Perhaps. Sometimes things happen for reasons beyond our control. She was lucky to have ye there to help her."

"I am lucky to have her. And you're right, I suppose. Although sometimes I cannot help but wonder what those reasons are."

"We are all often left with questions in life, aye?"

"Aye."

A sound up ahead had them all pausing. But the noise turned out to be a herd of deer crossing over their path. They continued riding on in silence, and Eva wondered if Strath's mission to fight Belfinch could be put under that same adage of everything happening for a reason? Things did happen for a reason sometimes. And the Laird of Dornoch traveling weeks from the north of Scotland all the way to Northwyck was starting to feel like the best thing that had happened to her since before her mother passed.

A fierce gust of wind blew chilly air down the front of her gown, cooling the necklace that was still buried in her bodice. A sign from her mother perhaps? Eva smiled into the dark. They soon came to the village edge and were greeted by the night watchman who recognized Strath and opened the gates for them.

The roads to the castle were empty of people, and many of the lights in the village houses, taverns, and shops were extinguished, though the torches on the wall were well lit, allowing them to see the path as they went. A dog barked from somewhere, answered by another hound a short distance away, and the warhorse's ears flicked back and forth.

A tingle of nerves slid along Eva's skin. Being in the woods with a dozen Scots was quite a bit different than being inside a fortress with hundreds of them. What would happen if one of them turned on her? What would happen if Strath couldn't protect her? She tried to calm these thoughts, to push them aside. But it was a hard thing to do when she knew she had no control over her own situation, other than how she reacted, which she vowed would be peaceful and also true to herself.

"Are ye all right?" Strath asked softly.

Eva let out a long breath, trying to understand how he knew her so well, even guessing how she felt by her body language. "Just a bit nervous."

"Dinna fash, Princess. All will be well."

She prayed he was right.

They crossed through a stone arch with its portcullis raised and doors open, and entered a bailey. Tomaidh leapt from his horse to rouse the stable master, who came out with several lads to take their tired mounts. The poor beasts deserved a rest. Strath swung down from the horse behind her, then reached up and grasped her around the waist. Just the touch of his fingers around her middle had her body humming in pleasure. As he pulled her down, their bodies slid momentarily together, torso to torso. He held her aloft a moment longer than necessary before setting her feet on the ground, and she didn't mind. In fact, she wouldn't have minded if he kept her like that a little longer. Their eyes locked, and her heart skipped a beat. Did he have any idea how being so close to him affected her?

For the briefest of moments, she thought he might kiss her. His gaze slid to her mouth, and her heart pounded so loud in her ears she felt like the world around them disappeared. Nervously, she licked her lip, flicking her own gaze from his mouth to his eyes, silently begging for him to please, kiss her.

Strath tilted forward, dipping his head a fraction of an inch, and she clutched to his shirt, sucking in a heady breath.

"How long will ye be staying, my laird? Want to make sure I put the horses in the right places." The interruption by the stable master had them pulling apart, suddenly aware of where they were.

Strath cleared his throat and ran a hand through his hair. Eva kept her gaze on his boots, counting the speckles of mud on the leather. Heat flushed her cheeks and laid a path down her neck to her chest. Goodness, had she really been about to kiss him in front of all these people?

Indeed she was. And the way her skin tingled, she suspected if he turned back to her and grasped her around the waist again, she still would.

"A few days," Strath answered, his voice more gravelly than normal. The very sound of it stroked the wanton part of her that still wanted to be kissed.

"Right, then. We'll take good care of the beasts." The stable master took hold of the reins of Strath's warhorse and led him away.

A few days... That sounded like a true respite to Eva. Almost too good to be true. Stopping for only a few hours at a time over the last week had left her quite weary, and clearly addle-headed with all these thoughts of kissing. But staying so long, wouldn't that allow time for Belfinch to catch up? As smart and prepared as Strath was, she had to trust that he knew best.

Strath took her elbow gently, and she suppressed a shudder of pleasure at his touch. He slid his hand down her forearm, grazing his palm along and wrapping his fingers around hers. They were holding hands. A move that was both intimate and natural. Oh, saints above, save her...

"Let us go in. My uncle should still be awake, as he normally doesna sleep until the wee hours."

Before they even reached the stairs to the keep, the doors were thrown open and a man perhaps twice Strath's age came out with a large smile on his face. Black hair streaked with gray hung around his shoulders. He was about the same height as Strath, with a shadow of a beard on his jaw.

"Uncle Jamie." Strath marched toward the man, tugging Eva with him.

Her knees trembled, knocking together as they went. Was this the point at which she'd turn from whatever she was to Strath into a prisoner? Her palms grew slick, and thankfully, Strath let her go before he could feel the moisture.

He embraced his uncle, and they patted each other on the back, talking at the same time and over each other. If she weren't so nervous, she might have actually smiled at their warmth and obvious pleasure at seeing one another. Instead, she wiped her sweaty palms against her gown and told herself to get a handle on her nerves.

"What brings ye to Glasgow?" Uncle Jamie eyed Eva over Strath's shoulder with open curiosity. "And with a lovely guest, no less. Ye didna get married without telling me, did ye?"

Eva was thankful for the dark, because her face flamed red at the suggestion. Married? Was that what he truly thought? Perhaps he'd spied them out the window about to kiss. The idea of marrying Strath...of being bound to his side for the rest of her life... Her mouth went dry, and this time when her heart skipped a beat, she felt it all the way to her toes. Marry Strath... Saints, but it would be heaven compared to being married to Belfinch. She stared at his profile, the long line of his nose, the strength of his jaw, and the high arch of his cheek. He was without a doubt the most handsome of men. Strong and kind and caring. She would be proud to call him her husband.

Strath let out a short laugh and then cleared his throat, breaking whatever spell she'd just been under and popping the bubble of her unrealistic dream. Why would she ever think he could marry her? She was a lowly English traitor in his eyes, no matter how much he flirted with her.

"Nay, not married," Strath sad. "'Tis a bit complicated."

"Well, she looks sweeter than that last wench ye were betrothed to."

He was betrothed before? Eva shot Strath a glance. He'd not mentioned it when she'd asked before if he was married. What had happened? Was it painful? At the shadows that crossed his eyes and the way his jaw tightened, she supposed it was. But that momentary reaction was quickly replaced with something she'd seen often in him —humor. He made jests of things that he found too serious or disconcerting.

"Aye. A goat would be better," Strath answered with a chuckle.

Eva tried not to be offended at that, muttering, "I'm better than a goat."

The men must have heard her, because Uncle Jamie stopped in his tracks, turned around, and held out his hand. "Apologies, my lady, I did not mean to offend. Ye are without a doubt much better than a goat."

Eva's lip quivered as she tried to hold in a laugh. "But am I better than a horse?" she teased, gifting him her hand.

"Och! Ye brought us a *Sassenach* with a sense of humor." Jamie burst out laughing, kissed the back of her hand, and tugged her into his side, all but knocking Strath out of the way. A flash of what could only be jealousy crossed her companion's face. "Come inside, and I'll get ye a bite to eat. My lady wife will be pleased to meet ye. She only has one daughter and the rest sons. The more women on her side to boss us men about the better."

Eva's eyes widened, and she stopped short. She had to explain her situation. That she wasn't a guest, else he become angry when he found out the truth. "I do not think you understand. I'm—"

Strath was there then, taking her elbow and giving a subtle shake of his head. "Lass, ye dinna want to deny my aunt the pleasure of your company do ye?"

Eva took a step back. Did he not want his uncle to know what her role was? Why she was here... Confusion warred inside her, along with it a deep longing to go along with his plan.

Eva licked her lips nervously. "It seems only fair to share—"

Again, Strath cut her off. "Aye, share her company. Let us go inside. Your hands are freezing, and the temperature is only dropping."

Unsure of why he was hiding her situation, and taking note that Jamie was now eyeing them with suspicion, Eva flashed the older man a brilliant smile. If she could simply be herself and not be the labeled prisoner of war she was, she would gladly do so. "I am getting a bit chilled."

Uncle Jamie laughed at that. "Ye *Sassenachs* may not all be alike, but the lot of ye canna handle Scottish weather."

If only he knew she was part Scots, he might be interested to know that not all of their breeding were immune to the cold.

He led the way inside. While the houses they'd passed in the village were dark, the castle was lit up as though they were expecting a caravan of guests for a feast. Candles dripped from iron chandeliers and carefully placed candelabras, and torches were mounted on the stone walls.

A fire blazed in a massive hearth. The scent of herb-strewn rushes and flowers filled the great hall of Glasgow Castle, and indeed there were filled vases lining two tables and propped on the mantle—a feminine touch to the starkly masculine room. Tapestries of great battles covered the walls, along with mounted heads of massive bucks, a bear, and a few wolves. Weapons were anchored in the stone as decorations, but also as a reminder that war was never far off.

"Frances," Jamie called. "Bring food and drink for my guests."

A harried-looking older woman appeared in the doorway from the kitchens. She emerged as though she'd been roused from her bed, and Eva felt immediately guilty.

Without thinking, she rushed forward. "Allow me to help you."

Frances gaped at her, and Eva wasn't certain if it was because she was English or because she'd offered to help. The woman didn't respond and looked to Jamie for an answer. Jamie, in turn, looked to Strath, who nodded. Eva followed the woman to the kitchens, glad to be found useful—and glad to be away from Strath and the strong pull to touch him, to admire him. She needed space to breathe, to think.

In the kitchen, sleepy scullions and spit-boys had risen and were in the process of preparing what looked to be a feast. Eva's guilt grew ten-fold.

"Oh, I do hope you don't mind me saying so, but the men would be happy with something simple. No need to go to too much trouble. Some bread, cheese, cold meat if you have it."

"Aye. Are ye certain?"

Eva nodded confidently. "I've been cooking them stew on the road with game and wild vegetables, and before that they were existing on dried venison and bannocks. They'll be very happy indeed. Besides, it will be quicker, and then you all can go back to sleep. I must extend my apologies for waking you."

The cook eyed her as though she'd grown two heads. Indeed, it was her position to prepare meals and serve her laird, but Eva had always found that common courtesy went a long way with those at her father's household.

Finally, Frances agreed. She waved to two young women, who quickly put some rising dough into an oven to bake.

"What can I do to help?" Eva asked.

"Nothing, my lady."

"Please, I want to be of use."

Again, Frances eyed her as though it were a test, but then her shoulders seemed to relax, "If ye want to gather the cheese and make a platter, I'll prepare a trencher of cold meats."

Eva went to work, cutting slices of cheese and arranging them on a large trencher, her mouth watering. It had only been a week or so since they'd left Northwyck, and before now, she'd never realized how much she actually liked cheese. She took a tiny nibble, savoring the creamy, sharp flavor. Saints, but the taste left her weak with pleasure.

Lads were already funneling out of the kitchen with empty trenchers, cutlery, mugs, and ale for the men. When she finished the cheese platter, Frances wouldn't allow her to do anything else but sit by the hearth and drink a cup of wine while breathing in the heady scent of the baking bread. By the time the bread was finished baking, Frances had assembled several platters of cold mutton, cold chicken, strips of venison, stewed fruit, and cold peas covered in melted butter. The wine had warmed her insides and made her feel more...alive somehow. Excited. And the scent of the food made her heady with hunger.

Eva liked that Strath had not told them she was essentially his captive, because it felt like she belonged here. Or that she was playing a part she was comfortable with. Home had been so cold over the last two years since her mother died and her sister moved away. Many of the servants who had a choice had left in the recent year because of her father's new taxing laws and treatment. And those that remained were standoffish with Eva for the same reasons. The offenses of her father had indeed trickled down to her, however unfair that was. To make matters worse, her father had been so distant with her too, that Eva hadn't realized until now how very lonely she'd been.

"Are ye nae hungry?"

Eva snapped up her gaze to see Frances staring at her expectantly, waving toward the door leading toward the great hall.

"Oh, aye, I am."

"Let us go. The lads have already taken everything out."

Frances waved Eva out of the kitchen before her, and the first thing she saw was Strath standing before the hearth as though he'd been waiting for her to come back. His gaze raked hungrily over her and heightened the tingles she'd been able to bank while away from him. She swallowed, fearing that her own desire was reflected back at him. If there were no one else in the room, would she walk right up to him and run her hands through his hair, tugging him down for a kiss?

Oh my...where did that idea come from?

Mild embarrassment washed over her at how closely he watched, and then more when she caught sight of his uncle elbowing him in the ribs and muttering some jest that made Strath laugh. Heat covered her cheeks, and she tried to hide a smile.

The next thing she knew, two women were rushing toward her, arms outstretched. It wasn't hard to guess that one was Jamie's wife and the other their daughter, for they looked very much alike and dressed as she'd expected ladies would. They both had silky blond hair fashioned into long plaits down their backs, and eyes the same blue-green she imagined the sea to be.

"Welcome to Glasgow," the older woman said. "I'm Lady Montgomery, but ye must simply call me Lorna."

"Thank you for the warm welcome. Please, call me Eva."

"This is my daughter, Isobel, and we welcome ye to the castle. I didna realize ye were in the kitchens."

"I didn't mean to step on your toes, but I really wanted to help."

Lorna laughed. "I'm surprised Frances allowed it. She is constantly shooing me out of her kitchen."

"She tried," Eva said with a smile.

"Eva," Isobel gushed. "'Tis not often we have lady guests being so far from our family, ye must sit by me."

"I am happy to join your ranks, but I must apologize if we woke you."

"Och, nay, we love a surprise."

The ladies each took one of her hands and led her to the table where they quickly surrounded her. Eva glanced over her shoulder to see that Strath was following her with his gaze.

"So tell us, how did ye meet my cousin," Isobel said.

"'Tis a rather interesting story, really. Long and complicated." Eva stared toward Strath, who was walking across the great hall with his uncle and some other men closer to his age she'd not seen before, who must be his cousins.

He sat across from her at the table, his foot nudging hers underneath. "What is long and complicated?"

Eva bit the inside of her cheek. She was unable to pull her foot away and wanted to nudge him back but didn't dare in case it had been an accident. Warmth flowed from that spot, all the way up to her core, and she fidgeted with her cuff to distract herself.

"The story of how ye met," Lorna filled in.

"Ah, aye, 'tis." He winked at her.

"Why don't you tell it?" Eva challenged him.

Strath's eyes sparkled with mirth as if to say, *I deserve that*. "All right then, I shall share it."

"Please, do." Eva poured him a cup of wine and they all served themselves from the trenchers.

"The long and complicated part of the story is that the Bruce sent me to England. The interesting part is that while there, I came across a lass in need of saving."

"Oh, that's so romantic," Isobel said, pressing her hands to her heart and glancing over at Eva with fascination.

Is that how he saw it? That he was saving her? Because that is exactly how it felt. And heaven help her, she'd let him save her every day for the rest of her life, even if he laughed at the idea of marrying her. That was how she knew for certain she was in trouble of falling hard.

"Why was she in need of saving?" Jamie asked.

Eva sat just as captivated but also a little scared. Was he going to tell them she'd been about to wed Belfinch?

"An evil bastard had dragged her to the aisle and was preparing to force his will upon her by claiming her as his bride." He glanced at her, his grin widening. "And she begged me to take her away from the land of heathens. So here we are."

Eva nearly choked on a bite of cheese at that last part. The land of heathens? That's what she'd called Scotland, and now he'd turned it around and called England thusly. Oh, the rascal...

"Well, 'tis good to see ye've been able to find love once more," Lorna said to Strath.

Now it was Strath's turn to choke. Tomaidh gave him a hard slap on his back and winked at Eva.

Love... Nay, it wasn't that. Not quite... Was it?

Isobel leaned close. "Ye're much better than his last betrothed." There was a murmur of agreement among those at the table.

"We're not betrothed," Eva tried to explain, her voice sounding breathy at even the thought of love and marriage all mixed up with her name and his.

"Not officially," Isobel said.

"Nay, not at all," she insisted.

At that, the table went quiet as everyone stared at Strath.

"Ye canna be serious," Jamie said, hard eyes on his nephew. "Ye'd best not be taking advantage of Lady Eva, lad."

"I promise ye, on the contrary," Strath said. "I've made it verra clear that she's not to take advantage of me."

Chapter Nine

Strath was in trouble.

He knew it the moment he watched his uncle kiss Eva's hand when they'd entered the castle. Perhaps he'd known it before then, too, when he'd nearly kissed her in the bailey. The feel of her warm body against his, the look of passion and courage in her eyes, the little flick of her tempting tongue as she tried to regain her sense.

The stable master interrupting had been irritating but necessary, and when she'd disappeared in the kitchens, he'd hoped the time away would give him a chance to cool down, a chance to get his head back in the right place.

But it hadn't been enough. In fact, the separation had only heightened his awareness of her. Everybody that ducked beneath the kitchen doorway had his anticipation perking to see if it was her, and then plummeting when he realized it wasn't.

There had never been another woman that had captivated him the way Eva did. Which made his interest in her dangerous. He'd learned the hard way with Jean what it meant to completely trust a woman. But this wasn't just simple desire. This was something compounded and infinitely more complicated.

And so he'd devised a test, one he was certain she would fail.

When he'd recklessly tapped his foot against hers under the table, he'd expected her to pull away. If not for propriety's sake, but because she thought it was an accident. But she'd not. Their feet had remained touching for the entire meal. Their gazes had met over the table, and the sensual tension between the two of them could not have been severed even with the sharpest of swords. His entire body was on fire.

And when she'd played along with his jest about not taking advantage of him, he'd wanted to swipe the table of its contents, reach across, and kiss her. The desire to do so had been swift and intense, and it had taken every ounce of willpower he had to finish their meal and not do just that. Not lay claim to her. Not crush her to him and ravish her.

The meal lasted another tortuous hour or so, and it was now well and truly the middle of the night. Thankfully, Lorna and Isobel showed Eva upstairs to a chamber, his aunt pausing to give him the eye when he automatically followed. What was he about to do? Tuck the lass into bed? He'd grown so accustomed to sleeping beside her he'd followed without a thought. Dammit!

Instead, he whirled around and followed his uncle to his study. Despite being exhausted, it was imperative they speak before he sank into a mattress. And Lord knew, he needed the distraction.

"Whisky?" Uncle Jamie asked.

"Aye."

He poured them each a dram while Strath went to the window and peeled back a corner of the skin that covered it to peer outside. Nothing seemed amiss. Men walked the wall, the roads were still deserted. There were no unusual sounds. Even the weather appeared to be cooperating.

Jamie handed him the cup, and they clinked them together, each saying, "*Sláinte*," before they swallowed the contents.

Strath relished the burn of spirits sliding down his throat. But one dram didn't dull the buzzing in his veins, nor the restless energy he felt.

"Another?" his uncle asked.

Hell aye, he wanted another. But drinking himself into oblivion wouldn't help. In fact, it might make it worse. It might make the idea of finding out where Eva's bedchamber was make sense. And if he made it that far, kissing her was a definite. So in spite of his desire for another, he declined. "Nay, I thank ye."

Jamie raised a brow but said nothing. He took Strath's empty cup and set them both on the sideboard, then leaned against it and crossed his arms over his chest. "Tell me, lad, what has brought ye to Montgomery lands?"

"We've been traveling over a week from the north of England, Northwyck." He told his uncle of the Bruce's order for him to find and contain Belfinch and what had happened when he'd arrived. How the lady had offered herself up in her father's place. But kept to himself the king's directive to find out about her. He showed his uncle the key he'd taken from Belfinch and they both speculated on what it could be for, each of them determining it had to be for some sort of treasury.

"Belfinch is the bastard who was forcing Lady Eva to wed?"

"Aye." Strath shook his head. This was going to be the hard part. "Turns out her father has been funding Belfinch's dealings. I'm not certain of their arrangement, but from what I gather, it appears that Northwyck may have been coerced somehow."

Jamie gritted his teeth. "Even still, ye've no proof of that for certain. Can she be trusted?"

Strath rubbed at the tension in the back of his neck. "Aye. She's a good lass with a big heart, and when I told her some of what Belfinch had been up to with her father's coin, she was devastated."

"She does seem to be a sweet lass. And I'd never have guessed that she was at all connected to anyone such as Belfinch. She reminds me of your aunt." A nostalgic smile crossed his face.

"Which part? Her willfulness?"

Jamie chuckled. "The sweetness, too."

An image of Eva flashed before Strath's mind. God, how he wanted to protect her. "Aye. She would have been crushed under that whoreson's boot. And I think part of her nature was already stifled by her father's dealings."

"How much of it did she know?"

"Not much. Nothing more than what I've told ye. I am under the impression her father was keeping a lot from her."

"That wouldna be unusual. Isobel doesna know much of what I deal with behind closed doors."

"Aye. And from what I gather, she wouldna have approved."

"Explain."

"The lass was overwhelmed, brought to tears when I made her see one of the burned out villages. She may be English, but she cares for all people. She also mentioned she used to take great care of those in her own village, even when they started to distance themselves from her."

"Aye. So what are ye going to do?"

"Belfinch should be traveling north by now, to Dornoch. And I intend to meet him there with my army."

"We'll keep an eye out for him here as he crosses. But what if he doesna make it all the way?"

"Ye mean, what if he's attacked on the road?"

"Aye. We can arrange that to happen, if ye like. Happens to bastards all the time." Jamie winked.

"While ordinarily I'd join ye in seeing his blood run into the earth, I dinna know how many men he'll be traveling with. Additionally, his fighting tactics will not be fair. Best if your scouts can send word north when he passes. I'd not want ye to be involved should it turn ugly."

"Have no doubt, lad, it will be ugly. Ye want him to go that far north? Are ye not worried about any damage he might cause on the way?"

"I am hoping he will stick to our bargain. That her father will reason with the man and keep him in line."

Jamie shook his head. "I think counting on a man as vile as ye say he is will prove to be a problem. As of yet, her father has done nothing."

Strath nodded, irritated, even though he knew his uncle was right. This mission had been risky from the beginning. Changing tactics midway had not been the best idea, though he had the best of intentions. It reminded him of another time altogether.

Negative thoughts came crashing into him swiftly. This was the second time in less than a year that he'd led danger to his family's doorstep, albeit unknowingly the first time.

Both times a woman had been involved.

"I canna ask ye to join in my mission, uncle. To endanger yourself and your men." He gritted his teeth. "But ye are right. I canna allow him to go farther north. Will ye keep the lass safe while I take my men to meet Belfinch on the road?"

Jamie shook his head. "Strath, ye're like a son to me. Lorna would have my head if I agreed."

Disappointment flooded Strath's veins. "I see. I'll send Eva with an escort north to my castle in Dornoch and leave at once with my men. Forgive me for bringing danger here."

Jamie narrowed his eyes. "Ye misunderstand. I canna allow ye to go off and find this bastard, and most certainly not alone. I invite ye to stay here. To give him time to come to us. We'll send out scouts. Maybe even leave him clues to come this way. Either way, the bastard will not be a problem long. And then when it is over, ye can take the lass north to Dornoch yourself."

Take Eva north after dealing with Belfinch? Was that even possible? But he wasn't going to argue with his uncle about it now. When the time came, he'd explain that despite what it appeared, Eva was not going to remain in Scotland. She had to go home to her own family, her people. Rebuild the life that her father had nearly destroyed and find a man stronger than himself to marry. But even the thought of her marrying someone else sent a hot wave of jealousy through his gut.

He cleared his throat. "Thank ye. I will owe ye much."

Jamie clasped his hand on Strath's shoulder. "Ye will owe *me* nothing. But ye will owe the lass your honor."

"What?"

"Marry her."

Strath shook his head. "I'm nae certain she'll have me."

Jamie chuckled. "Dinna be blind to what's in front of ye. Or to the truth."

"Mayhap there is a better man out there for her than me." Strath shrugged, uncertain how to explain to his uncle that he couldn't very well marry the woman when she might be an enemy to Scotland.

"Aye, 'haps. But ye know what? What could be better than a man who will love her as much as ye will? One who will protect her with their life? Can ye say there is another man out there who would be more willing to spend the rest of his days proving that to her as much as ye would? If ye can answer aye, then ye're right, she is not the one. The love of a good woman is a special gift. One worth fighting for."

Strath ran a hand through his hair. If he were so lucky as to be connected to a woman like her, he would indeed show her every day for the rest of their lives that he was deserving of her. And nay, he didn't believe there was anyone else out there good enough for her, not even himself, but he'd be damned if he would ever let her down.

"Ye know who told me that?" Jamie asked, refilling their cups with whisky.

"Who?"

He chuckled. "Your da."

Strath drank to that. "He's a wise man."

"Aye. And he believes in ye. Dinna forget it."

"I have disappointed him much lately."

"Only in your own eyes. If ye're speaking about your betrothal, and the eh...incident...dinna fash. He never blamed ye."

"I could have stopped the attack from even happening, or at least been there to help fight off the men."

Strath thought back on all that had happened. The clues he'd just been too stubborn or too stupid to see. Or perhaps he had and that was why he'd insisted on the one year handfast before pledging themselves fully in matrimony. The lack of emotion in Jean's eyes whenever he lay with her had been a sign. The overly friendly way she behaved with her personal guard. Luckily, the incident hadn't caused his people at Dornoch to lose respect, nor his father's men at Sutherland.

Jamie shrugged. "Mayhap. Mayhap not. No one would have believed the Guinn capable of attacking your father, and he did, proving their alliance was not a strong one. The truth came out, showed your father who he could trust."

His uncle had a point there. "'Haps."

"In any case, there is no use in worrying over it. Ye're a great warrior. A great man. And worthy of respect. Your people trust ye, and so does your da. Your whole family. Mistakes happen. But I tell ye what, King Robert would not have sent ye on a mission if he didna trust that ye could complete it."

"I appreciate that."

"Believe it."

Strath nodded. "I will."

"Good. Now, let us prepare for Belfinch's arrival. The sooner we deal with this bastard, the sooner ye can tell the lass ye love her."

"I dinna..." His voice trailed off, because even as he was denying it, Strath knew it for a fact—he *did* love her.

Holy shite.

He loved her.

If there'd been time to lose his mind over that realization, he would have, but instead, he had to concentrate. And so thoughts of Eva and love had to be put aside.

They worked into the night, rousing the steward, Tomaidh, and Jamie's master of the gate to make lists and plans. When the sun rose on the horizon, they slept for a few hours, but only after sending out scouts to spot Belfinch and leave clues as to where he should head. This had involved convincing a maid to go into Eva's room while she slept to take out her gown, which was then torn into pieces to be left scattered along the road. A trail of fine wool would lead straight to Glasgow Castle.

The trap was set, now Belfinch just needed to fall into it.

A BANGING on his door had Strath sitting upright in bed, the cobwebs of sleep instantly clear. Having slept fully dressed in case this happened, he rushed to the door and tugged it open, prepared to hear the battle was soon to begin.

But instead, he was met by an incensed Eva, arms crossed over her breasts, made more visible by the impossibly ill-fitting gown she wore that looked to be that of a servant's. "What have you done with my gown?"

"What?" He raked his gaze over her form and his body instantly hardened. With an arm overhead on the doorframe, he leaned against it casually, trying hard not to grin too much like fool.

"Don't play dumb with me, you heathen. The maid told me you

stole it. Was your purpose to have me parade around in my chemise all day, or to keep me locked in my chamber?" Her hands flew to her hips, and she pursed her lips as though she were preparing to give him a tongue lashing—and not the kind he preferred.

A night of sleep had not lessened his desire for her. Strath perused her form, wishing she were indeed wearing only a chemise. A well-worn one that allowed him to see just the faintest outline of what he was certain were flawless, creamy curves. Dark curls at the apex of her thighs—or nay, they'd be light. Golden as the hair on her head and just as fine.

Ballocks—he was growing hard as stone.

Trying to distract his growing desire, he cleared his throat and asked, "Where did ye get that getup?"

She opened her mouth and then shut it again, looking perplexed, as though she'd not been prepared for his question. "My maid. In her distress at having allowed you to steal my own, she let me borrow it."

"It fits ye...well."

That was an exaggeration. The fabric clung to her breasts, which were bigger than the maid's, but pooled around her feet, as she was obviously much shorter than the original wearer.

"Oh, please do not try to distract me with flatteries. It will not work. I'm irritated with you, and I don't find your jest to have been funny. Give me back my gown."

"I canna, and it was no jest, lass."

"What? Why? Explain."

"I dinna have it." He shrugged. That was the simple truth.

"Where is it?"

"Likely strewn about the Lowlands."

Indignation rippled across her features. "Strewn about the Lowlands? What the devil does that mean? Is this some form of torture?"

"Nay, nay." He wanted to reach for her, to pull her into his arms, and say he wasn't torturing her the way she was torturing him. Instead, he forced his arms to remain where they were and gave her a truthful explanation. "We tore it up, and I sent scouts about the land to leave it in specific places."

Her face flamed all the redder, eyes flashing with anger. "You're jesting with me." A tiny finger poked out from a too-long sleeve to jab at his chest, burning him in the spot.

"I assure ye, lass, I dinna jest." He caught her hand and flattened her palm to his chest.

"Why would you do such a thing? That is cruel."

At first, he thought she referred to where he held her hand over his heart, but even when he eased his grip, she didn't remove it, and he realized she was talking about the gown. "To lure Belfinch here."

"Lure him here? Why on earth would you lure him here...?" Her voice trailed off. "We are not leaving?"

He traced his thumb over her knuckles, finding he liked it all too much. He should let go. "We will eventually, but only when I have him in my custody."

"In your custody..." All the red drained from her face then, and she wavered on her feet.

Strath reached out to steady her just as her knees buckled.

"Will you use me as bait as you have used my clothes? Leave me lying naked in the field for him to find?"

"Nay, never, lass. I vowed to protect ye, and I meant it."

She clutched at him, fear flashing in her pinched, pale features. He hated seeing her like that.

"I don't want to... I can't..." She shook her head, fighting with her emotions. Her words. Him.

"I will never let any harm come to ye." His gaze fell to her lips. He wanted nothing more than to kiss her then. To put them both out of their misery. To forget why they were here. To at last claim her as his own.

But to do so when she was in this state was wrong. She needed to come to him of her own free will, for he'd already taken her against her will once when he'd taken her from her home. He would never do it again. Despite how much he wanted her. Despite the pounding in his heart that told him he would never be whole without her in his life for all time.

"He will have many men," she whispered. "He will not cease until you are dead."

"He canna hurt me, lass."

"He can do whatever he wants." Her voice was quiet but confident. "He has done whatever he wants before."

"Not when he is in chains. I will stop him. The world need never worry about Belfinch again."

"Will you kill him?" Widened eyes gazed at him in horror.

"Only if he forces me. I plan to give him over to my king, and perhaps his life can be exchanged for one of our own prisoners of war." His voice softened as he said those words, realizing she might consider herself to be that. "What—"

Strath couldn't continue, was unable to ask her what she wanted to do when Belfinch was detained. He didn't want to know her answer. Because right now, holding her against him felt like the best thing in the world, and to let go, to let her slip away, would be utter hell. Already, his chest hurt from the thought of it.

And yet, if that was what she wanted…

That was when he knew for certain it had to be true love. Because he was willing to let her go, even if it caused him pain.

"When he is captured…" Strath paused, afraid his voice would crack with the force of emotion running though him. He touched two fingers to her chin and tilted her face toward his. "Ye will be safe. Ye're not an enemy of Scotland."

The lass blinked up at him, a flicker of some deeper emotion in her eyes. Before he could identify what it was, and what it might mean, her eyelids dipped closed, and a tear fell unmistakable on her cheek.

She wiped it away and shook her head, avoiding his gaze. "Do you plan to give my father to the king?" There was no inflection in her tone. "And…me?"

Strath gave a subtle shake of his head. "I was not sent for your father." He couldn't bring himself to say aloud that he should be presenting her to his king. At first he was going to present her as a prisoner. A suspected enemy of the Scots, but now he knew differently.

Eva straightened and backed away from him. "And will you present me to the king in this maid's gown?" She held out her hands, running them through the air in front of her, and his gaze followed the movement.

He grinned slowly, teasing, incapable of not adding a little humor to the situation. The tension between them was so thick, he desired to lighten the mood. "While I wouldna mind ye remaining dressed like that just a wee bit longer, I wouldna dream of presenting ye to anyone with it so taut against your…" His gaze lingered on her breasts until she let out a huff and crossed her arms over her chest. Strath chuckled. "I jest with ye, lass. Your maid was supposed to have found ye a new gown, she must have forgotten as it was so late in the night. I will talk to my cousin, Isobel, and make certain ye have one of hers."

"Thank you."

"Ye needn't thank me, it should have been done already. I did not wish to cause ye distress."

Eva nodded, biting her lip. It seemed as though she wanted to say more, so he waited, memorizing the way her eyes looked with the sun filtering through his window.

"You have been so kind to me, my laird."

Strath blew out a breath, reaching forward to tuck an errant lock of hair behind her ear. He changed his mind and twirled it about his finger. "Ye need not address me as such when it is just us in private. And lass, ye deserve nothing less than kindness. Nothing less than happiness. I'm only sorry ye were tangled up in this mess as ye were, and that I did not meet ye under different circumstances."

Chapter Ten

Eva wanted to kiss him. Because everything he was saying sounded like goodbye, even if he didn't say it outright. And as confused as she was, there was one thing she was certain of. She didn't want this to be the end.

In the next few days, if not sooner, her father and Belfinch would be here. They would fight. They would lose. She knew that, even if Belfinch was too arrogant to believe it. The Scottish warriors were bigger, stronger, braver. They had more heart. And heart went a long way when it came to winning.

Was that not the reason why after so many years of war for their independence the Scots still got up every morning and fought? Was it not also why mothers and governesses told children the horror stories of the Scots, because in some part they were true? Only now, Eva knew there was another side to all of that.

She stared up into his stormy eyes, seeing a mixture of longing, pain, and determination. Determination to do what? Push her away?

His heart pounded beneath her hands, beating the same rhythmic tune as her own. No matter the words that came from his mouth, no matter that he implied he would be giving her over to his king. The truth was she had to find a way to stay with him, because she couldn't imagine it any other way. If she explained about her mother's family, about her desire to find out the truth behind her situation, he could help her. But there was more than that... she *wanted* to stay with *him*. Eva's chest swelled with unspoken emotion. Emotion she wasn't certain what to do with.

Despite what she saw in his eyes, what if he still rejected her?

They had been dancing along a path of uncertainty for days now. And all she knew was that if he was going to push her away, if he was going to give her up, then she was going to at least go after having kissed him. For if she did not, she might question for the rest of her days whether or not what she'd seen in his eyes was true. And how could she go the rest of her life not having felt his lips on hers?

Without hesitating any longer, Eva leaned up on her tiptoes and pressed her lips to his. At first, it seemed as though he were going to pull away, but then he snaked his strong arms around her back and pulled her tautly to his form. With decadent satisfaction, he kissed her back. He kissed her with all the passion and longing she'd seen in his eyes, with all the pent-up desire they'd both shared for days. Kissed her with heat and heart and left her body so filled with hope and happiness she thought she might burst. He teased the crease between her lips until she parted on a sigh, and he could slip his tongue inside. He was tender as he tasted her. Tender as he stroked her back, tugged on the length of her hair.

She clung to him, not wanting this kiss to end. Wanting to remember everything about it—about *him*. His scent of pine and spice. His taste of whisky and cinnamon. The feel of his warm, taut body against hers. The way his muscles rippled with every movement. Incredible. Decadent. Unforgettable.

She threaded her fingers in his hair, marveling at the way the softness tickled her palm, and tentatively stroked her tongue against his. At the low growl in his throat, she grew bolder, daring to swirl her tongue in a rhythmic fashion as old as time. Her body swayed into his. The whole world could have floated away for all she knew.

At last, this wondrous moment they had come to so many times...

Why had she waited so long? Everything would change now. And she was willing to give up any life in England just to remain here with him, to kiss him every day.

Someone cleared their throat behind them. Who could possibly want to interrupt such a perfect moment?

Strath stiffened, and sense returned to her brain.

Someone is *here*.

"Oh," she cried out, feeling heat rise to her face as she whipped around to see Tomaidh.

The warrior stared at his laird with raised brows. Thank heavens, he did not look at her at all, for she was certain she couldn't bear the humiliation of being caught in such a compromising position.

Strath eased her behind him in a protective gesture, stretching up his hand to grip the door near the top, but he didn't shut it.

"What is it?" Strath's voice was gravelly, tight.

"A scout has returned."

"I'll be right down."

Tomaidh left quickly, and Strath turned to face her. His lips were still a little wet, slightly swollen from the depth of their kiss, and she reached up to touch her own lips, sensing they must look the same. For a breath or two, he simply stared at her. Both of them were speechless. Was that regret in his eyes? Disappointment? Was it directed at her, or at their moment being interrupted?

She didn't regret what had just happened for a second, but she was positive she couldn't handle the rejection she felt certain was coming.

"We shall talk more later," he said, running a hand through his hair, and then stroking her cheek.

Oh, how she wanted to lean in to the tender gesture. Was that a sign he wasn't rejecting her? Or another way of saying goodbye?

Eva nodded, unsure of herself. She wanted to ask so many questions, to know if she'd pleased him, to tell him he'd pleased her. That she'd liked kissing him, and that...

But then he was tugging on his boots, and she stood there feeling a fool as he laced them up. When he was done, he let out a long breath and gazed at her in such a way she was certain she could see his thoughts. There was regret. There was trepidation. He rose from the chair, sauntered slowly forward. Again, he touched her cheek, looked as though he wanted to say something, but in the end, not a word left his lips. Instead, he gave a subtle shake of his head, let out a disappointed breath, and exited the chamber.

Eva was crushed.

Standing in the center of his room, she felt alone. Cold.

Fool.

Always the fool. Always putting her heart out there only to have it stomped on. Always seeming to be the last to know what was going on around her.

He'd not said anything, but he'd not had to. That look in his eyes had told her everything she needed to know.

Eva wrapped her arms around her middle, feeling vulnerable and disheartened. She'd put herself out there, given herself to Strath in that kiss in hopes that perhaps he might return the feelings.

There had been passion. There had been need and longing and deep emotion. She'd felt it. But no matter, he was not going to accept it.

Standing up straight, she smoothed out her hair, feeling ridiculous in the ill-fitting gown. What had she been thinking? She should have just waited for her maid to bring her one that fit. But she'd been so angry, so frustrated, she'd acted without thinking. And not once had she considered there'd be any consequences. And there hadn't been— not for wearing the maid's clothes. Nay, the only consequence had been a pleasurable kiss and a broken heart. And despite the pain cracking her ribs, she'd do it all over again.

She slipped from Strath's chamber, closed the door behind her, and made her way back to her room, which was on an upper level, praying she didn't meet anyone along the way. In her anger this morning, she'd not even considered the fact that she'd be marching in full view of everyone, wearing this ridiculous gown.

Luckily, she'd not met anyone on the way here and didn't come across anyone now. The maid waited patiently in Eva's chamber, and when Eva entered, she leapt to her feet.

"My lady." She pointed to the made bed and a beautiful gown the color of heather placed there. "Lady Isobel came by to see ye and left this. I hemmed the bottom so it willna drag."

Relief flooded Eva, and also a little guilt at having deprived Isobel of a beautiful gown. She'd make certain to thank her later. "I must express my apologies for taking your clothes. I was in a state, and it was unkind of me."

The maid shook her head and giggled. "'Twas the most excitement I've had all year. I'd do it again in a heartbeat."

Eva grinned. "I'm glad you enjoyed it."

"Did ye find out what he did with the gown?" The maid came forward and helped Eva undress.

"It's all over Scotland. Apparently, I'm to be used as bait."

"Oh." The maid frowned and looked away, not divulging whatever it was she'd wanted to say.

When the maid lifted the gown from the bed, Eva shook her head. "You dress first, please."

The young lady smiled and nodded. "Thank ye."

When she was done dressing, she helped Eva into the soft gown and then left. Not too long after, Lady Isobel came by to take her down to breakfast.

"Thank you so much for the gown."

"It looks lovely on ye."

"If there is any way I can repay you, please allow me. I feel bad that I've taken your clothes."

Isobel waved away her words. "Dinna feel bad. I have plenty, and the color of this one looks much better on ye than it did on me."

Eva smiled, smoothing her hand over the soft skirts. "Thank you."

"It was my pleasure. Are ye hungry? The men are meeting in my father's study, so my lady mother has set up breakfast in her salon, and we'd love for ye to join us."

"I would be delighted." And that was not an exaggeration. She longed for female companionship, and at the same time, it made her miss her sister all the more.

Since it had just been the two of them, and they were so close in age, Eva and Jacqueline had gotten along quite well. They had shared a chamber until Jacqueline was wed. And every night, they'd fall asleep telling each other stories. In the morning, they'd get ready for the day together, help each other with chores and their studies, knowing the sooner they were both done, the sooner they could explore.

Eva had begged to go with her sister when she married, but her father had forbidden it, saying that Jacqueline needed time to adjust to her new married life, that she needed to obey her husband, focus on his needs, and not those of her younger sister.

If she didn't know already, Jacqueline would be horrified when she found out what had happened. How Eva wished she could comfort her, tell her that all would be well.

Isobel linked her arm with Eva's and led the way up another flight of stairs and into the lady of the castle's salon, chattering all the way. The floor was strewn with rushes and tapestried carpets. Chairs and chaises with embroidered cushions were in the center of the room, and the walls were hung with soft wool drapes and tapestries.

In the corner, a harpist played soft music, and along one wall was a trestle table, not quite as long as those in the great hall, but still large enough to seat eight people easily, though at the moment it was only set for three.

"My lady," Eva said, ducking into a curtsy as Lady Lorna greeted her. "Your salon is beautiful and so welcoming."

"I'm glad ye could join us. 'Tis not often we have guests in here." Lady Lorna's eyes were bright with merriment, and it almost broke Eva's heart how welcoming they truly were.

Mostly everything she'd ever learned about the Scottish people was wrong.

"This is my mother's favorite room in the castle," Isobel said with delight. "And no lads allowed."

"Aye, a room for ladies only." The two of them laughed and gave each other a conspiratorial look that made Eva's heart ache for the loss of her own mother.

How would things have been different if her mother had not disappeared?

They led Eva to the table, and all three of them sat down. The harp music, soft candles, and sweet smells gave it an air of tranquility that calmed Eva's nerves.

A moment later, servants laid out platters of roasted ham with gravy and raisins, poached eggs, stewed fruit, and scones.

Eva's stomach rumbled. The aroma had her mouth watering, and she couldn't wait to taste each thing. "I've never seen a spread like this so early in the day."

"Well, we do love our breakfast," Lorna said, serving Eva and Isobel. "Truth be told, we love every meal."

"And you can barely tell. How do you keep your figure?" Eva slapped her hand over her mouth. "I should not have asked. Please accept my apologies."

Lorna waved away her apology with a laugh. "'Tis nothing. I enjoy daily exercise, mostly riding and walking."

"Oh, mother, ye are being modest now." Isobel took a gulp of milk. "Mother does tricks on her horse."

"Tricks?" Eva's eyes widened.

"Aye. She stands on them as they ride. Has even started to hang from the side upside down. My da is quite against it, but he still lets her do it." The way Isobel said it so casually, as though she were talking about her mother taking up sewing, made it seem so normal.

"That is incredible. I would love to see you do some tricks."

"Och, well, 'haps when the lads say it is safe to go outside, we can."

"Safe to go outside?" Eva paused in buttering a scone.

"Aye. The scouts have returned with news that they've spotted the English. Though they are nae close yet, it will only be a matter of days before they are upon us."

Eva's appetite fled. If the English had been spotted and a scout believed it would not be too long until they arrived, she would soon be reunited with her father and her future revealed. It was too soon! She'd not been able to find out anything about her mother at all. To ask now would only bring on suspicion, undoing any progress she'd made in gaining their favor. Eva swallowed back tears. Soon enough these two lovely women would possibly believe her to be an enemy; for they still did not know the truth of how she'd come to be with Strath.

"I see," was all Eva could manage. For the rest of her meal, she cut her food and moved it around the plate, barely eating anything at all. She laughed when appropriate, smiled, and tried to remain as cordial as she could, but if she had been asked to repeat anything that was said, she would know nothing, for her mind was very far away.

Chapter Eleven

After breakfast, Lorna and Isobel broke away to do their chores, leaving Eva on her own. With all the hustle and bustle going on in the castle and grounds, she thought for certain they'd want to keep an eye on her, to make sure she didn't sneak away. Then again, they didn't know she was Strath's prisoner and were supposed to be keeping their eye on her.

Eva had offered to help them with their duties, practically begged, but both of them declined, with Lorna insisting she take some time to rest, having so recently been on the road.

But Eva was not one to rest. She never had been. When she was a wee thing, her mother had often complained about her not napping. There was too much to see and do, not enough time in the day to do it, and who would want to waste such precious time on sleep?

Besides, even if she were tired, Eva was pretty certain that sleep would not come to her just now. It wasn't that the bed they'd given her was not comfortable, for it was. Nor was it that the sheets were not soft enough, for they were. It wasn't that her room was too drafty or loud, it was perfect. When she had fallen asleep the night before, she'd practically passed out. Nay, the problem did not lie with comfort itself. Her uneasiness lay in the impending battle, and with the sadness that filled her heart over Strath. When she closed her eyes, she saw Belfinch's twisted, ugly face, his weapon raised, prepared to strike at Strath with all his might. In her imagination, Strath didn't notice, he couldn't see, and the blade cut deep.

Though she'd never seen Strath fight, as she'd been inside the chapel when he'd taken Northwyck, and Belfinch had injured himself, she knew he had to be capable, else how would he have claimed victory? Besides that, he was built like an ox, made for storming doors and taking down his enemies. She was not fearful he wouldn't be able to fight back. And she was not fearful he wouldn't win.

What scared her was Belfinch's tactics. They would not be fair. How did a man of honor fight against someone without any?

She slipped out of her bedchamber, down to the great hall, and then through the kitchen doors into a well-tended vegetable and herb garden. The garden here rivaled that of her mother's, which had been extensive and a source of great pride. Eva had tried her hardest to keep up with it, and hoped her mother would look down on her with pride for what she'd been able to accomplish.

Her feet crunched on the gravel, startling a couple of women who were picking herbs and putting them in a basket. Eva waved and smiled. They waved back and then whispered to each other. She didn't recognize either of them, but that didn't mean she hadn't seen them in the kitchen the night before. She didn't begrudge them their gossip. Eva was a newcomer, and English, and she guessed if she were in their shoes, she'd probably be doing some whispering too.

As she walked, she felt their gazes on her, even though every time she looked back, they appeared to be busy with their herbs.

Beyond the garden was a grove of trees that promised the solitude she craved. Even the guards on the wall wouldn't be able to see her if she hid herself well enough.

Eva continued on to the orchard, where fruit trees had yet to flower, though their leaves were bright green against the cloudy sky. She touched the silky leaves, feeling the rough edges with the pad of her thumb, upsetting a finch who'd rested on a branch. Watching the bird flutter away, she remembered how she used to climb the apple trees in her mother's orchard and then peer into the birds' nests perched so high up she couldn't see from the ground. How year after year, she watched eggs hatch into tiny birds that then populated their gardens, returning every season.

Peering behind her and seeing no one in the vicinity, she grabbed hold of a branch, propped her foot on the trunk and prepared to hoist herself up when overhead, thunder rumbled, followed by a loud boom. It was deafening enough she might have guessed the castle keep was collapsing. She leapt back from the tree, knowing that climbing and storms did not go hand in hand unless one wanted to be struck by lightning. Which she did not.

Eva looked up into the sky where the dark clouds pushed into each other violently. They'd been without a storm their whole journey; perhaps this was how Mother Nature intended to pay them back for the reprieve.

Without warning, the skies opened up, fat droplets seeming to materialize out of nowhere, splashing on her face. She gasped and searched the orchard for the smallest tree to take shelter under. Then she caught sight of a thatched roof. A shed. She rushed toward the gardening shed that was thankfully adorned with an overhang. However rickety it looked as it leaned slightly to the left, it would do. She covered her head as the rain splashed on top of her and ran under the overhang.

Rain pelted the shed, but mercilessly, the thatch saved her from the majority of the drops. Eva stared up at the gray skies with fast-rolling clouds, hoping it was a quick storm. Thunder rumbled again, but with it, an odd sound. She tilted her head, listening more carefully. The noise was coming from inside the shed.

A frightened yowling. A cat mayhap?

Eva pushed open the wooden door. The iron hinges groaned, and she peered into the musty darkness. She could make out stacked tools, a few wooden buckets, a pile of wood, and shelves with various jars and baskets.

"Kitty, kitty," she called.

The frightened animal's call came again, and this time it was answered by a few tiny mewls. A mama kitty and her babies?

Her eyes adjusted to the dark, but still she didn't see them.

"Come out, I won't harm you," Eva cooed. She knelt down and held out her hand, wiggling her fingers to entice them out of hiding.

At Northwyck, they'd had many barn cats, and most were frightened of storms. As a girl, and even as a woman, she'd spent many hours lying in hay with the cats, trying to keep them calm with cups of milk, cuddles, and bits of fish she'd sneaked out of the kitchen.

A gray striped cat slunk from behind a pile of wood and sauntered toward her, tail swishing in agitation, meowing insistently. But not in warning, rather voicing its displeasure over the storm.

"Has it frightened your babies?"

The cat sniffed her fingers and rubbed its face against her palm.

Meow.

Two tiny kittens tumbled out from behind the woodpile, falling on each other, only to begin wrestling. Mama kitty ignored their play, preferring to rub her head on Eva's palm before sliding her body along Eva's side, allowing her to stroke her back and tail. Then with another meow of worry, the cat walked to the open door, poked her head outside, and gave another loud yowl.

Thunder cracked, followed by a gash of lightning that lit up the shed as though a thousand candles burned inside it. The two kittens ran back behind the woodpile, whimpering, and the mother cat leapt into the air, hair standing on end. She looked up at Eva and then back outside, almost frantically.

"The storm will be over soon, kitty."

Eva stroked the animal's back. But that didn't seem to calm the sweet thing. It didn't even purr. Instead, the yowling sound grew more frantic than before, and Eva could swear she heard an answering call somewhere in the distance.

"Is that it, momma? You have a baby out there in the storm?" Eva stood and walked out of the shed under the overhang, squinting her eyes as she peered out over the garden. The wind blew the tree branches, grass, and garden vegetation, causing everything to sway in the breeze like long green and brown tails. The rain pelted against leaves and stalks, and the dark clouds made visibility most inadequate.

But the cat did not stop her calls, and the tiny cries from outside the shed grew louder, sounding forlorn and scared. Eva's heart lurched.

She was going to have to walk out into the rain and search through the grass to find the wee kitten. Shielding her eyes from the rain, she stepped into it, and was almost immediately soaked to the bone. What was the point in trying to stay dry now?

She walked along the paths, rain dripping into her eyes and making her dress heavy. She searched in the grass and up in the tree branches but continued to come up empty. It seemed like the kitten's calls drew farther away with every step she took, and eventually, she felt like she was turning in complete circles, no closer to finding it.

"Eva!" Strath's voice cut through the thunder and pelting rain as he ran toward her. Concern etched his handsome wet face, and his dark hair was soaked and plastered to his forehead. "What are ye doing out here in the rain? Ye'll catch your death. Come inside." He reached for her hand.

"There is a lost kitten." She pointed toward the shed, stepping out of his reach in case he tried to force her inside. "Its mother is looking for it."

"What?" He stared from her to the shed as though she'd gone mad. "The kitten will find its way back to its mother. But ye will end up dreadfully ill."

"I've a stronger constitution than that," she countered. "I've slept outside in the rain and mucked about in the forest for days on end when it stormed."

He stared at her, rivulets of water dripping down his face in a pattern that almost looked like art. If it were possible, the rain made him look all the more handsome, sculpted, like a statue of the perfect man. Not to mention it caused his shirt to mold to his body, turning the white linen practically transparent, and causing every line and ripple of muscle to be visible. Good heavens. Her breath quickened, and she found it hard not to stare.

"I shouldna believe ye."

Eva jolted from her lusty stupor. "And why not?"

"Because lassies dinna do such things."

Eva rolled her eyes. "I'm no ordinary *lassie*."

"This I know." His tone had turned soft, and he stepped closer. "'Tis why I canna seem to get away from ye."

Eva's lips parted as she sucked in a breath. In the coldness of the rain, she could feel the heat radiating from his body, enough to cause a little steam to rise from his shirt.

"I've tried to keep away from ye. It's only been a few hours since ye barged into my bedchamber demanding your clothes, and yet with every moment I spend trying to forget about ye, I am only reminded of how verra much I want to kiss ye again."

Eva was in complete shock. Was she hearing him correctly?

"Kiss me?" Her words were almost lost in the hammering of the rain.

"Aye, sweet lass. I want to kiss ye more than I want to breathe."

He cupped the sides of her face with both hands, stepping close enough that the tips of their boots touched. Rain slid down the slope of her nose, dripped from her lips and chin, wetted her eyelashes. But she didn't care. She only had eyes for Strath, for how close he was leaning, the anticipation of his lips on hers.

Kiss me.

"Don't make me wait," she whispered.

A ragged breath escaped him, and his eyelids dipped as he closed the distance between them.

Eva held her breath, her entire body reaching toward him, even the hair on her arms. She closed her eyes and parted her lips, and time seemed to stand still until at last, his warm, rain-soaked mouth touched hers, sliding over her lips in delicious, decadent strokes. She sighed into his mouth, accepting the gentle touch of his tongue and demanding he taste her. Eva wrapped her arms around his middle, her fingers clutching at his back. Her nipples hardened, and the scrape of the wet fabric and his hard chest was almost more than she could bear.

Was this really happening? Had he truly come looking for her? Been thinking about her all day? About kissing her?

Strath slanted his mouth over hers possessively, more fiercely than he had that morning, and she thought she might faint from the pleasure of it. He slid his hands from her face, one cupping the side of her neck, and the other wrapping around her waist to tuck her impossibly closer. He backed her toward the shed, out of the rain, and her spine pressed to the wood, his hard body capturing her in a world of sensual hunger.

"What am I going to do with ye?" he asked between nips at her lips. He rested his hand on her ribs, brushing his thumb along the underside of her breast.

Eva gasped, arching her back as she instinctively craved more of his intimate touch.

"Keep kissing me. Don't stop."

"Och, lass," he said, sucking on her lower lip. "Dinna say such things. For if I knew I could keep on kissing ye and never stop, I would..."

Zounds!

Eva exhaled in silent, and sometimes not-so-silent, moans. Thunder cracked overhead, but even that couldn't drown out the pounding of her heart, and the heady sound of Strath's demanding growls against her mouth.

Abruptly, he slapped his hands on the shed above her head, ending the kiss on a ragged drag of breath. He let out a low curse, their foreheads pressed together, and his stormy gaze locked on her.

"I shouldna be doing this," he murmured.

Eva didn't have to ask why. "Sometimes we do things we think we shouldn't because we cannot live with ourselves if we don't."

"That is exactly right, Princess. And yet, if I continue, it will lead to a place neither one of us is...prepared for."

"Prepared?"

"Ye're a lady. I canna simply take ye against a shed."

"Oh..." She breathed out a sigh, realizing just now that he was speaking about making love to her. That was where kissing could lead. And her wicked mind immediately pictured the two of them without clothes, their bodies sliding together. But not in a bed; instead they were on the forest floor, or in a beautiful meadow surrounded by flowers, or right here in front of this shed.

"Och, lass, dinna look at me like that."

"Like what?"

"Like ye're thinking about..."

"But I was." *Oh, saints!* She'd not meant to admit that.

"Ye're too honest for your own good." He let out a groan, and his lips claimed hers once more.

There was an urgency when he kissed her this time, and it left her breathless and mindless. If he laid her down on the garden floor in the rain right then and there, she would surrender wholeheartedly.

It was only the yowling at her ankles and the scratching of the cat against her leg that brought her somewhat back to the present.

"Mama cat has come to our rescue," Strath breathed out on a laugh, parting from their kiss once more.

Not wanting their time together to end, Eva slid her hand into his and tugged him back out into the rain. "She wants us to find her baby. Help me?"

"Aye. Of course."

She was relieved when he agreed without hesitation. Who would have thought the mighty Strath would spend his time searching for a kitten? They combed the gardens some more, finally finding the tiny gray kitten trapped beneath an overturned bucket.

Eva lifted the poor soaked creature against her chest. The kitten immediately tried to burrow into her wet gown, seeking warmth and dryness.

"Poor thing," she cooed.

"The sprite is a fighter," Strath said, stroking his finger over the kitten's head.

Eva stared at him for half a breath, mesmerized all the more. She could remain this way all day, staring at him, marveling, falling for him...but they needed to get the kitten back to its mother.

They jogged back to the shed and reunited the pair. Mama Kitty immediately tried to lick away the rain from her babe's head and back, then she clamped her mouth on the kitten's neck and dragged it behind the woodpile, perhaps to nurse the sweet thing.

"Now that Mama Kitty's babies are all safe, let's get ye inside and dry. Ye'll need another gown." His gaze raked hungrily over the sodden gown that clung to her like a second skin.

Eva waved away his suggestion, not wanting to deprive his cousin of another gown. "This one is fine, I'll just let it dry before the hearth."

Strath's nostrils flared, and a heated look flashed in his eyes as he dragged his gaze leisurely over her form. "I dinna think I could stand it if ye walked around in that ill-fitting maid's gown again."

Eva laughed. "Oh, I wasn't planning on walking around in anything." As soon as the words were out of her mouth, she knew exactly how it sounded—and she certainly had no intentions to walk about the castle naked. She'd simply meant she'd stay in her chamber.

A low rumble sounded in his chest, and he swiped his hands over his face, looking as though she'd just dangled a sweet in front of him and then yanked it away. "Ye're a tease."

"I'm not teasing." She laughed. "I meant to stay in my bedchamber."

"Exactly. Come on. I'll see if Isobel has something else for ye to wear."

A thrill of excitement passed through her at the notion that Strath couldn't even bear to think of her undressed in her room. The tension that had been building between them for days, the passion in that kiss, had pushed them into uncharted waters. Excitement and curiosity coursed through her. Was this what it felt like to fall for someone? Oh, how glorious it was.

Inside the castle, they found Isobel easily enough. Her mischievous gaze shifted between them, but she didn't say anything about the fact they were both soaked and slightly disheveled. Eva knew how it looked, and really, what was there to deny? If anyone had come upon them in the garden, they would have seen exactly what they were all thinking anyway.

And she was not ashamed. Which of course, made her feel guilty. She should be ashamed for having acted like a wanton with no morals twice in one day.

Nay, she wasn't ashamed at all. In fact, she was smiling. Broadly. And a side glance at Strath showed he looked the same. For the past several days, every time she'd peeked at Strath, she'd wanted to be wanton. She wanted to forget her morals. Wanted him to kiss her. Touch her. Wanted to find out what would happen if she pushed him just a little bit more.

Good God, who in the world had she become?

This was wrong. They shouldn't. Couldn't. And yet, she had no desire to put an end to whatever it was that was developing between them.

Ever since she'd met Strath, she'd felt more alive, more like herself than ever before.

And if she was being true to herself, how could that be wrong?

How could he simply let her go?

They headed toward the stairs, Isobel's arm linked in hers and Strath following behind. When they reached the foot of the winding staircase, Isobel turned around, and Eva followed her gaze.

"I'll take it from here." Isobel gave her cousin a knowing look.

"Aye, right." Strath stammered, raising his hand in an awkward wave and backing up a step. "I'll see ye at supper then, my ladies."

Eva boldly met his gaze, despite the heat in her cheeks. "Thank you for helping me find the kitten."

"'Twas most certainly *my* pleasure." He bowed slightly and winked at her, a wicked grin flashing her way.

Oh, a pleasure indeed...

Heaven help her from being a wicked fool.

Chapter Twelve

The men gathered in the barracks, sharpening their weapons and drying their feet by the braziers. The rain had sent miniature rivers of mud rushing through the bailey, and walking the wall had left all of their boots thoroughly sodden.

Thankfully, hours after Strath had been in the garden with Eva, the rain had stopped, though the sun had yet to emerge from behind the clouds.

The warriors passed around jugs of whisky and ate hunks of roasted meat and bread.

Strath joined them for a while but refrained from eating as he planned to take his meal with his family and Eva. Tomaidh, too, would join them inside. He'd invited the men to join him, but they had their evening ritual down and wanted to stick to it. In fact, they'd even invited Jamie's men to join them, so the barracks were now even more crowded than before.

After their hard ride to England, the battle at Northwyck, and the journey back to Scotland, the men deserved a bit of respite and entertainment. Besides that, soon there would be another battle. And men in high spirits fought harder than those who were downtrodden.

Nodding to his men, he slipped out to the stables to visit Beast, wanting to brush the horse himself, and do some thinking. In just a short time he'd have to make a choice. Present Eva to the king and walk away, or ask the king for permission to keep her. To wed her...

Wee Duff was in the stables too, tending to his mount. He nodded to Strath as he approached.

"Wee Duff. Did ye get some meat?" Strath took hold of a brush and stroked it over his warhorse.

"Aye." The warrior was unusually terse and didn't meet his gaze.

"Something bothering ye?" Strath asked Duff.

Beast turned to nibble his thanks at Strath's shoulder as he continued to brush him down.

"Aye." Still Wee Duff did not meet his gaze.

"Tell me." Strath leaned against the stall, running the brush over his mount's flank.

"I saw ye in the gardens. With the lass." His tone was accusatory.

Strath stiffened for just half a breath and then continued brushing. "And?" Strath didn't keep his irritation from his voice. He didn't approve of his men spying, any more than he approved of them questioning his motives and actions.

"What are your intentions with her?"

"Is that any of your business?" Strath asked, feeling his nerves prickle.

This time, Wee Duff did look up from what he was doing, and anger blazed in his eyes so abundantly that Strath nearly took a step back.

"Aye. Ye've not told your uncle or his men the whole truth—that she is your prisoner. And now I see ye mauling her against a shed like she was a common whore and ye nothing more than stable hand."

"Dinna call her a whore. And I was not mauling her." Strath bristled, flexing his fingers. Beast, sensing his irritation, flicked his ears and tail.

Duff jammed the brush he was using back into a bucket. "Whatever ye might call it. But it was not a friendly kiss. Nor was it playful. Ye wanted to—"

"I'll caution ye not to finish that thought." Strath straightened up now, setting his own brush aside. He was so close to putting his fist through Wee Duff's nose.

"Noted," Duff said, sniffing with arrogance. "I want to know what your intentions are."

Strath narrowed his eyes. Was he truly having this conversation? "I dinna have to answer to ye."

"I think ye do." Duff was serious, accusation dripping from every word. "We all know what happened the last time ye let your guard down with a woman."

"This is not the same." Strath took a step toward Duff, wanting to shake the bastard for even attempting to compare the two situations. "Jean and Eva are two different people."

How could Duff even begin to compare the two? Jean was a scheming wench who'd tried to pass off another man's child as his own and then riled up her father enough to have him attack. Eva was a victim in her own home and would never harm anyone, let alone plot to have her father come and attack them. The lass had given herself over to them, not knowing what could happen to her, putting her life completely in his hands. When had Jean Guinn ever done anything for anyone without benefit to herself?

"Ye believe 'tis not the same, but I dinna see it that way, and neither will the men when I tell them." Duff puffed out his chest. "Her father is on the march, coming north, and ye think ye've got him pegged as weaker than Belfinch. What if that's not true?"

Rather than the heat of fury, a coldness gripped Strath at the base of his neck. Duff was treading in dangerous territory. "Are ye questioning my authority? My judgment?"

Duff blew out an angry breath, crossing his arms over his chest. "I'm questioning whether or not we're about to go into battle for the right reasons."

"Did ye see those burned villages? Would ye say that was the right reason? Or 'haps ye want to take it up with our king, who ordered us into England in the first place. Because if ye question my reasons for doing so, then ye must also question our king."

Duff paled a little at that. "I dinna question the king."

"Then dinna question *me*. I am your laird. And I'll not hesitate to have ye whipped for disobedience."

Duff clenched his hands at his sides. "I dinna want to see another wench bring ye down low. Ye'll not survive it the next time."

Strath narrowed his eyes. "Ye let me worry about the lass. And ye keep your nose to your own business. Follow my orders, or take yourself somewhere I willna be able to find ye."

Duff glowered at him for a few breaths before finally grumbling something inaudible and storming out of the stable.

Strath muttered an oath and kicked at a wooden post in the center of the barn, feeling the ricochet of it all the way up his leg.

What the bloody hell was that all about? Duff accusing him of not putting the clan first? Fury raced through Strath's veins. By breaking the handfast with Jean he had been thinking of the clan. It would have been a detriment to them all had he married a woman without morals who lied and schemed. How could Duff see it any other way?

"Dammit!" He kicked the post again. Hit it with his fist. Was ready to shake it hard enough to yank it out of place and cause the whole stable to collapse in on him.

The worst part was that if Duff was thinking this, other warriors might question him, too. He shouldn't have to prove to them he had their best interests at heart—because it was a fact.

Strath was first and foremost their laird, their protector, their leader, and all that came with that duty. He was also a loyal vassal to his king. He was not distracted by Lady Eva. All right, perhaps he was a little distracted by her, but not enough to shirk his duties. Not enough to put his men at risk.

Maybe he shouldn't go inside for supper. Perhaps remaining out of the castle and away from her was the best way to prove to his men he wasn't distracted.

It was frustrating that he even had to deal with this. Before Jean, no one had cared who he kissed. Who he rutted. In fact, his men would often pound their hands against his back in congratulations for his conquests. Was Jean's treachery, her father's betrayal, forever a stain on his reputation?

"Damn ye, Guinn," he growled.

"Who is Guinn?"

Strath jerked around to see Eva standing in the opening of the stables, eyes wide as she flicked her gaze from him to the post and back again. A plaid cloak was wrapped around her shoulders, and she pushed the hood back to reveal tiny golden curls framing her face, a hazard of the wet air, he assumed. A tiny smile jerked at her lips.

Strath pulled away from the post, his arms falling useless at his sides. The wrath drained from him as soon as he saw her.

"Are ye sneaking about, my lady?"

"Well, you might have heard me if you weren't so busy attacking that post. What did it ever do to you?" Her tone was teasing and light-hearted, and it was hard not to smile at her.

"I fear ye've caught me in a fit of temper."

"Don't be shy on my account."

"What are ye doing out here?"

"I went to check on the kittens now that the storm has calmed and decided to walk about the perimeter of the bailey."

"'Tis too muddy for a lass to traipse about."

"They've laid out hay." She eyed him for a moment longer. "Your warrior, Wee Duff, said you were looking for me."

Strath scowled. That *bastard*. When Duff had left him, Strath had wrongfully assumed he was going to let it go, follow orders as he should. How wrong he'd been to make that assumption. It would appear that Duff was more interested in causing trouble than peace, which Strath should not be surprised about at all.

"I wasna." He straightened. If Duff had sent her here, no doubt the whelp was going to try to send someone else, perhaps hoping to find them in a compromising position. By doing so, Duff had tossed down his gauntlet, challenging his laird, and he would have to be punished for it. The sooner Strath laid this bit of trouble to rest, the better. "Ye should go back inside, my lady."

"Why?" She cocked her head and studied him. "Are you not going to tell me about Guinn?"

"Nay, Princess. Go back inside, please." He added the last part in hopes she would understand how very serious he was.

He'd hoped wrong. She crossed her arms over her chest, standing rigid in place. "Why not?"

She wanted to question him, too? Strath gritted his teeth. Dammit, he didn't want to fight with her. He tried to remain calm and leveled her with a serious gaze. "I've ordered ye to go back inside."

Eva humphed and tapped her foot, clearly not backing down "Am I to be your prisoner now for all to see? Is this where it changes?"

"Nay. But Guinn is none of your concern."

"None of my business, maybe, but it is my concern."

Strath ran a hand through his hair; the lass would not budge, and short of tossing her over his shoulder, there didn't seem to be another way of getting her out of here. "Ye're trying to bait me."

"Maybe."

"Why?"

"I'm curious." She shrugged. "I've not much to do beyond walking about and spying on angry warriors. Indulge me."

Strath groaned on the inside. She was baiting him for...*entertainment*? "What about the kittens?"

"They were snuggled up sleeping with their mother. I left a bowl of cream, but I fear they are not as intrigued with me as I am with them."

"That is a shame. Ye're a fascinating woman." Perhaps changing the subject and flattering her would be enough to get her to go inside.

Eva laughed at that. "Flattery will not distract me, warrior. So, tell me. What could it hurt? Who is this Guinn?"

Strath let out a breath that bordered on a growl. Maybe if he told her, she'd listen and go back inside. "Guinn is the chief of the clan just north of my father's holding in Sutherland."

"And what has he done to make you so mad? Is he here?"

"Nay, he isna. 'Tis a long story. Dinna make me toss ye over my shoulder and carry ye inside, lass."

Her mouth fell open in mock outrage. "What would your aunt think if she were to see such a thing?" She winked, knowing she'd gotten the better of him. "Do you think it will take you longer to tell me than it will take for Belfinch to finally arrive?"

He frowned. "Nay."

"Then it is not *that* long of a story."

"Ye're right." He walked over to a bench along the wall, sat down, and patted the seat beside him. Across from them, tack and saddles and other staples were hung on the wall.

Eva sat down, thankfully with enough space that they weren't touching. Then he thought the better of it. If Duff's plan was to find them alone together, best they not give him any fodder, even if it was just the two of them sitting beside each other.

Strath stood and held out his hand, which she took without hesitation. He helped her up and then dropped her hand again, though he desired to bring it to his lips. "Let us take a turn about the bailey. The air in here is stifling."

She regarded him with eyes partially squinted, probably trying to read deeper into what he meant, but he moved toward the door, opening it to the cloudy afternoon sky. The rain had stopped, and the brisk wind blowing made it a bit chilly. Eva pulled her hood back up, shivering as she stepped out beside him.

"We could go inside if ye're too cold," he said.

"Nay, it is good to get some fresh air."

Their boots sloshed in a few unavoidable puddles. The grass in the bailey was patchy in places, and straw had been laid out to soak up some of the rainwater, but all the same, mud was unavoidable. Eva lifted the hem of her slightly too-long gown as they walked over puddles and then let it back down to cover her boots.

"Well, are you going to tell me or make me guess?" she asked.

Strath chuckled. "I was hoping ye'd forgotten."

"I love a good story, and yours has already left me in anticipation. What could possibly have the great and mighty Strath pounding his fists and boots on a poor defenseless stable post?" She laughed softly, and he wanted to gather her up in his arms, tickle her, and kiss that laughter away.

Instead, he crossed his arms over his chest. "Och, but now I fear ye'll be disappointed."

"Try me." She spoke softly, passing him a conspiratorial grin.

He was comfortable around her. Outside of his family and Tomaidh, he'd never felt this way about anyone before. Jean had not even come close, and neither had any of the other women he'd been in a relationship with. What was it about Eva? Her disarming smile? The genuineness about her? The fact he didn't feel as though she'd judge him? Whatever it was, she made him forget all the vows he'd just made to stay away from her.

"'Tis no secret I was betrothed to Guinn's daughter, and the two of them betrayed me."

"Ah, so this is why you did not wish to speak about her when we dined."

He slanted a glance at her, recalling how his family had made mention of his betrothal at dinner several times, and each time, he'd skirted around it. "Ye picked up on that, aye?"

"How could I not?"

He grinned and glanced across the bailey to see a few of his men had come out of the barracks with Duff. They started to head toward the stables. Strath stopped in his tracks, and Eva stopped, too. The men had yet to spot the two of them. It would appear that exactly what he'd thought would happen was coming to pass.

"Do ye trust me, lass?"

"Aye," she said without hesitation.

"Good. I'm going to point toward the castle, and I want ye to look, as though ye're concerned. I'll have on a stern face."

"What?" She frowned, and he hated what he was doing.

He jabbed his finger toward the castle, his face a mask of irritation he did feel, but not toward her. "Duff saw us in the gardens. He sent ye to the stables in hopes of catching us at something. He's now brought a few of my men in hopes of finding us in a compromising position as well. He worries I've been distracted from my mission."

"Oh." Dutifully, Eva looked toward the castle and then back at him, screwing up her face into one of concern.

"The men? Are they...worried?" she asked.

"Nay. But Duff likes to cause trouble. He believes... Och." He muttered a curse under his breath. "I'm going to take ye by the elbow and lead ye inside. They are watching us."

"All right." She nodded and cast her gaze toward the ground. "I will look dutifully upset."

"My thanks." He took her elbow gently and led her inside. "I will owe ye a favor for this."

She exaggerated tripping as he did so, and then had to hide her face in her hood to keep her smile from showing. "And another favor for that."

Once inside, she burst out laughing. He couldn't help but smile, not at the situation, but at her. He wanted to pummel Duff, and he knew he'd have to make his punishment public.

Strath led her toward the great hall, which was thankfully empty at this time of day. They took seats opposite each other in an alcove that was not hidden from view should anyone follow them inside, and then he continued his story.

"It was an arranged marriage to benefit our clans. Probably more so hers than mine, but all the same, since she was the chief's eldest child and he had no sons, I would have inherited his lands, bringing them into the Sutherland fold." He cleared his throat, thinking about the niggling in the back of his brain that had him encouraging his father to insist on a one year handfast before the official wedding ceremony.

"Did you love her?"

Strath grunted. "Nay. Not in the way I... Not in the way I've seen others." He'd almost let slip that he loved her. He was mostly certain that was what the feeling cramping his chest was. The reason behind his desire to ask the king if he could wed her. "Needless to say, I was a fool. When I returned her to her father, he plotted his revenge, but took it out on my father instead of me."

Eva's hands came to her mouth as she gasped.

"The Sutherlands prevailed, but my humiliation was out there for everyone to witness. Duff fears..." He cleared his throat. "Duff fears I'll fall once more for a woman who has ulterior motives."

"Oh..." She glanced out the window. "And when he saw you with me, a woman you'd captured, he believed you were going to make the same mistake again."

"Exactly." He couldn't have appreciated her astuteness more than he did right at that moment, because he didn't want to have to say the words aloud.

"Is he..." She bit her lip and glanced back at him, her eyes crinkled with true worry. "Is he right?"

Strath stiffened, not having expected that question.

"Am I compromising your leadership, my laird?"

Ballocks, but he hated to have put that worry in her head. With confidence, he answered her, "Nay. There may have been a brief moment where I thought it could be true. But I know for certain that ye have not. The only thing that compromises my leadership is when I dinna have the full trust of my men." He paused, running a hand through his hair. "There is something else, lass."

"Tell me." Her gaze searched his.

"I was not only sent to stop Belfinch's attacks on our border. The king sent me to... find ye."

She paled, drawing in a deep breath. "You were sent to find me, and yet you let me believe I was your prisoner? Why?"

"When I found that ye were to marry Belfinch, I believed ye to be an enemy to my king. The Bruce did not ask me to take ye back to Scotland, only to find out if ye were alive. But when ye offered yourself, I took it. It wasn't until later I realized ye were no enemy. Is there a reason ye could think of why the king would be concerned for your welfare?"

She shook her head slowly, but there was a flicker of something in her eyes that made him wonder if she was telling the truth. He'd have to worry about that later. For now, he had to take care of the situation Duff had created.

Strath stood abruptly, renewed anger surging in his veins. "I must extend my apologies to ye. I should not have used ye just now as a ruse. I need to go set things to rights."

Eva nodded, her throat bobbing as she swallowed. "You needn't apologize to me, Strath. Even if I shouldn't, I trust you. Besides, it was fun making mischief with you—even if it was for a rather wretched purpose. Your men do trust you. Don't let one troublemaker shake your foundation."

He could have kissed her then, but he refrained.

"I will see ye at supper." Duff be damned.

Chapter Thirteen

E va couldn't breathe.

Well, perhaps that was an exaggeration. She *could*, but it felt like all the breath had left her, and drawing it back in was taking every effort. She sat numbly rooted on the bench in the alcove of the great hall, watching Strath's retreating figure. His green, blue, and red plaid swung wildly against his powerful, sun-darkened legs with each lengthy, purposeful stride.

The king was concerned for her welfare. That could mean only one thing—that her letter to her mother's family had been received and they had implored their king to seek her out. That was how he'd guessed her name. She'd nearly forgotten that part.

There were so many questions she had, wanted to shout for him to come back so she could figure out all he knew.

But Strath did not turn around. And she did not expect him to.

Though she'd not known him long, there was only one other instance where she'd seen him walk with such intense resolve. And that had been in the chapel at Northwyck a few seconds before he'd tossed her over his shoulder.

The memory of that, of the strength and determination of him, had another gush of air rushing out of her. Duff was a fool to have gone against his laird.

What was Strath going to do?

Strath ducked beneath the arched opening that led toward the main entrance, and a moment later, the loudness of the bailey filled the castle, only to be cut off abruptly by the sound of the door closing. It was eerie to have heard the noise and then nothing. Eva suppressed a shudder.

Duff was certainly going to get a severe punishment for attempting to start an uprising, for that was what he was doing. A little part of her was also embarrassed. Duff had somehow watched that kiss she and Strath shared in the orchard. That deliciously wanton kiss. Eva pressed her hand to her heart, feeling it pound. That had not been an innocent kiss. The way he'd claimed her, pressed her up against the shed... Sensual didn't even begin to describe it. As she reimagined the entire scenario all over again, her body heated, nipples perked to life, and there was what she could only describe as a pulsing need between her legs.

Her body craved him. And Duff had been witness to all of that. Because of it, he'd determined his laird was not capable of leading the men. Was that a logical conclusion? Perhaps she might have thought so had she been on Duff's end. Perhaps not.

In any case, the fact this was happening at all was her fault.

Well, partially. She, Strath, and Duff had all played a part in what was happening now. But would Duff have taken those actions if she'd not thrown herself at his laird on two different occasions?

That remained a serious question. Duff had already started to question her on their journey, loudly, when she'd tried to cook the men stew. There was a chance he had been looking for an excuse to put down his laird. Eva didn't fully understand all the interworkings of a clan, but she did know what it meant when a leader was undermined.

She'd never forget being a young girl of perhaps eleven, and watching her father take a lash to one of his knight's backs. It had not been about a mutiny, but it did have to do with respect. These were harsh times. Men had to count on each other to stay alive, when one false word could prove to be life or death... Well, that called for a heavy hand.

Perhaps she should not feel bad for Duff. He knew what he was getting into. She couldn't imagine that Strath would surround himself with imbeciles, because while his men had to trust that he would lead them, he had to trust they would have his back. So while Duff might have feared his leader was going to be taken advantage of again, he could have gone about it a different way than the one he'd chosen.

Her mind flitted back and forth between the situation outside, her mother and the news of the king's inquiry. All of it made her a little dizzy.

Eva sat against the cool stone, leaning her head back and looking up toward the timber rafters crisscrossing in an arching pattern. A bird flew from one end to the other, probably had a nest up there. Whatever was happening between her and Strath was confusing. Not to mention overwhelming. Of course, it would be puzzling to his men, too.

And they might even perceive it as a weakness.

Eva didn't want to be anyone's weakness, especially not his.

But how could she prove that she could be his strength? There was so much she had against her. Being half English. Being daughter to an enemy of his country. Not to mention she'd been about to wed a man their king had sent him to battle—the very reason Strath had determined to take her prisoner. The list went on. The men would see their passion as Strath abusing his power. And she supposed she could see their point, and how it would look on the outside. But Eva didn't see it that way.

When he'd burst into that church, right after her initial fear, she'd experienced clear relief. She'd told him to take her. Offered herself. Known the consequences of doing so. She'd wanted protection from Belfinch, wanted to find out what happened to her mother, even if that had meant putting herself in Scottish hands.

Eva had chosen the lesser of what she'd thought at the time were two evils. Perhaps Fate or God had interceded to keep her safe. That she'd come to fall for the man who'd taken her.

If only they'd met under different circumstances. Then none of this would be happening.

Eva pushed herself up from the bench. Outside was eerily silent, at least none of the noise filtered in. Being alone in the great hall, surrounded by silence, she could almost imagine she was completely alone in the world. The sensation of it was overwhelming, pulsing in on her in a moment of sudden panic. She took a few hurried steps toward the entrance, an intense yearning to see what was happening flooded her, but she knew that would be a bad idea. She didn't want to watch a man be punished. She didn't want to hear it, either.

There was only one thing to do. This morning, she'd seen Lady Lorna exit the family's private chapel off the great hall. Finding the entrance was easy, and once inside the empty chamber, Eva closed the door. Candles were lit on the small altar. She went forward, knelt before it, and pressed her hands together in prayer.

She stared up at the carved stone statue of the Virgin holding her infant son. A mother whose only wish had been to protect her sacred child. What any mother would want. What her own mother had desired. And if Eva was ever blessed with a child, she would do the same.

Words escaped her as she stared at the tilted head, the carved lips, the emotion the artist had captured in their stonework. How did one pray for guidance? She'd not often been one to pray other than when she was told to. She'd confessed her sins to their family's priest, her list undoubtedly lengthier than anyone else's. But never had she asked for guidance. She'd always preferred to do things her own way.

"What should I do?" she asked the statue. "I think I love him. And it seems as though a love between us is wrong. For hundreds of years before us, people from different countries have wed. Uniting nations in matrimony. But have people that should be enemies married across borders for other reasons? For love?"

Eva sat back on her heels, recalling how Strath had said his own parents had done just that, and they were happy. Was that a sign she could try? That love and happiness were a possibility?

The door handle rattled, and a swish of air flickered the candles. But no one came in, and the candles flared back to life. She stared into the center of the orange flame of the candle closest to her, making out the faint lines of blue where it burned hottest.

What should I do?

No answers came to her, but a memory did, of her mother sitting behind her and brushing out the knots from her long hair. Her mother had always been so tender in her ministrations, and kissed away Eva's tears when the knots were extra bold. On that particular morning, Eva had been asking questions like any seven-year-old might. Why this, and why that, but then she'd asked her mother if she could live with her forever, and her mother had answered that one day, she would grow up and marry, and that she would have her own household to run. Eva hadn't wanted her own house. She'd wanted to stay with her mother. And her mother had said softly in her Scottish brogue, "*I pray for ye, my love, that one day ye find a man who takes away your breath, and when ye do, ye will know where home is.*"

But what was home? When she was a child, home had been love, her mother and father and sister. Home had been where she laid her head. Where she ate her meals. Where she played. Home had been safety. Home had been hope and happiness.

Eva sighed, understanding now what her mother had meant.

Whenever she looked at Strath, or indeed thought of him or sensed him near, her breath hitched. He took her breath away. When she was with him, she felt hope and happiness and anticipation for things to come—and that extended beyond kissing.

Strath was home.

"I want to stay," she said to herself. "I love him."

STRATH MARCHED out to the bailey, uncertain of what he was going to do until he saw Duff standing in the center of half a dozen Dornoch warriors. His men looked up at him warily, perhaps in that moment regretting having listened to any of the damning words Duff might have uttered.

"Duff," he bellowed.

The scorned warrior slowly turned around, and those who'd been surrounding him backed away, flickers of apprehension mixing with the dawning knowledge they'd been caught.

Upon hearing his bellow, Tomaidh exited the barracks with the other men.

"Ye want to challenge me." It was not a question, but a statement from Strath. He stopped about six feet from Duff, keeping his face emotionless, his stance rigid, strong. From this, he would not back down.

Duff puffed out his chest, thrusting his jaw forward in pigheaded-ness. "Perhaps ye need to be challenged."

Strath took note the man conveniently left off *my laird*.

"Does anyone else feel the need to challenge their laird?" Strath asked the crowd, scanning his men, especially those who'd been gathered with Duff to begin with.

No one stepped forward.

"Duff here believes me incapable of leading my men." From the corner of his eye, he saw his uncle approach from wherever he'd been. "For some time after the attack on Dunrobin by the Guinn clan, I felt to blame. Perhaps there were signs I should have seen from my betrothed, I readily admit that. But I am not to blame for the betrayal laid on our clans."

The men nodded in understanding.

"Who among ye would judge me for believing the woman I was to marry was faithful? I was a fool, aye. But I have learned my lesson. I also know that Guinn would still have attacked Dunrobin. All he needed was a push. If I'd not discovered her sins, we'd be married, and despite the attack, she would still be my wife to this day. And I'd be raising another man's bairn." Strath stared at each man, challenging them to speak up. "She would be your mistress, and ye would have to be loyal to her, protect her with your lives. After she'd betrayed us."

They'd not thought of that, not the way Strath had. Hell, until this very moment, he'd not fully thought about how lucky he was to have escaped that fate. By being married in the eyes of God, the only thing he could have done was lock her in a convent. And she'd still be his wife until the day she died. Not to mention the bairn. Even if it wasn't his, he'd not have tossed him to the wolves.

"Jean Guinn would not have made ye stew in the woods, because she thought ye might enjoy it over dried venison. She would not have laughed with ye to break up the monotony of a long journey. She would have put her *sgian dubh* to your throats while ye slept." Strath glanced at his uncle, about to reveal the truth for the first time. "'Tis true that she was at first my prisoner. That the king asked us to find her. But Eva, she has won ye all over, not just me. She has proven more than once she is not our enemy, but one of us."

The men called out a forceful, *Aye*. But the only reaction Strath cared about for that moment was his uncle's. To his relief his uncle nodded.

Strath pinned Duff with a glower. "Raise your sword, or strip off your shirt. Either way, I'll be giving ye a lashing to remind ye who is your laird. And I'll remind ye that I could have tossed ye in the dungeon for trying to start a rebellion."

Duff touched the hilt of his sword, clearly contemplating pulling it from its scabbard. *Mo chreach*, but Strath prayed the man did not go through with it. If he did, Strath would disarm him and put him down before he had to draw blood, but if the man pushed him to it, he could quite possibly take his life. No one would question him on it.

Aye, it would be his right if the man raised a weapon toward him. But even still, that was not what Strath wanted. Duff needed guidance, assurance. And he needed to understand his laird would show him mercy. Once.

By going behind Strath's back, Duff had made a mistake. But like Strath, mistakes were lessons that one learned from, that made a person better, which was why Strath was willing to show him clemency.

Nevertheless, Strath couldn't make him strip off his shirt to take his punishment. Strath couldn't force him not to draw his weapon. Those were decisions Duff had to make on his own.

They stayed still like that for many moments, Strath counting the seconds as they stared at each other. The wind picked up, and the sky overhead darkened when clouds passed over the dull sun. Rain would soon be upon them again. He would count to sixty, letting Duff have a full minute to make the choice for life or death.

Twenty-seven, twenty-eight, twenty-nine... The seconds dragged on with an agonizing stillness.

Finally, Duff took his hand off the hilt of his sword and moved it to the pin holding his plaid in place. Jaw tight and eyes never leaving Strath's, he unpinned his plaid and pulled off his shirt. He stood naked from the waist up in the bailey, and turned his back on his laird, prepared to take his punishment.

A collective breath was released from the crowd. Thank the heavens, Duff had chosen a thrashing instead. Strath's lungs were tight, almost bursting with the tension inside him. He glanced down at his hand.

Ballocks. Strath didn't even have a whip. He'd not been prepared.

"My laird." Tomaidh appeared at his side and handed him a horse whip he must have gone to get from the stables.

Strath took it with a nod of gratitude and approached Duff. He glanced behind him at his uncle, who gave a subtle nod. Had Uncle Jamie ever been in this situation before? Strath had certainly punished men before, but not many, and never with a whipping. Each lash would tear into Duff's flesh. And yet it was unavoidable.

Strath cleared his throat, feeling how dry it was. Lord, he could use a flagon of whisky right now. "Duff of Dornoch and Sutherland, ye are hereby charged with an attempt at mutiny and will receive a punishment of twenty lashes. Do ye confess?"

"Aye. I confess, and gladly take my lashes, if my laird will forgive me for being a fool."

Strath gripped the sturdy handle of the whip and heard the leather creak. "Aye. Ye will be forgiven."

And with that said, he raised the whip.

Chapter Fourteen

Eva found him in his chamber, sitting in the dark and nursing a flagon of whisky.

When he'd not joined them at supper in the great hall, she'd thought at first he must be late. Servants brought out trenchers of lamprey pie, roasted venison, green peas in garlic sauce, turnips in cream sauce, and fresh baked brown bread. Food was placed in front of her. Wine poured. The aromas and taste of the meal were delectable, better than anything she'd had at Northwyck. By the time everyone was served and had taken a few bites, the empty place across from her where Strath was supposed to sit stood out like a sore thumb.

She'd determined he was not coming to supper, and this was made even more clear when Tomaidh returned and gave a subtle shake of his head after having volunteered to go and find out, at Jamie's request.

After that, the food tasted a little duller, and the conversation grew quieter, everyone consumed by their own thoughts.

Eva couldn't imagine what kind of pain Strath must have been enduring at that moment. If she were in his situation, she probably would have declined to dine too. In fact, she almost had. When she'd come out of the chapel, Duff's lashing had ended, and she only knew that because she'd seen an ashen-faced Strath enter the castle and go up the winding staircase toward his chamber. He was so lost in thought that he'd not even glanced over to see her standing just a few feet away.

Oh, but how her heart had lurched to see him in such pain. Having to dole out the punishment must have been hard on him, no matter how deserved it was. Duff was not an enemy that had to be vanquished on the battlefield, but a man he'd fought beside. And that's when she determined to put aside her own confusion and fears so she could sit beside him at supper. Only, he wasn't there.

The situation was even harder on Duff, who'd had to give in and risk humiliation, risk being tossed out of his clan and be forever labeled a traitor.

Which was why after finishing supper, Eva excused herself and gathered a few provisions from the kitchen larder where she'd seen a shelf devoted to healing supplies. She exited the castle, marching with purpose toward the barracks where she was certain the warriors would have taken Duff after his punishment concluded.

Two men stood outside the barracks, leaning casually against the wall. They straightened to their full heights when she approached, giving each other side-eye glances as though they weren't exactly sure how to react. And that was all the more evident when she was within feet of them, and they simply stared at her, speechless, as though their tongues had been cut out.

"Good evening, sirs. Please, allow me inside." Eva squared her shoulders, the basket of supplies balanced on her forearm.

Finally, one of them spoke. "We canna, my lady. This is the soldier's barracks. No women allowed."

"I know exactly what it is," she said in her most authoritative tone. "I have come to tend to the warrior, Wee Duff."

At that, their eyes widened, and as though they'd passed some silent message, they moved closer together, shoulders touching, completely blocking her way.

"Definitely not, my lady," the second one said.

Eva raised her chin and pursed her lips. She would not allow them to thwart her in her task. She used a soothing tone when she answered. "I will not harm him. I want to help." She indicated the supplies she carried.

They eyed the basket, and one of them poked his finger inside to move the contents around, not finding anything that would cause harm to his fellow warrior. "We are nae worried for his safety, my lady."

She opened her mouth and then closed it again, understanding he meant Wee Duff might hurt her. Or someone else. But it didn't matter. She wasn't afraid. Narrowing her eyes, she said, "Allow me to pass. I'm not worried for my safety, and if you're so worried, you can escort me inside like true gentleman to make certain nothing happens to me."

While one shook his head, the second said, "I'm not certain the laird would approve of this."

"He would not approve of a man with a wound seeking attention from a healer?"

"Well..." They eyed each other once more. "Ye're a healer?"

Eva blew out a disgruntled breath and stomped her foot. This had taken quite enough of her time. "Move out of my way." She didn't give them a chance to respond. She pushed her way forward, knocking her basket into their joined elbows.

It was clear from their body language they considered blocking her and pushing her back. They resisted her for half a breath but then moved, choosing instead to follow her inside. Although the courtyard had been cloudy, inside the barracks was even darker, and she needed a few moments to let her eyes adjust to the lighting. The air was smokier than inside the castle, the ventilation for the fires not as good. She made out men surrounding several braziers. A few warriors were curled up sleeping on cots or just directly on the floor. Weapons lined the walls.

The building smelled faintly of sweat and musk and the fires.

She scanned the men, looking for Duff's familiar face, but she didn't see him. "Where is Wee Duff?" she asked them.

No one answered, but plenty of them stared at her, perhaps wondering if they'd consumed too much whisky.

Again, she was forced to show off the supplies she brought. "I've come to help him."

Tomaidh stood from where he'd been sitting in the shadows and approached her. Eva was grateful to see him. He'd been kind to her from the very beginning, and she considered him a friend.

"My lady." He glanced down into her basket, doing a similar perusal as the warriors had outside the barracks. When his eyes met hers, they were filled with questions. "Why would ye offer to do this?"

Eva hadn't realized how much questioning she would get for doing something kind. Were they all so cold in the Highlands that they didn't help a man in need? "He is hurt, is he not?"

"Aye. But by his own design." He regarded her without revealing his impression. "He was punished, as I'm sure ye must know."

"Aye. But even the punished deserve to heal, no?" She wasn't going to back down, no matter what they threw at her. Helping Duff was something she had to do.

The room had grown very hushed, only the sounds of the crackling fires breaking the silence. Tomaidh pursed his lips, deep in thought. "Does Laird Dornoch or Laird Montgomery know ye've come?"

She shook her head. "I came of my own free will. I did not think I needed permission."

Again, Tomaidh studied her, and Eva started to feel self-conscious. Was she supposed to have gained permission? She shifted on her feet, still confident in her own choice to help. "Certainly it is not unusual to care for the wounded in Scotland?"

"'Tis unusual for someone in your situation to care for our wounded, aye." He gave a curt nod, as if that explained it. That she was a simpleton for not understanding this, and perhaps now she would simply go away since he'd given her that information.

"My situation is this, Sir Tomaidh, and the rest of you as well," she said, looking pointedly about the barracks. "I am English, but I also have Scottish in my blood. I am the daughter of a man you suppose to be your enemy." Why had she admitted the latter when she'd not yet found the will to tell Strath? Perhaps part of her wanted to see what the reaction would be? Whatever it was, she trusted Tomaidh, and she trusted these men who'd done nothing but befriend her and protect her. "I was to marry another man who is your enemy. But that was not of my own free will, for he is my enemy as well. I beseeched your laird to take me with him in place of my father, not only as a dutiful daughter, but to escape my enemy. Your laird and I have become close. I am...fond of him. I care for all of you as well. So you see, to me, it is not unusual. Allow me to help, sir. Please."

She drew in a slow breath, counting the seconds as the silence dragged on.

"I've never met another like ye," Tomaidh said, and there was a murmur of agreement amongst the men, a newfound respect in their eyes. There was still a note of surprise in his voice, and perhaps a slight twinge of condescension. He likely thought she was an idiot. "Ye would offer your care to a man who might kill ye."

Eva had never been one to be fearful of the unknown. This was a gift her mother had taught her. Aye, she knew to be cautious, but to be paralyzed by fear? Never. And she was grateful for that now, as she kept her eyes steady on the warrior in front of her who'd just laid out the truth so bluntly. "He will not kill me. He's had plenty of chances before now."

Tomaidh grunted as he observed her. "All right. Ye may tend him, but not without me present."

Relief flooded her, for she was certain that even though she'd been able to push past the two guards outside, she'd not be able to get past all of these men. "I will not harm him, you have my word."

"I'm not worried about ye harming him. Duff is... Well, he will not be so kind."

Eva raised her chin. "We shall see."

With a slight shake of his head, as though he couldn't believe he was giving in, Tomaidh led her toward the back of the barracks and through a doorway to a small antechamber. There, lying on his stomach on a table, was Duff. He appeared to be sleeping. His back was laid open in fleshy, bleeding lines. Eva gritted her teeth at the sight. She'd seen worse, but even still, she knew it had to hurt something fierce. No wonder Strath had been so pale and deep in thought as he'd passed her. She couldn't imagine being the one to inflict such pain on another human, and not because they were threatening a life, but because it was a punishment that needed meting out.

Eva pulled a stool over to the table where he lay and set her supplies down on top of it. She withdrew a jug of whisky and poured a large cup.

"He's already had plenty of that to knock him out," Tomaidh said.

"All right." Eva nodded and slowly poured the contents of the whisky onto Duff's back.

That woke him up. The man bellowed, back arching, head swiveling to face her. Accusation was written all over his face as well in the curses he tossed at her. Eva stood her ground, even as the venom shot arrows through her belly.

"Get her away from me," Duff shouted.

"She has come to help ye, lad," Tomaidh said in a soothing tone. "Lie down and let her finish her work. Dinna act the fool."

"Traitor," he shouted at his mate and spat on the ground by her feet. "*Sassenach* bitch."

Eva drew in a deep breath through her nose and then let it out slowly, releasing with it the anger at his accusation. This was no less than she expected. The man had been beaten, and most certainly blamed it on her. On top of that, she'd just poured spirits on his open flesh. Well, perhaps she was willing to admit that pouring whisky on his wound to wake him was in bad form, but she'd call it even for him having spied on her. But instead of saying all that, which would only rile the warrior more, Eva schooled her features into calm authority.

"There has been no one to come and tend your wounds," she said softly. "Unfortunately for you, this *Sassenach* is the only one who has. So while you may be angry or offended by the nature of my birth and our connection, I can promise you I mean only to help."

Duff stared at her, seeming stunned she would not simply leave. That she had not exploded in a fit of rage at the way he'd treated her. She waited patiently, hiding her jumble of nerves and holding herself in place when she truly did want to run back to the comfort of her chamber.

She could smell the blood of his wounds mixed with the whisky. The sour scent of it was enough to make anyone gag, but she held it in.

In the dim light, she could have sworn she saw tears spark in his eyes. But before she could examine him closer, Duff dropped his head on his hands and muttered, "Get on with it then."

Tomaidh jerked beside her, no doubt stunned that the man had acquiesced so quickly. Eva had to hide her smile and the jig she wanted to dance at her victory, however small it was.

She winked at Tomaidh. Though she'd hoped this would be the result, there had always been the chance that Duff would deny her help. All wounded animals were reluctant at first. Usually, all it took was a strong yet gentle hand to show them you meant well. In most cases, anyway. Sometimes they did try to bite you, and then you needed to simply walk away.

"All right, then," she murmured, reaching into her basket for the remainder of the supplies. The sooner she got started, the sooner she'd be done, and the less likely he'd be able to change his mind.

Her hands trembled slightly when she grasped the clean linen, but she willed them to still. "Tomaidh, I need hot water to clean his wounds."

An hour or so later, Duff slept peacefully, his wounds cleaned. Eva had applied a healing salve topped by a poultice and gave Tomaidh strict instructions to keep the wounds cleaned and to find her if they started to puss.

Once it was complete, she went to the kitchens and fixed Strath a trencher of leftovers with Frances's help. Now she stood in the doorway of Strath's chamber and stared at a man who looked like he'd spent the better part of the last few hours in torment. His chamber smelled of whisky, but mingled with the spirits was the scent of pine and leather.

"We missed you at supper." Eva didn't close his door out of propriety's sake, but she did walk in and take the other cushioned seat on the opposite side of the table. She placed the trencher she'd gathered in the kitchen down in front of him. "I brought you something to eat. The lamprey pie was delicious. Our cook was not as talented as your uncle's."

He glanced down at the food. "Thank ye, lass." His voice was gravelly, as though he'd not spoken in a while. It sounded a lot like hers did when her throat was tight with emotion.

Eva cleared her throat, unable to meet his gaze. When she did chance a glance, he'd gone back to staring at his lap.

"I went to see Duff." There was no point in hiding it when he would find out sooner or later. No doubt, the men had spread it around the entire castle by now. What's more, they would soon tell Strath that she was part Scots, a fact she'd kept from him and now regretted. The timing just never seemed right. In fact, she wouldn't be surprised if they were interrupted at any moment by someone wanting to come and share the news.

"What?" He set the flagon of whisky on the table as he sat forward, blinking as if he wasn't certain he was seeing her there in reality. He looked as though he wanted to say more, to tell her how foolish she was perhaps, but he didn't.

"I treated his wounds."

Still, he said nothing. *Is he angry?*

Eva chewed her lip and then kept talking, hoping he'd respond. "He was not happy about it at first, but then he allowed me to do it."

"Why?" he choked out.

Eva blew out a shuddering breath. "I suspect because he didn't want an infection."

"Nay, why did ye help him?" Even in the dark, she could make out his pained expression.

"Because I am partly to blame for the situation, and because my mother trained me to care for others, and lastly, because I...care about you, Strath." She should tell him now about her mother, but... she hesitated.

At this admission, he sat back heavily in his chair, lifted the whisky and took a long pull. She was a little hurt he didn't respond, but knew that he would need to process through the haze of all he had going on in his head.

"Mind sharing?" she asked, leaning toward the table and extending her arm. Perhaps the whisky would fortify her.

Strath raised a brow but passed her the jug.

"I could have used this while I was dressing his wounds. I had some whisky with me, but it didn't seem prudent to drink spirits while trying to garner his trust." She let out a little laugh.

"Ye're amazing." He stared at her, his burr slightly breathy.

"Thank you, but I assure you, I am quite ordinary." She took a sip of the smoky-tasting whisky, impressed she didn't shudder this time. In fact, the warmth of the liquor as it slid down her throat was a welcoming comfort.

Strath shook his head. "Ye're too modest."

Eva passed back the flagon of whisky, and a shock of excitement raced up her arm as their fingers brushed. "I may not have a habit of self-congratulating, but I am by no means meek, and you must know this by now."

"I do. 'Tis part of what makes ye so fascinating to me."

Eva laughed. "All this flattery will give me a big head."

"Your head could be as big as that hearth over there, and I'd still find ye beautiful." He set down the whisky jug and caught her hand, brushing his finger over her knuckles. "I've never met anyone quite like ye, Eva, I'm serious."

Eva's gaze traced a path over the angles of his striking visage. "Funny, you're not the first one to say that to me today."

"We speak the truth. This world is full of selfish people, and I've only seen ye be honest and try to help others."

Honest. How could she tell him now that she'd kept a big truth from him? "I have helped myself plenty. With you, I helped myself."

He chuckled. "I wouldna consider kissing me as helping yourself, but if ye do, by all means."

That was not what she'd meant. Heat flushed her cheeks, and she thought about pulling away from his grasp, but he held her fingers fast. How easy it was for them to slide back into their routine. How easy it had been for her to pull him from his melancholy just by talking to him. Just by being there.

Eva smirked. "I meant by asking you to take me away from Belfinch."

"Ah." The humor left his face, and in its place, a dark look passed over him, as though until that moment, he'd forgotten all about the man.

Eva hated to think she'd spoiled what was proving to be quite a warm moment between them. Determining she wouldn't spoil it more just yet with her Scottish roots, she stood, circled the table, and came to stand in front of him. He still clutched her fingers. Her heart skipped a beat. A week, maybe even a day before now, she wouldn't be doing this. Wouldn't have been so bold as to take what she wanted.

Nevertheless, here she was. And not one ounce of her self-control wanted to put a stop to it. Without another moment's thought, she sat down on Strath's lap and wrapped her arms around his neck, pleased he didn't try to stop her.

He stared at her, but there was no surprise in his eyes, only desire, happiness, and pride. That was a mixture of expressions she would be happy to see on his face for the rest of her days.

"I want you to kiss me," she whispered.

"With the door open?"

She shrugged. "We have already been spotted before, what difference does it make?"

"In the dark?"

"In the dark, in the light, I do not care, as long as I'm in your arms. You say that I am amazing to you, but truthfully, Strath, I am the one who is in awe."

"Perhaps ye should be more cautious, Princess." His lip quirked in a wry grin.

"And why should I? Where has caution gotten me in the past?"

He chuckled, stroked a finger along the side of her jaw and splayed his other hand on the small of her back. "I want to know everything there is to know about ye."

"And already you know me better than most." *Save for one tiny part...*

"An honor 'tis."

She traced the outline of his mouth with the tip of her finger. "Will you make me wait forever, heathen?"

"I could never wait so long." And then he leaned up and pressed his lips to hers. The taste of whisky mingled with his own delicious flavor, and the stubble on his cheek tickled her fingertips.

Eva sank into his kiss, reveling in the passion of it, the way she floated away on a bed of heavenly clouds.

I love you.

Chapter Fifteen

E verything about this moment was wrong.

Alone, in the dark, in his bedchamber with a virgin lass betrothed to his enemy. A lass he loved. A lass he'd die for, and could very well be killed over.

In the eyes of the English, he'd stolen this woman. They'd say he'd abducted her across the border. Ravaged her without consent. Destroyed her soul.

And yet that could not be further from the truth. Well, most of it. Aye, she was English. Aye, he'd taken her across the border and she was betrothed to his enemy. But she'd come of her own free will. The lass's spirit was high, and her soul appeared undamaged. In fact, if someone were to ask, he might even call her happy. She'd not wanted to marry that bastard, and she had no problem with Strath luring Belfinch here to meet his doom. He'd not ravaged her—unless someone considered these powerful encounters to be ravaging.

Strath let out a groan, deepening their kiss. One word from her, and he would take her. God, how he would take her...

Ballocks! Nay!

He couldn't. Despite how she undid him with her kiss, he had to remember she was an innocent. That innocents had one bargaining chip in this world, and that was the fact they were untouched. Their virginity was essentially their way to buy a future. And, aye, how very wrong that was, when a man had the ability to forge his path without the cost of his body remaining pure.

Despite how wrong it was to continue kissing her, touching her, wanting her, how he felt about Eva could not compare to any other. So he continued to kiss her. To stroke her back. He took in her keening mewls, the desperate lash of her tongue against his, and kissed her back.

Her hands were in his hair, tugging loose the queue that held his unruly dark locks in check and threading her fingers in the tangles, massaging his scalp.

She was warm on his lap, her curves supple, and though he was cautious not to get carried away, he couldn't help but enjoy the soft swell of her hips and the way the underside of her breast felt against the pad of his thumb. Heaven help him, he was in trouble.

Eva's moans and the way she rocked in his lap were going to have him undone. Her legs were slung over the side of the chair, her bottom pressed to his hard cock, and her breasts crushed against his chest, nipples jutting through the fabric making him even harder.

She smelled heavenly, like flowers and honey mixed with the whisky she'd just imbibed. And all the more heady was the fact that she'd gone out to the barracks, knowing full well that Duff hated her to the core of his bones, and still tried to help, because she cared about him. Oh, did she even realize how intoxicating an admission that was?

Who was this woman? An angel from the heavens? If she wasn't, she was damn close.

There was no way on earth he could ever let her go.

Strath knew the difference between a woman who was worthy and a woman who was not. Eva deserved every bit of happiness in this world, and he wanted to give it to her. To give her everything.

"I love ye," he murmured against her mouth, the words tumbling out against her lips before he could halt them. As soon as they were out in the world, a moment of panic filled him, and then elation. He wanted to tell her. To tell the world.

She paused, one hand in his hair, the other on his shoulder.

Mo chreach. Would she rebuff him? Tell him he'd been a fool yet again? Strath squirmed, his stomach forming into knots. The seconds ticked by in echoing panic. But then she kissed him deeper, as though she were absorbing those words, sucking them from his very soul. She paused again, pulled away so she could gaze at him. Even in this dull light, he could see her beautiful blue eyes, pupils dilated.

"I love you, Strath."

Strath. The name that he went by, the only name so many knew him by. Suddenly, he wanted her to call him by his true name, for he'd never allowed another, not since he was a lad and his parents had given him this new name. "Magnus," he said. "Call me Magnus, sweet Princess."

She exhaled on his lips. "Oh, Magnus, I love you."

The moment the words left her mouth, Strath knew he'd never felt true happiness until now. Knew without a doubt that he would make certain his king knew Eva was his.

EVA WAS hot all over and so filled with happiness she could have leapt off Strath's lap and run twenty miles. Energy and joy thrummed in her veins. He loved her? He truly did?

Had she ever thought she'd hear those words? Not ever. And never from a strong and passionate warrior like him.

At first, she thought he was only saying it because he'd imbibed in more than his fair share of whisky, but then she realized that was not the case. If it were, he would not have asked her to call him by his given name. A name not even his aunt and uncle and cousins called him.

He loved her.

There could be no doubt about it. But where did that leave them?

Eva scratched lightly at the base of his skull, tugging on his hair. "What are we to do?"

"Well..." he drawled. "I can kiss ye here." He nuzzled her neck, nibbling at the place just behind her ear. "Or here." He slid his tongue on her ear, scraping his teeth over her earlobe in a way that made her shiver. "Or possibly here." His lips trailed a blazing path over her neck.

Eva sucked in a ragged breath. If she thought kissing him on the mouth could make her shiver, having his mouth on other parts of her was even better.

"Is this what ye meant, Eva?" he chuckled, lips grazing over her collarbones, hands massaging her back.

Was that what she meant? Huh?

And then she remembered her question. "Oh, no, I meant..." She tilted her head to the side, giving him better access to her neck. She really did quite like that. "I meant what are we to do about loving each other?"

"What is there to do but keep on loving one another?" he asked.

While it was a lovely answer, she was hoping for something more, and she wasn't afraid to say it. "We are going to soon be at war, Magnus." She ran her fingers along the collar of his shirt, wondering if he would shiver the way she did if she pressed her lips to his skin? "What are we going to do about a future? I love you. I don't want to leave you."

She leaned down to test out her theory, skimming her lips over the stubble on his neck. The corded muscles flexed at her touch, the pulse of his heartbeat against her mouth. He sucked in a breath. She would take that as an affirmative, that he did in fact feel it just as she did.

"I want ye by my side, always," he said. "Unless of course there is someone holding a sword at me, then I want ye as far away as possible."

"I would be willing to fight for you."

"I would never ask."

Eva touched her hand to his face and kissed his mouth lightly. "Loving someone means never having to ask them to protect you."

He grinned at her, his eyes intense. "God, I want to make love to ye."

"I want you to make love to me, too."

"But not until we wed."

"Then let us wed."

He stilled. And she wondered if he was thinking about Jean Guinn. "I am not her. I will not abandon you or betray you."

"I know. But..." His jaw tightened, and she felt him distancing himself.

Eva smiled and kissed him anyway. "I will do whatever you wish."

"There are more matters than just the two of us deciding. We must follow the orders of the king."

The king. The one who was looking for her. The swirling thoughts racing through her mind had the power to douse her elation at just having discovered he loved her. But she didn't want to think about them. She wanted to revel in this newfound awareness. Had to for her own sanity. "Then we must convince him a marriage between us is sound. How could he refuse?" She was aware of how naïve she sounded when she said it, but the warmth cascading through her filled her with a vibrant hopefulness.

He stroked the side of her face. "How could I ever deserve a woman like ye?"

"Don't say that. You deserve happiness. You're a good man, a good leader. I know we've only known each other a short time, but in that time I've seen into your heart, Magnus. I've seen the way your men look up to you. I've seen the way your family adores you. And the way you've conducted yourself with me..." She pressed her hand over his heart.

Strath shook his head and leaned his forehead against her so their eyes were locked. She giggled.

"Ye know how to pull a man from his misery."

"Only you, my love. And I can only pull you where you want to be pulled. You have to believe."

"Huh," he mused. "My uncle said the same thing to me recently."

"He's a smart man."

"Aye. The both of ye are right. And I do believe. I didna think it was possible, but I'd be a fool not to. And I've been a fool, blindly going through the past few months without seeing the truth for what it was."

"Good. I like the teasing, kissing Strath—Magnus—better. But I would be happy with whomever you are, as long as you're mine."

"Och, lass, ye dinna know what it does to me to hear ye say it. I will spend the rest of my days proving to ye that I'm worthy, if ye'll have me as your husband."

"Aye, a thousand times, aye."

He chuckled. "Not more than a thousand?"

She tickled his ribs, and he pretended it worked and then started to tickle her back until she fell off his lap. He caught her mid-air and fell onto the plush tapestry rug on the floor with her.

They were laughing so hard tears came to their eyes. His solid body was pressed into hers, sending spirals of pleasure rushing through her. All of the sudden, their laughing ceased, and his heady, heavily-lidded gaze met hers. Desire mirrored in his regard, and shivers caressed every inch of her skin. Then he was kissing her again. His hot, demanding mouth on hers, and she could have swooned from the passion of it. Heart pounding, belly wobbling, limbs trembling, she sank into the passion that was her warrior.

"I want to give ye pleasure, but I will nae take ye fully until our wedding night."

"Give me pleasure?" Her voice wobbled a little, filled with craving, nerves firing.

"If ye'll let me."

If she'd let him... She wasn't opposed to pleasure; in fact, she was so weak when it came to the way he made her feel that it didn't take more than a few seconds for her to say, "Aye. Show me."

"*Mo chreach,* will I ever." Strath kissed her harder, his tongue laying claim to her mouth, his solid body rocking against hers.

"The door," she murmured, somehow aware that if they were to do this, the door needed to be closed.

They were lucky that no one had come by yet.

Strath leapt to his feet and was at the door in two strides. He closed it tightly and put the bar in place. Eva sat up and lifted her hands to him, silently asking for him to pull her up, but he shook his head and lay down beside her on the soft carpet.

"If we're going to be scandalous," he said, "we'd best do it right."

"Oh," she gasped. "This is very scandalous."

He chuckled and reached for her, kissing her hotly as his hands roamed over her hips and her ribs. Her body strained forward, nipples tight, aching buds. She wanted him to touch her, and when he brushed the pad of his thumb over her nipple, she sucked a breath through her teeth, eyes popping open at the pleasure.

"I like the way ye respond to my touch," he murmured against her lips.

Eva clutched at his shirt, tugging at the ties, wanting to feel his skin. When she had it untied at the collar, the linen fell open enough for her to slide her hand inside, to feel the warm hardness of his chest and the tickle of hair against her palm. His skin was rougher than hers, fascinating.

Strath let out a ragged breath, much like the ones she was exhaling. These were small touches, nothing in the grand scheme of what she knew happened between a man and a woman, and yet they were already panting, and sparks of pleasure and keen wanting stormed through her.

Strath trailed kisses over her collarbone and then flicked his tongue over the place on her chest just above her breast. He skimmed his fingers along the inside of her gown, giving a little tug until the fabric slid lower and he brushed her nipple. Eva moaned, and he kissed his way lower, until his tongue replaced his roving fingers, and white heat shot from her breast straight to her core.

Good heavens. How would she survive this pleasure?

Eva tightened her grip and slid her other hand into his hair, not wanting him to let up from his ministrations.

"Do ye like it, Princess?" he asked and took a nipple into his mouth to suck.

Like? She wasn't certain there was a word for how much she was enjoying this. "Aye," she crooned. Heat pooled between her legs, and she moved her thighs together restlessly, wanting more. Something more.

Strath seemed to know exactly what that more was. He caressed her hip, squeezing gently and then moving from the back of her thigh over to the front. The back of his fingertips slid slowly upward until he cupped her sex through her gown, and Eva thought she would die from the pleasure of it.

Aye, this was the something more. Unable to stop herself, she tilted her hips forward into his touch, the pressure of his stroking hand almost too much to bear. Almost.

"Ye have so much passion inside ye." He leaned up and kissed her mouth, his hand still rubbing between her legs.

Then he replaced his hand with his thigh. The hardness of his arousal pressed to her belly, and he slowly slid himself against her, a groan on his delicious mouth.

"This is sinful," she murmured. "But I don't want to stop."

"Not yet," he groaned. "God, not yet. I want to taste every delicious inch of ye."

Taste...every inch... How sensual and...intoxicating that thought was.

"And I want to do the same to you," she replied, very much desiring to run her hands along the length of his body and kiss him from his ankles back to his lips.

"Och, Eva... Ye have no idea how verra much I want ye to do that." He slid a hand down to her knee, where he slowly started to inch the fabric of her gown up until his fingers grazed the laces of her hose. He caressed higher, touching her bare thigh. "Your skin is so soft."

His heated palm skimmed over the sensitive flesh of her thigh, and she quivered, holding her breath as frissons of pleasure flashed in the wake of his touch and found their way through her fevered body.

Slowly, he rose higher, his lips on hers as his fingers brushed the curls at the apex of her thighs. He slid a gentle finger between the folds, searching for something, and then she knew when he found it—a knot of flesh that when stroked had her body bucking with the intensity of the pleasure.

"Aye, lass, pleasure..." he crooned against her mouth. "Take it."

And she did. Writhing with every delicious stroke. How had she not known that such feeling, such decadent pleasure could be had? Her body bowed, hungry, striving for something higher, more intense.

With every rise of her hips, every moan from deep in her throat, Strath answered with a groan of his own. His fingers increased their pace, until Eva could no longer think of anything save pleasure and him.

Then what her body had been racing toward was there, shattering her in breathless pulses of ecstasy.

"Och, princess, ye climax so prettily," he murmured.

"Climax... That is the perfect word for it."

He chuckled.

"I want to do the same to you. Will you teach me?"

Strath fell to the side, rolling onto his back with a groan. At first she thought he was distraught, but his eyes were filled with desire, and the curve of his mouth told her everything she needed to know.

He wanted her.

"I fear I may scare ye," he said.

"How could you ever scare me?"

"A man is different than a woman."

She gazed down over his plaid, making out the jutting fabric where his...man parts...must be. "I know that," she said quietly.

Curiosity coiled inside her. Oh, how she wanted to touch.

She trailed her fingers over the crisp hair of his muscled thigh, beneath his plaid. She stopped when she reached his hip.

"Teach me," she said.

Strath pulled at his plaid, revealing himself to her. An engorged shaft, thick and long with a velvety-looking head, jutted from between a thatch of dark hair. Goodness, it was...mesmerizing.

"That is your..." She swallowed, unable to say the word.

"My cock, princess, and now yours."

"My cock." She grinned down at him, and his smile widened.

"Ye really are a wonder, Eva."

She laughed softly and reached out to touch him. When he'd stroked her, it had been with his fingertips, but he didn't appear to have a button like her, unless the engorged tip was it. She touched it, and he hissed a breath.

"Am I doing it right?" she asked.

"Almost." He took her hand in his, moved her fingers to grip his cock at the base and then stroked upward and back down again. "Like this."

"Oh," she said, barely audible.

Stroking his velvet hot flesh sent frissons of desire careening through her once more. Giving pleasure gave pleasure; how incredible.

She explored him stroke after stroke, watching his face, watching the way his belly rose and fell in jagged breaths. His gaze never left her as they continued, and she thought she might burst from wanting to… to see him climax.

"Lass," he croaked. "We need to stop before I…"

"Nay, I want you to finish."

"But it is…messy."

"Messy?" she asked before realization dawned. His seed.

She leapt up, located his wash basin, and returned with a linen. "Will this do?"

"Ye will be the death of me," he chuckled.

"Nay, I will be the climax." Grinning, Eva sank back down to her knees, took his cock in hand, without his help this time, and then leaned over him to kiss his mouth as he'd done to her when he brought her to fruition.

Taking notes from what he'd done to her, she quickened her pace, and Strath groaned into her mouth, his breath fanning quick and hot over her cheek. Then he groaned, and warm liquid spilled over her hand.

Climax… She kissed him one more time and pulled back to take in his flushed face and the cloudy look in his eyes.

"You climax just as beautifully, heathen."

"God, I love ye," he said in reply.

He used the linen to clean himself up and then pulled her down beside him to kiss her tenderly.

"It is a wonder there are any virgins at all," she mused.

Strath burst out laughing. "*Mo chreach*, lass, ye think the funniest things."

Chapter Sixteen

Eva woke with a start, her body cramping on one side, and she realized she was still inside Strath's room, lying on his floor, with his body curled around her back.

They'd fallen asleep on the carpet at some point, after hours and hours of discovering each other and surrendering to pleasure. She'd felt safe and happy in his arms. And once again, she was reminded of those moments in the chapel when she'd realized that to her, Strath represented home.

How she would have liked to remain like they were for the next twenty years. Alas, the aching in her side and the very real need to use the chamber pot forced her awake.

Gently, she removed his arm from around her waist and stood, stretching out the kinks from having slept in the same position on the floor for nearly the whole night. How quickly she'd gotten used to sleeping in a bed.

Gray light filtered through the shutters of his windows. With morning came the stark reminders of what she'd not told him, and what his mission from the king could mean. Eva glanced down at him, wondering if she should wake him. Tell him now.

But her maid would have noticed she hadn't sleep in her room, and at any moment, a search could be called. While she hoped the woman was discreet enough to not tell anyone, there were no guarantees. Alas, no one had come looking for her yet, so it wasn't too out of the realm of possibilities. Unless of course, her maid had guessed where Eva was and had chosen to keep it a secret.

Even with no one looking at her, she felt her cheeks heat. Well, it was time to face judgment. Eva tiptoed over to the door, wincing when she stepped on a board that creaked loudly. She glanced back to make sure she'd not woken him and saw he was in the same spot as before.

Eva raised the bar on the door and opened it, breathing a sigh of relief that it made nearly no sound. She didn't want to wake Strath, or anyone else in the castle.

"Where are ye going?"

Too late, the sound of his groggy voice reached her, and she turned around to smile down at him. He'd rolled over to face her and propped his head up on his bent arm.

"I was going to wash up and prepare for the day. And also assure my maid that I am still an innocent, though she probably won't believe me. But I must try."

He grinned lazily, got to his feet, and came toward her. "Ye're no innocent, Princess."

Eva laughed softly. "Perhaps not in my head, but certainly as far as any priest is concerned." She bit her lip. "Well, mayhap not. I should probably pray on that. Confess."

"Will ye tell your confessor every detail?" He nuzzled her neck, pulling her into his embrace. "Do I need to refresh your memory?"

"Oh." She gave a gasp of mock outrage and playfully slapped at him. "You're a rogue."

"And ye fell in love with me that way." He softly bit her earlobe.

"That is true." She wrapped her arms around him and sank into his solid warmth. "Maybe I do need to be reminded..."

"Reminded of what?" The gruff sound of Uncle Jamie behind them had Eva springing away from Strath, her face flaming red as she took sight of Laird Montgomery in the dimly lit corridor.

He was fully dressed and eyeing them both with barely concealed amusement. She was certain her hair was a disaster and her gown was wrinkled enough to alert everyone to the fact that she'd slept in her clothes. But she thought he might be most amused by the way her face had gone from flushed with desire, to pale white, to flaming red again.

Thankfully, when she peeked between her lashes, Laird Montgomery was no longer looking at her, but at Strath. What excuse would he, *her lover*, come up with? And would his uncle believe him?

"Reminded of why she loves me." Strath's voice held the same note of teasing that it had the first night they'd arrived and he'd told the entire table about how he'd had to get her to agree not to take advantage of him.

"I see," Uncle Jamie said, rocking on his heels with his hands clasped behind his back.

Eva's tongue was paralyzed. By now, Jamie had to know what she'd told Tomaidh and the men. She should declare the truth now. But how could she say anything? She could barely think. And the warrior standing before them blocked any escape she might make. She was well and truly trapped. Whatever shame she was supposed to feel in this moment, she didn't. If anything, she wanted to staunchly support their relationship. To fortify that she meant to make a life with Strath. She raised her head, trying to find the courage to speak up.

"And are her feelings returned?" Jamie asked.

Eva's gaze swept to Strath, wondering if this would be the moment he denied her.

"Aye, uncle." Strath glanced at her, eyes glittering with amusement. "Verra much."

He was finding humor in this. It took a good measure of her will not to stomp on his foot and wipe that smile off. The warrior wasn't taking this seriously at all.

Eva straightened her shoulders and regarded the older laird. "I love your nephew, my laird, and I'm not ashamed of that."

The older man smiled at her with genuine affection. "Well, then," Uncle Jamie said with a very distinctive note of authority. "Now that it is settled, nephew, ye'd best inform your Da and Ma. I'm certain they'll want to know ye've found yourself a bride. And your Da can plead your case to the king. Of course, ye have my blessing. Ye'll make my nephew a good Scottish wife." He left no room for argument, not that he'd get any from her. And then she realized what he'd said—*Scottish*.

She had a sudden panic that Strath would argue. An irrational fear that he'd change his mind when he found out the truth.

"Aye." Strath touched her elbow, and she blew out a sigh of relief. He'd not mentioned his uncle's reference to a Scottish bride. Had he not heard him? Saints but she'd dug herself into a corner. How was she going to make this right?

"Strath, I need to tell you something." She flicked her gaze at Uncle Jamie who didn't seem to catch her hint that she wanted privacy.

"Can it wait, lass? I'd like a moment alone with my uncle. I'll come find ye to break our fast in a little bit."

Eva hesitated. And he smiled encouragingly, fortifying her. "Nay, it cannot." She swallowed, keeping her eyes locked with his and pretending his uncle wasn't standing there. "My mother was...is a Lindsay. I was told she was dead by my father, but I believe her to still be alive. She was abducted by Belfinch's father, and... Part of the reason I offered myself to you in Northwyck was in hopes I might find out what really happened to her."

To his credit, Strath did not react. He nodded curtly, then cleared his throat. "Why did ye wait so long to tell me?"

Tears threatened and she wrung her hands in front of her. "At first I thought it best to protect myself, and then when I determined to tell you, the timing just..." She swallowed, knowing her explanations were only excuses. "I made a mistake."

"I see."

"Please forgive me."

He nodded. "I'll come find ye shortly."

Eva could have burst into tears right then, but she managed to stand up tall. "Aye, my laird." She curtsied to his uncle and took off at a near run down the corridor, feeling the niggling sense of mortification at having been caught in such an improper encounter, and a fear that soon she would find herself back to being a prisoner.

Strath had no comment on what she'd revealed other than to ask why she'd not told him sooner. How would he trust her again after she'd proven to be a withholder of the truth? She wouldn't blame him if he didn't.

Her maid stood in her chamber, face pale, hands wringing, while Lorna paced in front of the hearth. A low fire was lit, and Eva's bed was still made from the day before.

"Oh, thank God." The lady of the castle rushed forward to grab Eva by the shoulders and examine her. After searching her person and finding nothing harmed, she regarded Eva's face with motherly concern. "What happened?"

Eva cleared her throat, trying to find some of the strength she'd had with Laird Montgomery. Why was it harder with Lorna than it had been with him?

"I was... Well, Strath and I..." Eva's face was so hot, she was pretty certain it was going to burst into flames.

"Oh." Lorna's eyes widened with realization. "No need to say more." She turned to face the maid and nodded her heard toward the door. "I've got it from here, thank ye for coming to find me."

Ah, so her maid had gone to look for her after all. But at least she'd waited until morning. Once the maid was gone and Lorna had shut the door, she indicated that Eva should follow her to sit in a chair before the hearth.

"When I was about your age, I found myself in a similar situation." The older woman arranged her skirts around her feet and then leaned back, rather more relaxed than Eva would have guessed a lady could be.

"You did?"

"Well, as far as a man is concerned, aye. Jamie was visiting our castle in Sutherland. We fell for each other, harder than I thought possible. My brother, Magnus, Strath's father, found us one morning in the stables...quite in a state of undress."

Eva's mouth fell open. "Really?"

Lorna chuckled, nostalgia making her eyes misty. "Aye. I suspect that Jamie will be quite a bit kinder to Strath than my brother was to us. Though I could never fault Magnus for what he did. He was only trying to do the right thing and take care of me. Our parents died when he was only a lad, and he's been in charge of all of us ever since."

"What did he do?"

"Well, what any protector of a maiden might. He took Jamie to task. Left him bloody, and then sent him on his way, forbidding us from seeing each other ever again."

Eva gasped, her hand coming to her mouth. What would happen if she were sent away? There was no way she wanted to live out her days without Strath. Every minute would be misery. God, she prayed he forgave her.

"How did you...come to be together?" Eva asked, wanting to hear a happy ending to what could have been a disaster.

Lorna sat forward and tucked an errant lock of hair behind Eva's ear in a motherly fashion she ached for.

"I was with child. My brother had no choice but to let us be together. We were so in love, but Magnus didna believe in such things. Of course, the irony of that was he found Arbella not too long after."

"Strath's mother?"

"Aye. A lovely lady and a true, genuine heart. Everyone that meets her loves her, and you will, too. Besides, she's also English, so ye've already got that in common. She will be a good mother-by-marriage to ye." Lorna frowned and pursed her lips. "That is, I assume ye'll marry."

"We said as much to each other last night. And he confirmed it once more this morning when Jamie found us." *But that was before...*

"I hope ye werena too embarrassed to see my husband." Lorna bit her lip. "But he insisted on investigating when your maid woke us to say ye were not abed. We worried something had happened to ye."

"I'm sorry to have disturbed your sleep. That wasn't my intention, I assure you. I fell asleep and didn't wake until just before Laird Montgomery arrived. However, I was fully dressed." Eva smiled through her worry. "Though that hardly made a difference at the time for how embarrassed I felt."

Lorna laughed. "Ye're a sweet lass. Ye'll make a great addition to our family."

"I would be honored to be a part of it. I..." She was about to confess how much she missed her own family, but her words got caught in the emotional knot in her throat. Eva glanced down toward her lap where she'd wrung her skirt around her fingers.

"What is it, my dear?"

Eva gave a slight smile. "I miss my family."

Lorna reached forward and patted her on the knee. "I understand that, lass. My family is scattered across the Highlands. We do try to get together occasionally for a family gathering, usually around a wedding or the birth of a bairn. This past Yule, Strath's father held a massive feast that brought many clans together to celebrate. Where is your family?"

Eva looked down at her hands again. "My sister, Jacqueline is married to a lord who resides near London." She steeled herself. "Papa is…" She held her breath, unsure how to answer, because the truth was she didn't know where her father was exactly, but she could guess he was on his way here. Hiding the truth was difficult, and she might as well tell Lorna now before it came out. The woman had shared so much with her, and she felt they were growing close in the way friends and family should be. A lie would ruin all the good they had between them, and the truth was bound to come out soon. "My father is the Earl of Northwyck."

Lorna nodded slowly, the slight twitch at the corners of her eyes the only sign she gave that she knew who that was.

"He is probably on his way here now. With Lord Belfinch." Eva waited for the storm that was sure to come.

But it didn't. Lorna folded her hands together in her lap, and said calmly, "I see."

"I want you to know that I had no idea what Belfinch had my father involved with. I…"

"Ye needna explain yourself to me," Lorna said softly, kindness filling her features.

"But I do. And there's more."

Lorna's brows rose, but she remained quiet.

"My mother was abducted two years ago. I was told by my father she'd died of a fever. But, about a year ago I received a letter I thought was in my mother's hand. Part of the reason I wanted to come to Scotland was to find out what happened to her. She's a Lindsay."

Lorna let out a long sigh. "Ye're part Scots."

"Aye."

"The Lindsays are a powerful clan."

"Ye know them?"

"Aye, my dear."

"Will ye help me?"

"I will try."

Eva choked on a sob. "I hope you can forgive me for keeping it from you."

"It is easier to forgive than to foster resentment. So tell me, what of the story Strath told of how ye met? Was that also a falsehood?"

"It is mostly the truth. I did ask him to take me, but it was in place of my father. I...I didn't want to be left behind and forced to marry Belfinch. Which would have happened. I knew he was evil. He's been blackmailing my father for the past two years." She stopped abruptly, realizing she was babbling. Tears sprung to her eyes. *Stay strong!*

Lorna let out a long exhale. "Well, then ye're verra lucky my nephew listened."

"I feel terrible for not telling you everything before. And for not telling Strath sooner about my Scottish roots. When I arrived and everyone was so welcoming and kind...I got caught up in the web of being someone else."

"Dinna fash. Ye're not someone else," Lorna said. "Ye've been yourself the whole time, have ye not?"

"What?" Eva blinked rapidly, confused by the question.

"Well, we are not our parents." Lorna grinned, her features soft and her demeanor calming. "We are not the men who want to marry us. We must remain true to ourselves, no matter what."

"That sounds like something my mother would say." Eva brushed at the tears on her cheeks.

Lorna smiled. "I think I would like her verra much."

"And she would like you, too."

"Come, let me help ye get ready since I sent your maid away."

Eva agreed without hesitation. "How far is Dornoch from here?"

"A week, if the ride is fast, twice that, if ye're taking your time."

"Oh. So Strath is one of the family members who is scattered."

"Aye. Sadly. But for the men, it is even worse, because not only are their holdings scattered, but they are involved much with the king, so often on campaign."

"Is your husband gone much?"

"Not as much as he used to be."

Lorna pulled out of her wardrobe. "We had this one made for ye. Seemed unfair for ye to only have one gown."

Would their kindness never cease? Eva felt weightless, ready to collapse with gratitude. But she forced herself to stand strong against the tide of emotions sweeping her up. "Thank you, I can never repay you enough for all you've done for me."

"Loving our nephew is payment enough. The lad went through a lot with that last one." Lorna held up the gown, examining it with a fine eye and running her fingers down the side and along the hem.

"It is beautiful." She chewed the inside of her cheek. "I heard about...Jean Guinn."

Lorna nodded. "I think it goes without saying that if ye break his heart, ye'll have a lot of enemies." Lorna said it with a laugh, but the veiled threat was still implied.

"I swear I will not hurt him." Eva crossed her hands over her heart.

"'Tis ironic, is it nae, that his last betrothed was Scottish and an enemy of his clan? And now he has found ye, an English lass, who should be his enemy but is not?"

"Half Scots," Eva teased. "The irony has not been lost on me, either."

"I do love a happy ending."

"Me, too." Eva bit her lip, easily hiding her face as she slipped out of her old gown and washed up to put on the new one. Would theirs be a happy ending?

Why did it feel like they were all getting ahead of themselves?

"Do you think he'll forgive me for not having told him the truth sooner?"

"Oh, aye. He's a smart lad."

A knock sounded at the door.

"Go behind the screen, I'll see who it is." Lorna went to the door, opened it a crack, and spoke to whoever was in the corridor in hushed tones.

Eva stood still, straining to hear what they said, but she couldn't make out the words. Then the door clicked closed once more, she peeked around the side of the screen.

Lorna stood in the center of the chamber. There was a pained expression on her beautiful face. She didn't speak for several moments, so long that Eva wasn't certain she would.

"What is it?" Eva asked nervously, stepping out into the room.

"The scouts have spotted an English army headed this way."

Chapter Seventeen

Eva stood in the center of her chamber, staring at the closed door. Only moments before, Lorna had been there. She'd been hopeful of a future with Strath, and now she feared for any type of future she could have.

The English were coming.

Belfinch. Her father.

Eva swallowed past the knot of fear in her throat, her mouth suddenly dry. The idea of pouring herself a cup of water seemed an insurmountable task. Her feet were heavy. Her limbs paralyzed.

What was she to do? Should she pack? Prepare for...whatever was to come? There was nothing to pack. She'd come only with the ragged dress Strath had used for bait, and now only possessed the two gowns Lorna had gifted her. But she couldn't take both. Instead, she would leave with only the gown on her back.

She wasn't a warrior. She wasn't a leader. She didn't even reside at this castle. There was nothing she could do to prepare. Unless she put together another basket of healing supplies. That was something. If Wee Duff had let her work on his wounds, other men would too, wouldn't they? But the castle likely had their own healer, and Eva would only be in the way, and winning over one Scot was different than hundreds.

Eva took a few shaky steps toward a chair and sank heavily onto it.

The English had been spotted. There was no telling when they'd arrive. Could be in a few minutes, could be hours. Could even be tomorrow.

What would her future be then? When Belfinch arrived, what if he said he'd leave as long as they handed her over? Was her life worth more than a hundred men? Nay.

She would have to surrender herself. Because she couldn't bear the thought of being the cause of a war. The very idea of surrender had her belly heaving, and she rushed to a chamber pot, but nothing came out. She'd not eaten since the day before. But her body didn't get the message, and she heaved some more.

Eyes watering, she staggered toward her bed and lay down. She stared at the wall where the window let in sunlight, so different from the rain they'd been having.

Were the kittens all right?

All she could do was wait and try to figure out a way to say goodbye to a life she'd learned to love and people she'd come to like and respect in so short a time. To say goodbye to Strath...a man she'd envisioned spending the rest of her life with.

Some time later, noise from the bailey compelled her to rise. Eva went to the window, pulled back the skin that covered the arrow slit, and peered outside. Men stood on the walls, the spring sun glinting off their weapons. There were more of them than she'd seen the night they arrived, all standing straight and rigid.

Would they battle right there where she could see them? Would they simply take her and go? What if Belfinch demanded blood? What if Strath didn't win? What if Belfinch could not be subdued?

Fear struck her then, causing a cold sweat to bead on her spine. She didn't want to wed Belfinch. She didn't want to go back to Northwyck. She wanted the life she'd thought she'd have just that morning—a life with Strath.

"I won't marry Belfinch," she said to no one. Even if she had to go in order to save lives, she would find a way to escape that fate. She would find a way to go to her sister. To live near London, maybe even as a governess to her sister's children. Why wed anyone if she couldn't have the one man she truly wanted?

A horn blew a warning, rending the air. Dear God, it was happening now. Belfinch had arrived.

Eva searched out the source but didn't see any men on the wall with a horn or any riders yet on the horizon.

Had the noise come from the village? From a warrior at the top of the keep that she couldn't see?

The horn blew again, sending gooseflesh to rise along her arms. A knock sounded at the door, and Lady Lorna opened it softly.

"Eva, I must request ye remain in your chamber for your safety."

She nodded without question, knowing the order did not come from the lady herself. Besides, she was certain even if she could, she'd not be able to speak. For what could she say besides goodbye?

"Can I get ye anything?"

Eva shook her head, trying to find a voice. "Is it possible to speak with Strath?"

"I doubt it, lass. The men are putting on their armor. But I will tell him ye wish to speak to him."

"Thank you." Eva turned back to the window as Lady Lorna departed, her face drawn.

The men were donning armor. That meant Strath was in the barracks. She had to speak to him, to apologize once more and beg his forgiveness. She just had to pray he would return to her, that all would be absolved. And to tell him her decision and hope it would save blood from being shed.

Eva opened her door a crack, fearing that Strath might have put a guard on her door, but the corridor was empty. Lifting the hem of her skirt, she hurried toward the stairs, stopping to listen at the top of them. The sounds of people moving about did not appear to be coming from the stairwell. At each twist, she paused a moment to listen and finally made it the bottom.

The great hall held at least a dozen men who looked deep enough in serious conversation not to pay her any mind. She slipped past the great hall and was reaching for the wide oak door that led to the bailey when it was pushed open. There before her was the man she'd gone to find.

Strath looked magnificent and fearsome in his leather-studded armor and weapons strapped about his hips. The hilt of his claymore jutted above his shoulder.

"What are ye doing down here? Did my aunt not tell ye to remain in your chamber?"

Eva nodded. "She did, but I had to find you. We have to talk, it will only take a moment."

"Come, lass. 'Tis dangerous." He gently gripped her elbow and started to tug her back toward the stairs, but Eva dug in her heels.

"Please, Strath, I have to know that you forgive me for not telling you my whole story upfront."

He paused a moment, cupped her cheek. "Princess, I understand, and ye have nothing to forgive. I would have done the same thing."

Relief flooded her and she leaned against him, wrapping her arms around his middle and hugging him tight. He kissed her swiftly, and then said, "Come, it is not safe."

"Where are Lorna and Isobel?" If they'd been in the solar to wait out the battle, Lorna would not have requested Eva remain in her chamber alone.

He frowned. "As mistress of the castle, my aunt has duties to attend to when we're at war. And so does my cousin."

"I want to be a part of those duties. I can help them. And there is something else."

The muscle in the side of Strath's jaw ticked. He knew her well enough to know she would put up a fight. No doubt he was trying to come up with a resolution that would suit them both.

"What is it?" he asked.

This was the hard part. And she'd not realized just how difficult it would be. "I...I'm going to surrender myself."

"What?" Hardness glittered in his eyes, and she realized what those very words would indicate to him. That she'd used him. That all this time, she'd been a liar.

Eva was quick to recover before he could draw more conclusions.

"I love you, Magnus, but my life is not worth the lives of all your men. If I go with Belfinch, there will be no battle."

"Is that what ye want? To go with him?" Coldness infused every word. Already he was hardening his heart to her.

She reached for him, but he backed up a step. "That is not what I want."

"Then why would ye willingly go?"

"To save your men."

"Ye think I'm not capable of saving my own men?"

"That is not what I meant."

"Tell me, Princess, exactly when did ye decide ye'd go with Belfinch when he came for ye? Was it in the chapel, or when I had ye spread out beneath me?"

Eva gasped at the anger in his words. How quickly he'd changed from that morning. She blinked back tears. "You're cruel."

"I'm cruel?" He let out a sharp, disdainful laugh and backed up a few paces. "And what would ye call what ye've just accomplished?"

The pain in Eva's heart broke it apart piece by piece. "You're twisting my words. You think because I aim to help you avoid a battle that I'm somehow the same as Jean Guinn. I thought you knew me better than that, but it would appear all I was to you was a body to slake your lust on. And I told you that I love you. I opened my heart to you, and you have broken it."

Strath looked as though she'd slapped him, and she felt the pain of every metaphorical blow.

When next he spoke, his voice was calmer. "If there was a way to avoid battle and keep ye here, would ye choose to stay?"

"Aye," she answered without hesitation. "I thought you were smart enough to understand that. But is that possible?"

"I can try."

Eva bit her lip, the tears she'd been trying not to shed slipping out. "I cannot believe you thought I would betray you."

"I'm sorry, lass, I do know you better than that. It was a gut reaction." He came closer and gathered her into his arms.

At first, she resisted, but then she sank against his warmth. "I don't want to be the cause of your people getting hurt."

"Ye willna be the cause, Princess. Belfinch is wanted by my king for his crimes against our country. Whether or not ye were there or here, my duty has always been to take him."

Knowing that made her feel a little better.

"I canna allow ye to leave with him. I want to marry ye, Eva." He tipped her chin and kissed her gently. "I want to spend the rest of my days with ye."

"And I want to spend mine with you, too."

"So stop this nonsense about giving yourself over to that monster."

Eva nodded, swallowing hard. He was right. It was foolish to think that giving herself over would do anything but break both their hearts. Knowing Belfinch, as soon as he had her in his grasp, he'd attack anyway, just because he loved bloodshed.

"I want ye in your chamber, protected, because if for some reason the man breaks through our ranks, your barred door will be an added protection. Would ye like Isobel to stay with ye? I can make it so."

Eva nodded. "Aye. I don't want to wait alone."

"'Tis just a precaution, Eva. I will come for ye. By the time night falls, all this will be over."

IT WAS TIME.

For the first time in his life as a warrior, Strath was not ready. It wasn't that he wasn't ready to take on Belfinch, to lift his sword, or anything to do with that part of the battle. In those areas, he was completely confident.

What had his ballocks in a vice right now was the beautiful lass hidden in her chamber. If this didn't work out the way he'd planned, he might never see her again.

When she'd said she was willing to sacrifice herself, his mind had first gone back to those moments with Jean Guinn. Guilt riddled him for ever comparing the two of them. He'd known from the very start that Eva was different. And he didn't care that she'd kept her mother's heritage secret. Aye, at first he'd been disappointed, but when it came down to it, that truth altered nothing.

Jamie came to stand beside Strath on the battlements. "The scout saw two liveries in the English garrison marching toward Glasgow, which means Belfinch and Northwyck will be here within the hour, if not sooner."

Strath nodded. They'd had the horns blown so those in the fields and mountains would know to take themselves somewhere safe.

Only time would tell what kind of man Northwyck was. He prayed the man was kind to his daughter, that he listened when Strath told him to stand down, because he wasn't the one he was after. Because while he was prepared to fight the man, Strath would hate to explain that to Eva. Even if she didn't harbor the fondest memories of her father, to know the one she loved killed him would be hard. But Belfinch... He was going to have a hard time not running the man through. Eva's bruised face had healed, but the torment she'd been put through must still be raw, for he'd felt it all the way deep in his bones when she'd spoken of the bastard's treatment of her.

And despite what he'd told her, there was no way in hell was he going to let her leave with Belfinch.

The horns blew once more from the keep, a warning to those in the village that an enemy was near. Men, women, and children would be preparing for their arrival. The men with weapons, the women and children hiding.

As soon as the horn had been blown, Lady Lorna had taken in the villagers who needed a safe place, and he had to trust that Eva was still safely in her chamber with Isobel.

A warrior rushed up the stairs, panting. "My laird," he said to Jamie. "We've gotten word, English soldiers were seen in the woods."

"Let us prepare for battle."

Strath followed his uncle down the stairs to the bailey. The stable master had readied Beast, and Strath leapt onto his back and settled in the saddle.

Flanking him on horseback was Tomaidh and Uncle Jamie. Each of them wore their armor, as he did, and though they did not have their weapons drawn yet, they were ready for anything should they be needed.

His horse's flesh rippled beneath his thighs. The animal could feel his angst, and he loosened his grip and rubbed a gloved hand over his warhorse's mane. Beast sidestepped, mouthed his bit, sensing battle was near.

"Are ye ready?" Uncle Jamie asked.

"Aye."

"Is she?" Tomaidh added.

Strath shrugged, recalling how Eva had been willing to sacrifice herself. "What choice does she have?"

Immediately, he felt like a complete arse for saying it. Strath chalked it up to the cold sensation of fear that was trying to get a grip on his spine. The sensation was new, and he hated it. But dammit, he loved her and he didn't want to lose her.

Tomaidh grunted, and Strath could feel his judgment in that one sound.

They'd not spoken since he'd given Wee Duff a lashing, and Strath was glad of it, but at the same time also disappointed. He wished he'd had more time to explain to his best mate how much he loved her, even if it made him seem weak-kneed.

He wished to hell Belfinch was out of the picture.

Why did it feel like Fate and time had messed with his head? Was this God's way of telling him he'd not yet made up for the mistakes he'd made in his past? That in order to prove himself, he had to lose?

Because that's what it felt like. Even if he had Belfinch's neck beneath his blade, to lose her would be like that blade slicing into his own heart.

"I love her," Strath said to no one in particular. "I dinna want to lose her."

Jamie slapped him on the back and squeezed his shoulder. "I know that feeling verra well, lad. Fight like the devil, and ye'll come back to her."

"Thank ye, uncle." Strath cleared his throat, forcing himself to focus on things other than love. "If it comes to battle," he said to Tomaidh, "make certain the lass's father is safe. Though he is a blackguard and doesna give a damn about his daughter, I would like her to see we spared his life."

"Aye, my laird. I will personally see to it."

The men on the wall gave the signal. Belfinch was within sight.

"Ready?" Uncle Jamie asked.

"Aye."

The men rode through the village to the second gate, their army behind them. The houses were closed up tightly, candles extinguished, giving the village an eerie feel. Not even a lone chicken walked across their path.

"Open the gate and ready the archers," Jamie called up to the men on the outer wall.

The cranking of the chain as the portcullis was raised echoed in the silence of the bailey. Strath, Tomaidh, and Jamie went through the gate to wait for the riders to approach. They did not draw their weapons. They would meet the men on the field and would approach this civilly before calling out for battle. Waiting in the village bailey was an army of their men, and the archers prepared to shoot on Jamie's signal should negotiations fall through.

Across the moors, Strath took stock of the riders approaching. At the head were the liveries of Northwyck and Belfinch just as the scout had reported. Behind them rode their metal-clad knights, perhaps fifty of them. While it wasn't a massive army, it was big enough to set a tone for their intent. They would fight.

When they were half a field away, the two lords broke off from their army and rode toward them. Good. Strath had that worried the men would try to fight right then and there instead of waiting to discuss terms. Not that he wouldn't have enjoyed taking Belfinch's head, but he wanted this to go according to plan.

"You," Belfinch accused as he drew closer. "Where is she?"

"How is your head?" Strath asked, unable to stop himself from adding the jibe.

"Where is she?" Belfinch asked again, ignoring him.

Strath tilted his head from side to side, cracking his neck and trying to find the patience not to attack the bastard. "She is safe. We require that ye leave your army outside our walls and come inside to discuss terms. The both of ye."

Belfinch gave a subtle shake of his head. "Send her out. And my coin."

"I'm afraid that is not how this is going to work," Strath said.

"Ye will be safe inside the walls," Jamie added.

Safe until our king arrives to take ye hostage...

"Who are you?" Belfinch said with disdain.

"Laird Montgomery."

Both Belfinch and Northwyck nodded, having recognized the name. Strath stared at Eva's father. The man looked to have aged a decade since he'd seen him a little over a week before. What was it about Belfinch that held him captive?

"Your daughter will be pleased to see ye are alive," Strath offered.

Northwyck cocked his head, looking momentarily confused, then he nodded and flicked his gaze toward Belfinch.

"His daughter belongs to me. And if you don't present her within the next five minutes, I will order my men to attack. Given the way you attacked the castle of Northwyck in England, we cannot trust that we'll be safe behind your walls."

"Fair enough," Strath said, having expected that. He'd made an attempt at decency as he'd promised Eva he would. But decency had no place with these men. He withdrew his sword. "I'll take pleasure in a bit of exercise."

There was a flash of fear on Belfinch's face. Perhaps he thought that by bringing his army with him, Strath would show fear, but he'd clearly not learned anything from the first time they'd met.

"You will regret it," Belfinch hissed, yanking on the reins of his poor horse and turning in the opposite direction and kicking the sorry animal into a gallop. The whoreson would likely hide behind his army while they fought.

"I doubt that," Strath called after him and signaled to Tomaidh, who was quick to apprehend Northwyck before he could ride away.

"Please don't kill me," the old man whimpered.

Belfinch didn't even turn around.

"How did ye raise such a strong daughter considering ye are so weak?" Strath asked.

"My wife," he sputtered, "she is...strong."

Is? Was the old man confused? "I could have guessed. Take him inside—and keep him contained."

Tomaidh nodded, grasped the old man's reins and dragged him through the throng of Scottish warriors.

Jamie shook his head. "I could never imagine being that weak."

"Aye. To give one's daughter over to a monster."

"Aye, and to Belfinch, too," Jamie teased.

"Let's show the bloody *Sassenachs* how a battle is won, and leave Belfinch to me." Strath raised his sword in the air.

Before Belfinch reached the rear of his line, Strath let out a war cry. The Montgomery and Dornoch warriors followed him across the field, hungry for a fight. They were hungry to practice their skills, hungry for triumph.

The English were slow, encumbered by their armor and too cold to be fueled by passion. Strath and his men put their fury at years of abuse and from the English cruelty into every swing and block of their swords. *Sassenachs* fell like iron flies, dropping left and right.

Belfinch hid at the back, using his men as shields and refusing to fight. Strath couldn't blame him for it. The stupid bastard had fallen over a pew in the chapel and knocked himself into a deep sleep in the process. What injury could he cause himself in the defense of his person?

The thought made Strath laugh. Perhaps the idiot would knock himself from his horse and break his neck, leaving the duty of taking him to the king a moot point.

The armored knight in front of him widened his eyes in horror at Strath as he brought his sword down on the flesh between his neck and shoulder.

The Scots pushed their way through the iron knights until Strath reached Belfinch, who was quick to drop his sword and hold up his hands. In his haste, he did exactly as Strath guessed he would, and tumbled backward off the horse.

Strath shook his head. "Ye have a big mouth but are nae so handy with a sword."

Belfinch gritted his teeth. "My life is worth more than my corpse."

"Who says I care?"

"All you Scots care. Besides, you would have killed me already."

"Aye. I would have."

"What will you do with me?"

Strath shrugged. "Dump ye in a dungeon? Let the rats feast on your toes."

"My king will send an army to find me."

"Will he? Do tell me, what was that key I took from around your neck for?"

Belfinch gritted his teeth but said nothing.

"Ye have a choice," Jamie shouted to the men not already cut down. "Die or surrender."

Iron knights dropped to their knees, their weapons clanging on the ground at their feet.

"I think the key hides your treasure. The things ye've been stealing from Northwyck."

Belfinch still said nothing. Strath grinned and shrugged as he reached forward and grabbed the man by his hair, pulling him up until he was standing. With a flick of his sword, he cut through Belfinch's belt and used it to wrap around his wrists.

"I wonder how quickly I can find your treasure," Strath asked, using a perfect English accent. "I am here on official business from his lordship, allow me entry."

Belfinch growled.

"Aye, that is what I'll do. I'll pretend to have been sent by ye. And I'll have ye sign a document. Oh, what fun it will be forcing ye to sign it..."

Strath continued to bait the man as he dragged him all the way back to the castle.

"Better still, perhaps I'll send a letter to Northwyck's other daughter, along with the key and the coin we took from ye, and let her distribute what ye stole to Northwyck's people. What hold did ye have over the man anyway?"

"He destroyed my life, and I destroyed his."

"Ah, a classic case of revenge. What really happened to Lady Northwyck? What could he have done to ruin your life?"

"He killed my father." The man conveniently did not mention the lady.

"Ah, I see." Strath let out an exaggerated sigh. "That will do it. I can understand why ye'd be so irate."

"You understand." Belfinch latched on to that. "See, he deserves to have gone bankrupt because of it."

"I have one question though. Did guilt over killing your father cause him to allow ye to blackmail him? Why did he not simply kill ye?"

"'Twas murder, and he blamed another lord for it. The other lord was beheaded, his property forfeit." Belfinch gritted his teeth.

"So killing ye would be in his best interest."

"Only if he had the key." The words came out begrudgingly, but Belfinch clearly wanted Strath to believe him.

Why else would he tell him that?

"Ah, I see. Your treasure also holds some documents to that effect."

Reluctantly, Belfinch grumbled, "Aye."

"Interesting. So all this time, ye've been holding that threat over his head?"

"And I will continue to do so if you'll return what is mine."

Strath tsked. "Why did he kill your father?"

Belfinch gritted his teeth, clamming up once more. There was more to the story, and Strath didn't believe for a second that the man didn't know the answer.

"Ye dinna have to tell me now, but in due time, I will find out. I'm thinking the lady has something to do with this."

"Why do you even care? Take me to your king and be on your way to stealing my coin. By keeping the key, you're only protecting a murderer."

Strath wasn't so certain about the latter. Men didn't simply go around murdering other men. And from what he'd gathered about Northwyck thus far, the man was a bloody weakling, even if he was capable of cruelty.

And Strath knew exactly why he cared. The answer was up in her chamber right now, waiting for word. She was waiting for information on her father. Her mother. On Belfinch. On what would happen to her. Perhaps even worrying over his own fate.

Mayhap, it would be easier to get the information he needed from Northwyck. He could give the bastard the key and send him on his way —but not with his daughter.

Nay, that notion left a bitter taste in his mouth.

Eva was his.

Chapter Eighteen

"Father." Eva walked slowly across the great hall to her father, who stood near the doorway with hands tied.

When she'd seen Tomaidh walk with him beneath the gate, head hung low, she wasn't certain how she felt, and she still wasn't. It was a mixture of trepidation and relief. Relief to know he was alive, but trepidation about what this meant for her. A jumble of emotions had flooded her system, enough so that her knees had nearly buckled and she'd had to catch herself on the stone windowsill. It was only because she'd had some time to calm down that she was able to walk straight now.

Despite Isobel's warning they were supposed to remain in her chamber, Eva refused. She had to stop halfway down to gulp in air, feeling like an invisible force held its hand tight around her lungs.

Isobel remained close behind her.

And now, here was her father, in the flesh.

He glanced toward her, sadness and confusion in his features, not at all the reunion she'd expected. It was almost as if...he didn't recognize her.

"Eva, my daughter," he said at last, his voice downtrodden. Scraggly locks of hair hung about his head. He looked as though he'd not bathed in weeks rather than days. Even his clothes were rumpled and covered in stains.

This was not her father. This was someone different, someone occupying her father's body.

"Father, are you ill?"

"Eva, my daughter," he repeated.

What was wrong with him? Something wasn't right. Out of duty, Eva contemplated whether she should embrace him. When she did, she felt the bones of his shoulders beneath her hands. His spine seemed to curve more, making him smaller. Because he was bound, he could not hug her back.

Eva pulled away, searching out a familiar face. Tomaidh stood not too far away.

"Please, sir, untie him."

"I canna, my lady."

Eva knew there was no use arguing. Her father was an enemy of the Scots, no matter how he'd gotten there, or how weak he appeared.

"Father, are you well?" Eva asked again, running her gaze over him, taking in the dark-purple smudges of exhaustion beneath his eyes.

"I am thirsty, girl, please get me a drink."

Eva looked to Tomaidh, and he gave a slight nod. If he'd not, she would have ignored him anyway. She went into the kitchen and poured her father a cup of ale. She took a long sip of it, hoping to bolster herself, and then refilled it and returned to the great hall.

The eyes of the warriors in the great hall followed her. They were not necessarily hostile, but neither were they friendly. Her father greedily sipped the drink, spilling half of it down his shirt.

"Eva, my daughter." Why did it sound like he was reminding himself of who she was?

"Aye, Father. I worried I'd never see you again."

"Where did you go?" he asked, confusing her with that response.

But before she could ask his meaning, Lady Lorna and Isobel entered the great hall. The younger of whom must have gone to find her mother.

Isobel looked worried, and her mother wore a stern expression. Would they send her back to her chamber? Was this when she would learn she was no longer a guest in their house, but the prisoner she should have been all along? Had the talk she'd had with Lorna this morning been a bad idea? Did the mistress of the castle now judge her to be false?

"I'm sorry," Eva said. "I should have..." She shook her head. "I needed to be certain he was unharmed. He may have had dealings with Belfinch, but he is still my father. I think he may be ill."

Lorna passed her a sympathetic look. "Untie this man," she told Tomaidh.

"But, my lady—"

"Ye're correct, I am your lady and mistress of this castle. Do as I've instructed and untie this man."

"His Lairdship—"

"Dear heavens, ye're a stubborn lad. If ye choose to disobey me and I ask ye a third time, it will not be without consequence."

There were a few murmurs of encouragement from the warriors in the hall that must have gotten in the way of their lady before. Tomaidh nodded curtly and pulled out his dagger to cut the ropes at her father's wrists.

"Please, sit down," Lady Lorna said to her father, leading him toward one of the cushioned chairs near the hearth. "Can I get ye something to eat?"

He stared up at her. "Eat."

Something was most assuredly wrong.

"Aye, my lord. Some soup?"

"Soup." He nodded and stared down at his hands.

Eva was ready to cry. What was happening? Why did her father seem to be forgetting simple words? Why did he seem so...off? She couldn't put her finger on exactly what was happening, but she knew without a doubt that something was seriously wrong.

Rushing forward, she dropped to her knees and pressed her hands to his. "Father, what has happened?"

"Eva, my daughter." A slight smile twitched at his lips. "How much you look like her."

Tears pricked her eyes. He spoke of her mother.

"Where is she? Is she out picking mushrooms again?" Her father laughed and looked toward the door as though he expected her mother to walk through it.

Eva gaped, his cruel joke like a stab to the heart.

"Eva, go and get your sister. Tell her this nice lady is making us some soup. Mother will be upset if I don't feed her supper."

Cold chills swept over Eva. Her father, the powerful Lord North-wyck, was losing his mind. It would appear that years had been stripped from his memory. At least two. But how? Why now?

"Father, mother is not here. You're in Scotland," she said softly, praying he wasn't playing a cruel trick, and yet also praying that he was. For if he wasn't making a jest, that meant there was something terribly wrong.

"Scotland!" His eyes widened, and he jerked his hands away from her, standing so abruptly that she fell on her bottom and the chair he'd been sitting on shot backward nearly into the fire. "Where is my wife? What have you heathens done with her?"

Was he admitting that her mother was in fact alive?

The warriors put their hands to the hilts of their swords and took slow steps forward. If he showed anymore aggression, they were likely to kill him.

"Father." Eva pushed to her feet with the help of Tomaidh, who in fact tried to shield her. "That's not necessary."

But Tomaidh would not let go, and several of the other warriors in the great hall had now come forward to restrain her father.

When Lady Lorna returned, she found him once more bound. Before she could demand his release, her father lunged for one of the men, demanding the return of his wife from the heathens who'd taken her. His wild eyes looked frantically about, seeing things they could not.

"I will get him a tincture," Lady Lorna said softly and then returned to the kitchen.

"I'm sorry, my lady," Tomaidh whispered.

"You needn't apologize."

"Has he always been this way?"

She shook her head, certain if she spoke, her voice would not come out clearly. Her throat was already tight with the need to shout and weep all at once. As she backed toward one of the benches and sank onto it heavily, she thought back over the years since her mother had been gone, about how her father had aged, how there had been some forgetfulness, but nothing more than she would attribute to his advancing years.

Isobel sat beside Eva and laced her arm around the crook of Eva's elbow. "Can I get ye a glass of wine?"

"Nay, thank you."

Isobel nodded, her gaze on Eva's father. They sat in silence, Eva's mind tormented as she wracked her brain for every odd instance over the last few years. Isobel sat silent and strong beside her, allowing her to lean on her.

Lady Lorna returned with a steaming cup of soup. With a few coaxing words, she had the Lord of Northwyck downing the contents. She issued orders for him to be taken to a chamber, and for guards to watch over him to make certain he didn't cause himself harm or attempt to escape.

"How long has he been like this?" Lady Lorna asked, concern in her gaze.

"I've never seen him this way. Forgetful maybe, but this...never."

"The stress of the situation," she said as the men led him away. "But I do believe he may be suffering from a madness that afflicts the older generations."

"Madness?" Eva stared at the empty place where her father had been only moments before. If she thought she'd been lonely before, now was ten times worse.

"I'm sorry, my dear. Perhaps some rest will help him regain his senses." Lorna's voice was soft, and Isobel had yet to let go of her arm.

Tomaidh reappeared but then ducked through the archway toward the main door of the castle.

"The men must have returned," Isobel said.

Eva's limbs prickled. In her rush to see her father, she'd almost completely forgotten about Strath and Jamie out on the field with their men. Had they beaten Belfinch? She'd not been surprised at all when the lying villain had chosen to fight instead of giving himself up. She prayed the casualties were not great, and that Belfinch had been apprehended quickly. Though she knew this fight had nothing to do with her, she couldn't help feel guilty about someone getting hurt or killed.

What if Strath had been hurt?

She was pulled in two directions—one upstairs to see that her father had calmed down, and the other to run after Lady Lorna to make certain Strath had not been harmed in battle.

How did one make a decision between duty and heart?

Strath made the decision for her when he ducked beneath the arch, searching out the great hall until his gaze fell on her. Relief swept over his features in much the same way it swept through her.

"Ye're here," he said, as though he'd imagined she would have floated away. She was relieved he'd not rebuked her for leaving her chamber.

"You're not hurt."

He shook his head. It took everything she had not to leap up, rush forward, and toss herself into his arms. Lady Isobel slinked away and somehow managed to silently tell everyone else in the great hall to disappear, too. The two of them left quite alone, the air in the room felt charged.

Eva rushed forward and tossed herself into his arms. She wrapped her arms around his neck, and he lifted her off the ground, burying his face in her neck.

"I was so worried," she said.

"Everything will work out."

"Where is Belfinch?"

"He is in our dungeon. I promise ye, lass, he'll never harm ye again."

She looked up at him through a sheen of tears. Despite the emotional turmoil raging in her head, she could sense he was hiding something from her. But before she could ask, he kissed her.

Eva allowed herself to be swept up for a few moments in his touch, his kiss, forgetting about everything that had just happened. But all too soon, it was over.

"Where is your father?" He frowned, almost as if he worried over the answer. "Tomaidh was supposed to bring him in."

"He has been taken to a room. He..." It was too difficult to say he was consumed with a madness she didn't understand. That he seemed to have almost forgotten who she was. "He is unwell."

"I see." He cleared his throat. "I've sent word to the king."

"The king?" She'd nearly forgotten...

"Aye."

"Will he...be coming here?" *Will he decide my fate?*

"Nay, not yet. Belfinch will likely be kept here as a prisoner. Or mayhap moved to Edinburgh."

"And you?"

"I will stay here for a short time. Once I hear back from the king, I will know my orders."

She nodded, wanting to ask about herself. What was she to do now that her father was...ill? What would she do if Strath had orders to go on another mission? She couldn't stay here. Up until that moment, she'd told herself that wherever Strath was would be her home, but he would never allow her to journey with him on a mission.

Staring up at him, his expression gave her no idea as to what he was thinking.

Finally, she asked, "What am I to do? Where am I to go?"

His eyes widened. "Ye'll go home."

"Oh." His words might as well have been a sword slicing through her belly.

"If I'm unable to do it myself because of the king's orders, I will have Tomaidh escort ye."

He was sending her back to England. Eva couldn't believe her ears. She stumbled back, feeling the room start to spin. When Strath steadied her, she jerked away from him.

"When will that be, my laird?"

"I have to question your father. There is information I need from him."

Eva shook her head. "I do not think you will gain the information you seek."

"Why is that?"

Why should she answer? He'd broken her heart so casually and then asked about information he needed.

"Because of the memory lapse ye mentioned?"

"Mayhap he is not the only one with a memory lapse," she retorted.

Strath frowned again, having the audacity to appear confused when he looked at her. Well, she wasn't going to remain quiet.

"How dare you rail at me this morning when I offered to sacrifice myself when you were planning to send me back all along."

Strath tilted his head, eyeing her as though she was the one to have gone mad and not her father. "Explain."

Explain? He would treat her like one of his underlings? Ha.

Eva crossed her arms and glowered at him. "Perhaps you ought to be the one explaining."

"I must admit, Princess, I'm confused about what we're talking about." He spoke calmly, rationally, as though he were mocking the very real emotion that made her voice waver.

"You are sending me back to England!"

"I am doing no such thing."

"You just said you were sending me home, that Tomaidh would escort me."

Understanding dawned then, and he shook his head, a soft chuckle on his lips. "I'm sending ye home, aye, but to our home, not back to England."

"Our home?"

"Ye're to be my wife, and my wife lives at Dornoch Castle, with me." He stepped forward, and she didn't retreat.

"I am sorry. I feel foolish for having assumed otherwise."

"The both of us have been doing a lot of assuming. 'Tis not good for us. Let us make a truce, here and now, no more assuming. We will clarify things of such importance."

"That seems like a good rule."

"And then also we must kiss and make up."

"An even better rule."

Strath bent to kiss her again, the stubble of his chin scraping over hers as he claimed her mouth. Eva sighed, their tongues dueling, and the hardness beneath his plaid pressing provocatively to the front of her gown. Quivers of desire lit up like a thousand candles inside her body.

Against her lips, he murmured, "I need to talk to your father, love. As much as I want to carry ye up to my room...I canna. Not yet."

"All right," she sighed, disappointed. "But as I said, it will be difficult. He appears to have suffered some sort of fit. He does not know what year it is."

Still holding her in his arms, Strath leaned back, his narrowed gaze on hers. "As evidenced by what?"

"By him believing we were at home, that my mother was with us. Then he started saying she'd been taken by Scots." Eva shook her head, still confused by all that still remained hidden.

"Och, lass, nay."

Eva nodded, forcing back tears that threatened once more. "I think this means she is alive as I suspected. Mayhap with her family. Or else another cruel trick."

Strath didn't say anything, but a light went off in his eyes that had her questioning what he might be thinking. He kissed her swiftly, then let her go and walked toward the door.

Before she could call him back, before she could wrap herself once more in his warm embrace, he left the great hall.

Chapter Nineteen

"Ye said he killed your da." Strath paced before Belfinch, who'd been chained to a wall in the castle's dungeon.

The man watched him, his expression blank, his lips unmoving.

"Why did he kill your da? How do ye know it was him?"

Still nothing. Strath refused to let the man's lack of response cause him to lose his temper. Strong and steady won every time.

"Why does he think his wife was taken by Scots?"

Belfinch winced.

"Ye know why. Tell me."

Still, he kept his mouth firmly closed. Strath seized the front of his shirt and lifted the bastard several inches off his arse. Belfinch gritted his teeth. He was scared but fighting it.

"I willna hesitate to beat the truth from ye, dinna test me."

"The old man is mad," Belfinch said through bared teeth, eyes cagey. "I've been dealing with his ramblings for months."

Strath regarded Belfinch skeptically. He was hiding something. And Strath was about to take a giant leap at knowing what that might be. There'd been two clues. One from Belfinch himself, and another from Eva's father. "Ye know something."

The man shrugged as much as one could in shackles while being pinned to the wall by a much larger warrior. "I know a lot of things." Spittle peppered the corners of his mouth.

"Why does Lady Eva believe her mother could be alive? Why did Northwyck say she died of a fever?" Strath kept his voice even, not displaying any outward sign of what he guessed.

The corner of Belfinch's eye twitched. "Why does anyone say someone has died of a fever?"

"Dinna answer my questions with riddles." The vein in Strath's neck throbbed, and he had to restrain himself from head-butting the bastard into unconsciousness. He kept his hands fisted in Belfinch's shirt rather than pressing his forearm to the man's throat.

In the dim light of the dungeon, Strath could have sworn the man paled a shade. And why shouldn't he? The fact he hadn't already pissed himself was either a sign he wasn't as afraid of Strath as he should be and was therefore stupid, or, well, really there was no other reason besides stupidity.

"We'll start with your fingernails," Strath said. "We willna tear them off at first. Nay, we've a lass who likes to jab her sewing needles beneath the nail. The pain will be excruciating."

More sweat beaded on Belfinch's forehead, and he bared his teeth but still said nothing.

"When ye're bleeding from your nails, we'll move to your toes. When we finish with your feet, we still won't tear off your nails. Nay, we'll save that for later. Instead, we will start to peel the skin away from your arms. Layer by layer, until we reach the bone."

Belfinch trembled with fear, the stink of his sweat pungent.

"Her mot-th-her—" Belfinch stuttered, his teeth chattering. "Eva has always believed her mother died of a fever because that is what her father told her."

"Is she dead or alive?"

The man's body strained, ceasing its trembling before letting out a great shudder. He was trying hard to be brave. Trying hard to hold on to his secrets, but Strath wasn't going to let him.

"Tomaidh, get Elsie, and tell her to bring her needles." Of course,

Strath was lying. There was no lass, and he'd made up the name. But often the threat of torture was enough to get men talking.

"Wait!" Belfinch shouted.

Tomaidh halted, and Strath nodded. "Go on then, tell me, else I will send for Elsie."

Belfinch's beady eyes flicked back and forth before he finally said, "Lady Northwyck...is not dead."

Strath stilled. "Say again?"

"She is not dead."

"Lady Eva's mother, the wife of Lord Northwyck, is not dead?"

Belfinch nodded emphatically. "Not dead." His eyes were wide, and he seemed to be telling the truth.

"Where is she? What happened to her?"

The man's shoulders slumped, as though he'd tried for too long to hold in the truth but had given up now. Once one part had slipped, what did it matter if he held in the rest?

"When we abducted her, we held her for months, nearly six of them. And she did catch a fever. But then, in the dead of night a load of you heathens descended upon our castle and took her into the Highlands," he said dejectedly.

"Explain." Strath's heart started to pound, and he tightened his fists on the man's shirt. Eva's mother was alive? She'd told him how much she missed her. How close they were. Even her father had said that Eva's mother was the strength in their household. God, what it would mean to Eva to see her again.

"We believed Northwyck to be behind our ruin. Our crops failed season after season. Our cattle and sheep died. And yet Northwyck thrived. There was no other reason for it other than he had to be stealing what was ours and poisoning our flock. So my father had Lady Northwyck taken."

"Who stole her from ye?" Strath demanded through gritted teeth. "Was it her family? The Lindsays?"

"I do not know."

"Liar." He slammed Belfinch against the wall.

"I swear." Belfinch's gaze was flying everywhere as though he couldn't find a place to focus.

The bastard was lying. He had to be. "How do ye know she's still alive?"

Belfinch swallowed, shaking now. "He wouldn't have killed her."

"Who wouldna?"

"I don't know!" he shrieked, squeezing his eyes shut, anticipating a blow that Strath did not deal. "Only that he wasn't paid to kill her."

"That doesna mean she did not die of illness, or by some other means."

Belfinch nodded, hurrying to say, "I retract my statement then. I *believe* she is still alive, for there would be no cause for her death."

"Is this why Northwyck killed your father?"

"Aye."

"And ye blackmailed him all these years, holding over his head the accusation of murder and his wife's whereabouts?"

"Aye."

"Ye're a bastard. And ye deserve a painful death." Strath pulled the *sgian dubh* from his boot and pressed it to the skin at Belfinch's throat.

"Please. I am the only link you have to finding her," he pleaded, licking his parched lips.

"Ye just said ye didna know the Scot who has her." Strath pressed harder, causing a droplet of Belfinch's blood to slide down the blade.

Belfinch winced. "I know who took her. Please don't kill me."

Strath could have pounded him for keeping the information. For making it such hard work to get out. "Who?"

"Your king."

Strath let out a growl, pushing the blade enough to sting but not cause any real damage. Belfinch howled all the same, wrenching against the shackles. If Strath weren't careful, the man would impale himself on the blasted dagger.

"Ye're a lying bastard! The king didna take Northwyck's wife! I'll give ye one more chance to explain."

"But he did! She's his cousin!"

"What?" At that, Strath's anger cleared. Had he heard correctly?

"Lady Northwyck's mother is sister to Robert the Bruce's mother."

"This is absurd."

Belfinch started to laugh, an uproarious maniacal sound. Mad...

"But it is the truth. And you know it. The Lindsays are powerful, and you know they are related to the king. Do you not see? The king sent you to stop me from tormenting his relation's husband. He sent you to find out whether the lass lived because we sent a rumor north that Eva was dead. That was what this was all about. "

"It was about the Scottish people," Strath insisted, tasting bitterness on his tongue.

Why could his king not have been honest with him? Did he not trust him with the truth? Why didn't Eva tell him she was a bloody royal—did she even know? So many questions swirled through his mind. And then he thought about the fact that his men had judged her solely on being wholly English when in fact half her blood was Scots.

And dear God, the lass didn't know the truth about her mother. The letter she'd received had been real. Her father had lied. So many questions... Burning most of all: why had her cousin, the King of Scotland, not sent for his relations in England?

Belfinch's laughter continued, and Strath's patience had come to an end. He shut the man up with a hard knock to the head. The English bastard slumped to the ground, laughter silenced at least for now.

"My laird," Tomaidh said.

Strath shook his head. "Not now." He left the dungeon by way of the ladder, and Tomaidh followed. They pulled up the ladder, leaving Belfinch where he was, unable to escape.

Mo chreach... His mind tumbled back to Eva.

She had no idea.

Strath wanted to punch a wall. He marched back toward the great hall but found it empty.

Tomaidh followed but far enough behind to give him the space he'd requested.

"Tomaidh," he said, turning around. "What am I going to tell her?"

"Tell her about what?" Uncle Jamie came toward them.

"Bloody hell," Strath grumbled. "We'd best go somewhere private."

In his uncle's study, he explained what had happened in the dungeon, and Jamie, too, was left quite speechless.

"The king not telling ye everything has nothing to do with trust, lad. There is something deeper here. Darker."

"Like what?"

"I dinna know."

"Do ye think my da knows?"

Jamie shook his head. "He would have told ye, even if the king swore him to secrecy. Your da trusts ye and wouldna have wanted ye to go into this mission blind."

Strath let out a breath. "That's true."

"When ye sent word to the king of Belfinch's capture, I sent word to your Da. He is not far, should be here by morning."

"Where is he?"

"Castle Buchanan. He had a meeting with your uncle Samuel and sent word he'd like to know when ye arrived."

"Ah." Strath nodded, wondering if that was his father's way of keeping an eye out for him.

"Lorna was hoping for a visit from your Aunt Catriona, but she and Samuel are expecting their first grandchild any day now, and she canna leave her daughter's side."

Strath did grin at that. "My mother will be much the same when my sister goes to her childbed."

"I suspect Lorna will, too."

Strath grew somber once more, thinking of mothers and daughters. "What should I tell Eva?"

"Do ye have to tell her anything?"

"If it were me, and I'd been unsure of whether my mother was alive, aye, I'd want to know. Besides, there is also the matter that she might be able to get some information from her da."

"Good point. I think when it comes to matters such as this, the straight truth is the best. Keep it simple, keep it concise. Dinna dally. Just tell her. And then answer the questions when they come. Shall I come with ye?"

"Nay, I want to tell her on my own."

"I'll sit with her da, then," Jamie said. "Mayhap I can make sense of it. My grandda was like that, and though jumbled, there is some measure of truth in what they say."

The men made their way up the stairs to the next level. A guard was stationed outside the chamber door, and he nodded as they approached.

"Is the lass inside?" Strath asked.

"Aye, she's not left."

"Thank ye." Strath eased open the door, not wanting to startle either of the parties inside.

Eva sat in a chair with her back to the door. She didn't turn when he entered, though he did see her shoulders tighten, and she sat up a little straighter. Her father lay on the bed, covered in a blanket and fast asleep. His face was flushed as though he had a fever.

Jamie stood by the door as Strath approached Eva. He placed a hand on the back of her chair, though he wished it were on her shoulder. God, how he wanted to offer her comfort.

"Lass," he whispered.

"You took longer than I thought." There was none of the joy or spirit in her voice he'd come to look forward to in their exchanges.

"May we speak in private?"

She hesitated in answering.

"My uncle will sit here with your da. If he wakes, he'll come and find us."

"All right," she said.

Strath held out his hand. She took it as she rose and followed him out the door and down the hall to an alcove covered with a curtain. Inside, were two benches that faced each other and an arrow-slit window that looked out over the bailey.

"This is cozy," she said, a half-hearted smile on her face.

Strath found it hard to return the smile. The news he had to impart weighed heavily on his mind. She sat across from him, making a bigger deal out of arranging her skirts than he'd ever seen before. Her hands trembled as she ran them over the fabric, making his heart lurch. He wanted to pull her into his arms, to hold her while he told her this dark secret.

"When was the last time ye ate something?" he asked.

"At breakfast."

"Ye should eat something."

"I'm not that hungry."

Damn it. Here they were talking about food, and if she wasn't hungry now, he knew as soon as he imparted this news to her, she would not be hungry at all. But he couldn't force her to eat, and making her wait to hear the news was cruel.

"I have discovered something today when speaking with Belfinch," he started, waiting for her to say something.

She bit her lip, eyes rounder than apples. *Mo chreach.* It was best she heard it from him.

"Don't keep me waiting, please, Strath. You're scaring me."

He nodded, recalling what his uncle said. Just as it was best to yank out a bad tooth rather than letting it fester, so too did he need to yank this truth from his heart.

Drawing in a deep breath, he let it all out in a rush. "Your mother did not die of a fever."

"So it's true? She's alive?" She narrowed her eyes. Her fingers clasped so tight in her lap, her knuckles had turned white. "Who told ye this? Was it my father? I'm not sure we can trust him." Her words came out in a tumble, like waves crashing on the shore.

Strath leaned forward, cupped her cheek, and met her gaze. "It was not your father, and I believe there is a great possibility that your mother *is* alive. And she is with my king. A relation of yours."

One minute she was staring at him incredulous and he was nodding his head, and the next, she was slumping forward, and he was catching her limp body against his.

"That could have gone better," he mumbled to himself. "Tomaidh?" The man was never too far.

From a distance, he could hear the clipped boot heels of his mate coming down the hall.

"Aye, my laird?" Tomaidh peered behind the curtain, brows rising when he spotted the lass.

"Bring me a wet cloth and some whisky."

Tomaidh gazed on with sympathy. "Did ye have a chance to tell her?"

Strath frowned. "Nay, she swooned because I'm such a handsome devil," he said sarcastically. "Of course I told her. Well, partly."

"I'll be back straight away."

Strath stared down at the lovely lass in his arms. The love of his life. The woman he desired above no other. When she woke and they found out what had happened to her mother, what then? Would she want to go be with her? Did that change things for the two of them?

Ballocks, he couldn't let her go that easily. He'd sooner give up his lands and castle than part with her. Even if he had to live in the land of heathens.

Chapter Twenty

"Lad."

Strath jerked his gaze toward the entryway to Eva's room. His father stood on the threshold, windswept hair more the color of charcoal than the black it had been in his youth.

"Da." Strath stood up from the chair he'd pulled to the side of Eva's bed where he'd been waiting for her to wake fully. She'd come to shortly after collapsing into his arms but had subsequently fallen back into a fitful sleep. It was as though her mind did not want to come to terms with what he'd revealed.

"Is this Lady Eva?" His father walked into the room, staring at Eva with a scrutinizing regard.

"Aye." Unconsciously, Strath puffed his chest, and he understood why. He would protect Eva, even from any judgment his father might pass down.

But there was no need. His father broke out into a smile. "She is bonny. What happened?"

Strath let out a low breath. He should have known his father would not find Eva lacking. No one could. And what a relief to know his father trusted his choice in a woman, given what had happened before.

"She swooned upon hearing some rather shocking news." Strath nodded his head toward the door. Though he hated to leave Eva, he didn't want to talk about her as though she weren't there simply because she was not awake.

His father followed him out into the corridor, where Strath explained all that had happened. From his arrival at Northwyck, Belfinch's fall, Eva offering herself up instead of her father. The journey to Scotland, their arrival. Her love of kittens, even. He told him everything. Well, not *everything*. There were some private moments he preferred to keep to himself. But he did tell his father he loved her and wanted to marry her. That he'd offered, and she had accepted. How Belfinch had arrived, and the lies that had come out of it. How the poor lass had believed her mother dead, and then came to be unsure, and how just today they'd found out that the lady was alive and in Scotland.

"I knew ye'd find someone," his father said with a smile, grasping Strath's shoulder and giving a firm squeeze. "Your mother will be excited to have another English lass in the family, even if she is only half."

Strath's gaze fell back through the doorway toward the bed where Eva lay curled up on one side, her hand fisted beneath her cheek as though even in sleep she was ready for a fight. "If she'll still have me."

"She will, son, she'd be mad not to."

There was a clatter of hooves in the bailey, followed by the booming of voices from the great hall. Hurried footsteps sounded on the stairs, and a moment later, Tomaidh came into view.

"The king is here." He drew in a ragged breath, looking nervous. "With...Lady Northwyck."

Strath glanced at his father, finding it hard to form words. Eva's mother was here? Several reactions vied for purchase inside him. He should be elated that Eva was going to be reunited with her mother. But he was also distraught over how Eva would react. She'd fainted upon hearing her mother was alive. What would happen if she saw her? He had to be there for her, of course. Help her see this through.

The Earl of Sutherland clasped his son around the shoulders. His dark eyes, the same shade as Strath's, bore into him. "Courage, lad. The king admires ye. Have faith in that."

But there was something he had to do before they went downstairs, before the opportunity was lost. Something he'd promised himself he'd do when he saw his father again.

Resolute, he glanced toward his mate. "Tomaidh, will ye sit with Lady Eva, and if she wakes, please come get me?"

"Aye, my laird. I'll keep her safe, and come find ye as soon as she awakens."

With Tomaidh in the room watching over Eva, Strath turned back to his father. He blew out a breath and ran his hands through his hair. This was a lot harder than he thought. But he could do hard things. He had done hard things.

"I want to beg your forgiveness, Da. For not seeing sooner what the Guinns were up to."

His father narrowed his eyes, crossed his arms, and waited.

"For rushing off and dumping Jean and her lover with her father. There was likely a better way to go about breaking the betrothal that did not involve publicly humiliating the laird, which caused him to attack Dunrobin. Though ye've forgiven me before, I'd yet to find the will to forgive myself until recently."

The elder Magnus pressed his hands to Strath's shoulders and looked him square in the eye. "I forgave ye before, and I'll forgive ye again. Dinna blame yourself. Hindsight always has us seeing different ways of doing things. If the man had been of sound mind, he'd not have attacked. What his daughter did, their attempt to cover it up, was enough to have me laying siege to his castle." His father chuckled. "And hell, we've all learned a hard lesson when it comes to women. But it seems like ye've been gifted with another chance." He nodded toward Eva, and Strath followed his line of vision.

His chest tightened with love and pride. Somehow, over the course of the weeks he'd known Eva, the armor he'd put up around his heart had melted. At his father's words, he felt like a huge weight had been lifted from his shoulders. Everything seemed to be right in the world. Well, almost. There was still the bastard in the dungeon to deal with, her addled father, and of course, her mother coming back to life. But those things seemed easily surmountable if he had her by his side and his father supported him. "Aye, and with your blessing, I'm going to marry her, Da. I love her."

Magnus grinned and clapped his son on the cheek. "Ye have it, lad. Even if she was not related to the king, I'd give ye my blessing. But as it is, 'twould seem we're gaining a better alliance than that of Guinn."

Strath chuckled and shook his head. "And a hell of a lot less treachery."

"Aye, there is that. Now, let us go and greet our king."

Feeling lighter than he had in a long time, Strath followed his father down the steps and into the great hall where servants ran frantically to and fro with food and drink.

Warriors, including those who'd fought in battle and sustained minor injuries, were waiting in line to greet their king, Robert the Bruce, who sat on the dais. Even in his advancing years, the king still cut an impressive figure. His hair was mostly gray, and so was his beard. Shallow lines creased the corners of his eyes, between his brows, and down the centers of his cheeks, making him look what he'd heard his mother call "distinguished". Despite the gray and wrinkles, the Bruce's body was strong, and his eyes sharp.

As soon as the Bruce caught sight of Strath and his father, he waved them forward. Strath bent a leg to his king and kissed the ring on his outstretched hand.

"Your Highness," Strath said.

"Strath, good work in England, and here. Two less *Sassenachs* to torment our people. And I hear ye found Lady Eva."

Strath bowed his head in subservience. His father might have a friendship with the king, having served him and helped him defeat the English more times than anyone could count, but Strath was still in awe of the king who'd brought this country closer to independence. So while his Da might clap the king on the back and tease him, Strath would remain where he was, head bowed, and offer up only his respect. "'Twas an honor to serve ye, Your Highness. I am as always your humble servant."

"Humble! Bah!" The king laughed. "Sutherland," he said to Strath's father, "Your son is funny."

Strath glanced up confused, seeing the king's mirthful grin.

"There's no need to be humble about having captured a menace, Strathnavor. Tell me how ye really feel."

He'd not heard anyone call him by his title in a long time. Glancing at his father who nodded with a wry grin, Strath said, "I was glad to have caught the filthy bastard. I hope he rots in the dungeon."

"Belfinch will be hanged in the morning for his crimes against Scotland," the Bruce continued. "And the other man, Lord Northwyck—"

"Your Highness, beg your pardon, but the man is not well," Strath interrupted. "An illness of the mind."

"How so?"

"The man canna seem to recall the last two years."

The king grunted, staring at Strath. "Mayhap that will change soon."

Strath knew he had to be referring to Lady Northwyck. Strath bit his tongue. He wanted to ask about Lady Northwyck but didn't see any ladies present, and he wasn't certain how to broach the topic. If he didn't broach it now though, there might not be another chance, and he had to do it for Eva. The lass deserved to know where her mother was.

Clearing his throat, Strath dove right in. "Your Highness, if I may, Belfinch told me about Lady Northwyck. When the lady was stolen and presumed dead, Northwyck killed Belfinch's father, at which point the newly titled Belfinch began blackmailing Northwyck."

Robert the Bruce nodded. "A messy affair. I'm glad my cousin is safe. We tried to get her daughters more than once, but then we found out about Jacqueline's marriage and Eva's death. She'll be relieved to know her daughter is still alive."

Strath tried not to be frustrated at the response. "Your Highness, with the blackmail in play, I am uncertain Northwyck was behind all the attacks on the border. There's no doubt he is guilty of funding Belfinch's assaults, but it is my opinion that a man under duress should not be held to the same level of accountability. This does not mean I think there shouldna be some form of punishment however."

The king studied him for several moments. Would the king be angry for what he'd said? Possibly. But it was the truth, and there was no one here to plead for Eva's father but him.

"Ye speak your mind with ease," the king responded. "I admire that. No more of the humble ballocks ye were spouting before. I am in agreement with ye. Though I think the reason ye pursued the topic is because of the lass, is it not?"

"Aye. I wish to marry her."

"I'll allow it."

Strath blew out a breath, having just experienced a moment of panic.

"And ye can assure her that her father will not receive the same punishment as Belfinch, though he will have to face his crimes."

"Aye, Your Highness, I thank ye."

Despite what he'd told the king he knew, there was one secret Strath kept to himself—the information regarding the key. The more he thought about it, the more he decided it was only right to send the key and the coin purse to Eva's sister, who could make certain the people of Northwyck were properly repaid. As much as he loved his king, Strath knew for certain he would want to take the bounty for himself. Wars were expensive, so Strath could not blame his king for wanting to garner more coin to pay for it. This, however, he needed to give back to Eva's people. Which brought him to the next bone of contention he'd been holding back from.

"Your Highness," Strath said. "May I ask where Lady Northwyck is?"

"I am here, sir." The voice was melodic, a fair mixture of English and Scots.

When Strath turned around, a beautiful woman who could have been Eva two decades from now approached them. She had the same silky golden hair, identical bright-blue eyes, and skin the texture of fresh cream. The resemblance was uncanny. The only difference he could make out was that this woman was at least six inches taller than his wee Eva.

"My lady." Strath bowed to the woman.

"Stand, sir, please. I understand you saved my daughter." She regarded him behind a serene mask.

Strath stiffened. "Aye." He had saved her from a fate this woman had left her to. "She was relieved to find out ye lived."

The woman's eyes glistened, but she didn't seem taken aback by his words. "I tried to tell her."

Strath held his tongue, wanting to ask a whole lot more, like why she hadn't she tried harder to get to her daughter? He felt the eyes of his king boring into his spine. He had questions for him, too. But alas, the tongue of a vassal must be held, and he'd already pushed too much when it came to his liege.

Clearing his throat, Strath returned to face his king. "If ye will excuse me, Your Highness?"

Robert the Bruce nodded, and Strath strode from the great hall, certain his father and uncle would keep the king busy. He had a very strong urge to gather Eva up and take her away from here. To hide her from the torment of knowing her mother was not only alive, but very well.

He trudged up the stairs, his foot hitting the seventh step when a voice stopped him from below.

"Sir Strath." It was her, Lady Northwyck.

He came down the steps to face her. "My lady?"

"Will you show me where my daughter's chamber is? I would like to see her. To speak with her." Though her face appeared calm, the lady clenched her fingers tightly in front of her waist.

"She is to be my wife." Strath offered, letting her know that he would protect Eva, even from her

"Ah, very good news." She looked sad though, but he didn't take it personally. She was probably more upset at all the time she'd lost. "I have missed her so much. Will you take me?"

"Aye." Strath offered her his arm and they walked together up the stairs. "I know it is bold of me to ask, my lady"—without the king present, how could he resist—"but I must know what kept ye from saving her yourself?"

"That is a question I ask myself every day." She shook her head. "When my cousin found out that I'd been abducted, he sent men to bring me north. I begged them to get my daughters, but the men would not deter from their plan. When I asked the Bruce to bring Eva to me, he agreed, but every attempt made was thwarted. And my husband...

Well, I think he was compromised enough to steal me away for a ransom. He stole me once, at the border when I was just a lass of sixteen. Soon after Jacqueline came and I couldn't possibly leave either of my daughters." She stopped walking, squeezed his arm. "Ironic isn't it? That I should be taken away from them? You were our last hope to put an end to it. There is only so much a foreign king can do on foreign soil. I will be forever grateful to you, sir, for what you've done for my daughter."

Though he hated all that she said, he understood it. "I would do anything for her." They continued walking up the stairs. "Why do ye think Northwyck claimed ye were alive when he spoke with Eva?"

"Belfinch could have told him, I suppose." She shrugged. "He did not try to find me."

"Do ye think he's truly gone addle-brained?"

"Nay," she said softly, her eyes cast toward the floor. "Northwyck is clever. He was weak when I met him, but he also has a mean streak. I used to escape into the woods with the girls when he was in a temper. I made a game out of it. I prayed every day when I was gone that he would keep his temper in check."

"He did not raise a hand to her himself, but he didn't stop Belfinch from doing just that."

"Oh," she let out a little whimper. "I will never be able to make it up to her."

"My lady, ye're coming back from the grave. I think begging her forgiveness will be enough. She's missed ye greatly."

Lady Northwyck patted his arm. "Thank you."

"Do ye want to speak to him? I'll hold him if ye wish to thrash the bastard?"

The lady smiled and patted him on the arm. "You'll make my daughter a good husband. I can tell. While the offer is strong, I'd rather not see him again. To give him an audience would only feed his power."

"If ye change your mind..."

"I won't."

Eva's door was closed with Tomaidh standing sentry. "My laird." He nodded to Lady Northwyck. "She's not yet woken."

Strath nodded. "Thank ye for watching over her. Will ye let my uncle know I need to speak to him?"

"Aye, my laird."

"He is still with Lord Northwyck."

Tomaidh gave a slight bow to Lady Northwyck and then disappeared down the corridor.

"Are ye ready, my lady?"

She looked paler than she had in the great hall, and her hand trembled slightly on his elbow. "Aye, I've been ready."

Strath opened the door to find Eva standing by the window, her eyes closed as she sucked in the fresh spring air. When she turned and saw him, her eyes brightened, but she paled when she saw who was beside him. He feared she'd swoon once more, but a resolute expression came over her.

The fighter he knew her to be came out, standing tall. She narrowed her gaze on her mother. "Mama, how are you here?"

"I'll leave ye two alone." Strath started to back toward the door, but Eva stopped him.

"Nay, you can stay. You are to be my husband."

Strath strode forward, pressed his lips to her cheek, and whispered in her ear, "I love ye, lass, but ye must speak to your mother alone."

She started to shake her head but then stopped, a resigned sigh escaping her. "You're right."

Strath bowed to Lady Northwyck and left the room. He met his uncle in the passageway and relayed his conversation with Lady Northwyck on the stairs regarding her husband.

"Ye think he's faking being of addled mind?" Jamie asked.

"Almost certainly. If we go to him now and tell him what we know, and give just one tiny falsehood that the king has ordered his execution tomorrow along with Belfinch's, I think we'll see a different side. If we don't, then we know he is ill, and for that reason alone it would be cruel to execute him."

Jamie agreed, and they hurried down the next flight of stairs to Lord Northwyck's chamber.

They found the older man sitting by the window, rocking back and forth.

"He's been like that since I came in," Tomaidh offered.

"Thank ye." Strath patted his mate on the back and gave his uncle a glance. Jamie nodded, giving Strath permission to speak first. "Lord Northwyck, your wife has arrived with King Robert the Bruce."

The rocking stalled a breath and then picked up faster.

"She is upstairs with your daughter. Naturally, Lady Eva was surprised to find out her mother is alive. It's a miracle. We shall celebrate tonight."

And still he rocked.

"In other sad news, I'm afraid ye'll not be joining us in the celebration. Ye see, the king has decreed that ye and Lord Belfinch be charged for your crimes against Scotland, and he has ordered your deaths."

At this, the man ceased moving once more.

"Ye'll be hanged tomorrow morning."

The rocking stopped completely. Northwyck turned slowly toward them, his gaze more lucid now than when Strath had first laid eyes on him. "You lie."

"I never lie." Strath's voice was hard. The bastard had tried to trick them all, including his own daughter, all for the sake of saving his sorry arse.

Northwyck stood in a flurry of rage and rushed at Strath, but Tomaidh stepped in, easily subduing the man with a hard grip on the back of his neck, lifting him far enough off the ground that he had to stand on his tiptoes. The English lord was not very tall. In fact, Strath would wager to guess he was shorter than his wife. At least this was the only thing that Eva had inherited from him.

"Are ye ready to tell the truth, Lord Northwyck?"

"What difference does it make if I'm to be executed?" the older man snarled.

Strath shrugged. "None, I guess." He didn't want to tell the man what punishment he would actually receive yet. Best to let him stew. His fate would likely be a lashing, and then imprisonment until an arrangement could be made with the English king to pay for his release. That would be years. Enough time to ponder all the wrongs he'd done and hopefully come out of it a better person. Strath directed Tomaidh to take him to the dungeon. With one last look at the man who would be his father by marriage, Strath said, "Say hello to your good friend, Belfinch. He'll be happy to see ye're feeling well once more."

Northwyck's screams of fury followed Strath into the corridor and down the stairs. While Strath wanted desperately to go see Eva and make certain she was all right, he knew she would need this time to heal and speak with her mother. Besides, he needed to go speak with his king, and let him know Northwyck's madness had been a ruse.

With the king here to collect the English traitors, there would be no more reason for the Dornochs to remain in Glasgow.

Home.

Strath longed to go home. He couldn't wait to start his life there with Eva.

Chapter Twenty-One

Just over one week later...

Eva stared across the hall of Dornoch Castle to where her mother sat talking with Lorna, Isobel, and her new relations by marriage, Lady Arbella and Lady Greer, and several aunts. In the short time since she had met Strath's sister Greer, she'd come to know her as quite a headstrong lass. Strath remarked on how much trouble his sister often got into. The youngest of his sisters was also there, Lady Blair, but she'd gone upstairs with the oldest sister, Lady Bella, who'd needed to change her dress after she'd turned abruptly and her large pregnant belly had bumped someone's elbow, causing a full cup of wine to spill down the front.

On the opposite end of the hall were the men, Jamie, Strath's father, his cousins, uncles, his brother Liam and Bella's husband, Niall.

Everyone had been happy to meet her, and she likewise. Of course, she'd been nervous, but they'd all welcomed her with open arms. When they'd arrived the day before, everyone had been gathered, and just that morning, Eva and Strath had said *I do*.

Her new husband sat beside her. They'd sequestered themselves near the hearth for a few moments, hoping for just the tiniest bit of privacy, for there was no way anyone would let them sneak away from the great hall or even duck into one of the window alcoves.

The servants bustled around them now, putting the finishing touches on the wedding feast. When they'd arrived the night before, Lorna and Eva's mother had worked together in the kitchens on getting the preparations just right, and Eva was glad, because she'd been so nervous she was certain to make a mess of it.

Great vases of wildflowers filled the hall, and the rushes had recently been replaced, herbs strewn in for a refreshing and soothing aroma.

"How do ye feel?" Strath asked.

Eva smiled, sat forward, and grabbed hold of his hand. "I feel wonderful. I am the happiest bride in all the world."

He grinned and kissed her hand. "I meant about your reunion with your mother."

"Ah." She watched her mother conversing pleasantly with all the other women. They looked like they'd known each other for years. Strath's family was so easygoing and kind. Just like him. They could be hard and brutal if need be, but when they were with family, they were all heart. Her mother and Lorna had grown close during their journey here, and Eva was glad of that.

Her mother had explained what had happened, and while it had been hard at first for Eva to accept, giving that she felt her mother should have tried harder to protect her, she'd forgiven her anyway. She was also grateful her mother had divulged to her the nature of the relationship she'd had with her husband. That the nature visits had been because of his temper. That they'd not fallen in love at the border, but that she'd been abducted. Eva would have never guessed those things.

When speaking with her mother, she remembered and held on to Lorna's words *"It is easier to forgive than to foster resentment."* Eva agreed wholeheartedly. "I am happy. I missed my mother so much, and to know that she is alive and thriving is all I could ever want."

"And your father?"

Eva pressed her lips together. That was another story. "I'm glad the king pardoned him, though I will never forgive him for keeping the truth from me, or for the way he treated my mother. I'm glad he's gone back to England."

Strath nodded, kissing her hand again. "I understand that, love. I would find it hard, too. Know that I will always support ye in whatever choice ye make. What do ye think your sister will say?"

Oh, her poor sister... She wanted to run to her and gather her up in her arms. "I think Jacqueline will be just as angry. She really needed our mother during the days leading up to her marriage and after the loss of her child. But she will do good things with the key and coin that you sent her." Eva's heart had melted even more, if possible, when her husband had told her his plans for the treasury Belfinch kept full of Northwyck coin and property.

"Aye. Perhaps ye can write her about coming for a visit."

"I don't think her husband would allow that."

Strath pursed his lips. "That is a shame. If ye like, I'd be willing to take ye to England to visit her."

"That is too dangerous. Strath, nay. I love that you offered, but I could never ask it of you."

"Ah, my lady," he said in an impressive English accent with not even a trace of a Scots brogue, "but it would be my pleasure, and a lovely honeymoon for us both."

Eva's mouth fell open. "You'd not be able to wear your plaid."

"An easy enough task."

She sighed wistfully. "But I may miss it. What will I do not being able to see your bare knees?" she teased.

"Och, lass, ye'll be seeing my bare knees, aplenty. Dinna fash about that."

Eva giggled behind her hand, hoping not to draw attention from anyone in the great hall, for she was certain the way her husband was looking at her like he wanted to eat her alive would give away their conversation.

"All jesting aside, love, I'd be happy to figure out arrangements for ye to see your sister."

"Are you certain?" Her heart was pounding, and she chewed the inside of her cheek, trying not to get her hopes up.

"I am. As long as your sister and her husband will have us. And as long as the king gives me leave."

"Perhaps I can convince her to travel north, so we will not have to go so far south. Besides, I'm not certain her husband will have us. He was not thrilled with the idea of having me visit before."

"I have an ally on the border, we could meet her there. I could arrange to make a delivery or some such for the king."

"Oh, Strath!" She leaned forward and pulled him into a hug. "That would be the very best of gifts."

"My laird." Maxwell, the castle's steward, approached. "We are ready to serve the feast."

Strath nodded, stood, and held out his hand to her. She took his hand, overcome by a fluttering in her belly. He was her husband. This strong, incredible man.

It was no lie that she really did feel like the luckiest woman. A month ago, if he'd not come into her life, everything would be completely different. She might not even be alive.

Strath let out a whistle, drawing the attention of everyone in the great hall. "If ye all would join us, my lovely bride and I would like to welcome ye to our castle, and to the celebration of our marriage."

A loud cheer went up, echoing in the rafters. Strath led her to a grand table, sat at the head, and scooted her chair beside him. At first, she was going to tell him not to, that she should sit in her proper place, but truth be told, she wanted to sit right beside him and never leave.

The aromas of the food made her mouth water. When they'd been on the road from Glasgow, she'd attended the cooking again, this time with her mother's help. It had been like old times, and Eva was pretty certain that had it not been for their weeklong trek to the Highlands, she might not have been able to forgive her mother as quickly.

Before their food was served, Strath's father presented them with a beautiful silver two-handled cup. The priest at their wedding ceremony had called it a *quaich*. The handles were carved with symbols, one of which was two hands gripping a crowned heart. Etched on the side, it said, "*With these hands, I give you my heart, and with this crown, my love.*"

Strath's father held up his cup, and the rest of the tables did the same. "A toast to the new bride and groom. My son, I am so proud of ye, and to ye, my dear, the one who stole his heart, I thank ye. *Sláinte!*"

"*Sláinte!*" everyone called out.

Eva and Strath sipped from the shared cup, their gazes connecting over the rim. Strath winked, and Eva returned the gesture, a shiver of anticipation racing along her spine.

"Kiss! Kiss! Kiss!" their guests called out.

Eva's face flamed red. The Scots were certainly much more comfortable with displays of affection in front of one another than the English were. And she liked that. So she grabbed the back of Strath's neck, tugged him close, and kissed him hard on the mouth, with the sounds of their guests cheering, laughing and a few bawdy jokes surrounding them.

When they pulled away, the blush had gone from Eva's face, and all she could do was smile at her husband.

"Let us eat," Strath called out, and then with a mischievous grin, he said, "lest my wife decide to take advantage of me early."

And just like that, the heat returned to her face. But she couldn't help but laugh, and she poked her husband in the ribs as he poured them each a cup of wine.

Placed in front of them were platters of fresh poached salmon topped with herbed cream, venison with currant gravy, mutton and pork pies, honey-glazed root vegetables, a selection of aged cheeses, honey-mustard eggs, sugared almonds, delicious smelling fresh baked bread with mounds of freshly made herbed butter and enough spiced wine for the entire country.

They dined until Eva thought she'd burst, and then Strath placed his hand on her knee, leaned over, and whispered in her ear, "I've been waiting for this moment since ye laid down on the soft rug in my chamber at Glasgow. Let's sneak upstairs so we can continue the path pleasure showed us before."

A tremor raced over her skin. Oh, how very much she wanted to do just that.

"Oh, aye," she murmured.

Strath stood abruptly, gripping her hand in his. "We bid ye goodnight."

"Not so fast!" called out his mother, followed by the agreement of the other women present. "We need to dress her."

"And we need to torment *ye*," Strath's brother Liam said to him.

"So much for a quick escape," Strath said with a wink in Eva's direction.

She flashed him a saucy grin. "I will try to hurry them."

"Same."

Eva allowed herself to be swept away by the women, their voices singsong as they talked of love and men and their own wedding nights. In her chamber, they replaced her gown with a sheer chemise with light pink ribbons that tied near her throat—which they of course left loosely tied. They tugged her hair out of her plait and brushed it until it crackled.

They asked her questions, most of which she couldn't remember, and she answered them quickly or not at all. She thought that perhaps they were more overwhelming than the wedding night itself.

Finally, her mother pressed her hands to Eva's face and bent over to look into her eyes. "Are you ready, my child?"

"Aye, Mama."

"Do you want to ask me, us, anything?"

Eva shook her head. "I'll be all right. Strath is... He is sweet." She didn't want to say that he'd already introduced her to pleasures of the flesh, and that the only thing she was pretty sure they'd not done, was the deed itself.

Which, instead of being scared, she was excited for. This was Strath. Her Magnus. Her love and her lover.

Eva beamed a smile at her mother. "I love him, Mama. I trust him. And I'm so happy."

The ladies in the room cooed at her for having said it.

Lady Arbella, as beautiful as she was funny, pulled her into an embrace. "I'm so pleased to have you as my daughter-by-marriage."

"That means the world to me, my lady."

"Oh, please, my dear. You married my son, you must call me Ma, as he does, or Arbella."

"All right, I will." Eva hugged her once more, and then every lady in the chamber wanted a hug, too.

At last, Lady Northwyck shooed them all out. "I love you, my child."

"I love you, too, Mama."

A few minutes later, Strath quietly entered the room, the grin falling from his face as his gaze swept the length of her. "Good God, lass... That gown is...my new favorite."

Eva blushed but didn't avoid his stare. Strath sauntered closer to her, eyelids growing heavy with that look she knew so well. His I-want-to-kiss-you look. When he reached her, he slid his fingers up her arm, dancing through the long locks of her loose hair.

"Ye're beautiful, and I canna believe ye're mine."

Strath cupped her cheek and bent closer to her, pressing his lips softly against hers. Not a demanding, nor a frantic need, but one that Eva felt was full of love and overflowing with promise. He slid his lips over hers, touched his tongue gently to the seam between. Without hesitation, she opened, allowing the warm velvet of his tongue to touch hers.

They kissed like that for some time, swept up in desire. Their bodies were flush against one another, and heat cloaked them. But when Eva untied the leather queue holding his hair back, threaded a hand in his locks and used the other to caress the muscles of his chest, their kiss took a different turn. Strath tickled a path up her ribs, leaving shivers of anticipation in his path. His thumb caressed the side of her breast, and she gasped, her nipples hardening into tingling knots. Oh, the things he did to her body. Hunger for him and knowledge of the pleasure he could bring made her ache with anticipation.

Eva arched her back, searching out the heat of his hand, nipples aching for attention. She wanted his touch...wanted him to put his mouth on her. Heavens, but she was a wanton. Wicked in every sense of the word. But even knowing that, she wasn't going to stop. She wanted him to touch her. To experience the pleasure she knew he could give her.

And Strath didn't deny her.

A gasp of pleasure fell from her parted lips when his hand covered her breast. Warm with just a bit of pressure, he massaged her. Her nipple was taut and rubbed against his palm. The friction of the sensitive flesh brushing against the material of her thin chemise and his palm was intoxicating.

"*Mo chreach*, lass..." he murmured against her mouth. "I love how passionate ye are, how your body reacts to just the slightest touch."

Eva gripped Strath's shirt while he kissed a heated path over the column of her neck. Her head fell back when his lips grazed her collarbone and then drifted over her nipple. She gripped him tighter, the wait near agony. Eva arched her back again, pushing her breasts up toward his mouth. The heat of his tongue flicked out over the fabric covering her nipple, followed by his lips as he nibbled and teased her. Eva's breath came in shallow pants, and she leaned up on tiptoe to get closer, unsure of anything and everything except for the heady bliss of his mouth at her breast.

"I've wanted to taste ye so bad I ache," Strath said, flicking his tongue over the tip of her nipple as he spoke. "Waiting has been torture."

"Oh, aye..."

His hardness pressed against her hip, and Eva knew exactly what it was. She recalled the way his soft velvet cock had felt in her hand. His arousal, thick and pulsing. She sank closer in his arms, loving the feel of that restrained passion pressed to her hip. Strath growled and gently nipped her flesh. Eva responded instantly, with a mewl of her own, her body bowing with the demand for more.

"Ye're driving me wild, lass..."

"I want you," she crooned, pressing both hands to the sides of his face, lips tingling and swollen from his kisses. "Dinna make me wait any longer."

Strath touched his forehead to hers. "Och, lass, nay..." He nibbled at her lips. "'Tis your first time, and we must take it slow."

They stared at one another, the crackle of the fire the only sound against the beatings of their hearts.

Eva pushed Strath back toward the bed until the mattress hit the back of his knees, and he sat. She stood quivering between his deliciously naked knees. Nervous and excited all at the same time.

With trembling hands, she circled her finger on the hard curve of his knee, trailing up just a few inches over his thigh until he groaned.

"I do love how improper you Scots are." She bent forward and pressed her lips to his knees.

Strath reached for her, gripped her hips, and massaged lightly. He tugged her closer so her knees hit the edge of the bed, and his thighs pressed to the outside of hers. And then he started to skim his own hands lower, over her rear and to the backs of her thighs. She shivered, sucking in a deep, heady breath of his masculine, spicy outdoor scent.

"I'm going to remove your night rail."

Eva swallowed. "All right."

Strath grasped the loosely knotted pink ties and unlaced them, sucking in a breath when the fabric fell to the side to reveal the swells of her breasts. "*Mo chreach.*" His gaze grew serious as his gaze hungrily roved over her. "I am the luckiest husband in Scotland."

Eva tugged the fabric off one shoulder and then the other, until it fell to her waist. Strath blew out another breath, its warmth touching her skin like a kiss. It was as though he'd not seen her breasts before. But she supposed he'd not seen them in the light, for when they'd lain together and he'd shown her passion before, they'd been in the dark.

Strath's desire for her was obvious, and it only urged her on.

"Will you make me the luckiest wife?" She shimmied so the night rail fell in a pool around her ankles.

Sliding his palms up over her bare bottom, he groaned. "Och, lass, I can promise ye more than luck. I can promise ye happiness, and bliss, endless hours of bliss."

Strath's pride and guarantee of pleasure only endeared him more to Eva. She loved his confidence, and she knew from experience he would make good on his promise.

"I expect nothing less, husband," she teased, running her hands through his hair.

Saints, but she'd been blessed when he laid siege to her father's castle—for it was then he'd laid siege to her heart. And now she was going to let him lay siege to her entire body. And as much as she teased him about her expectations, she was truly grateful. Not only because he'd saved her life when he'd allowed her to go with him, and not only because with one look he made her skin tingle with burning need, but because he encouraged her to be herself and loved her for it. It was a gift she couldn't be more grateful for.

Eva used to believe that it was a lie that every English lady looked forward to her wedding day. To her, marriage used to be a death sentence, but now it was a sentence of love. She wasn't naïve enough to believe they wouldn't have their ups and downs, but she was confident the two of them could conquer whatever life tossed at them.

Strath gazed at her with something akin to wonder. His lids were lowered, heavy with desire, and she was certain her own expression mirrored his.

He touched his fingers to her shoulder, skimmed lower over her breasts, around them, never quite touching her nipple. Her skin burned where he touched, and she shifted restlessly between his legs in an attempt to ease the urgent pulse between her thighs. Every inch of her skin was suddenly alive, over sensitized, and her mind hummed with a thousand incoherent thoughts.

Strath shifted her body around so that his thigh was now between her legs. He pulled her forward, and that place that pulsed slid deliciously along the length of his muscled thigh. Goodness... She slid closer, and their bodies molded together in a tantalizing mix of raw, potent sensuality.

Strath murmured as he nibbled her lower lip, hand cupping her breast, thigh rubbing the very heat of her. "I burn for ye."

Eva's eyes closed in pleasure as he teased a path with his lips from her shoulder to her neck, pausing just over her heart, which pounded frantically.

Eva tugged at the pin holding his plaid in place, and he eagerly tugged off his *leine* shirt and tossed it somewhere behind her. He was all glorious muscle connected in lines and dips and a sprinkle of dark hair.

Boldly, she traced her fingers over his collarbones, down the center of his chest, and over the thick muscles. Crisp hair tickled her palms as she explored, and the sudden need to taste his skin, to breathe in his scent, took over.

Eva pressed a kiss over his heart, feeling rather than hearing the pulse beating there. Strath sucked in a breath, his muscles rippling beneath her kiss. He cupped her face, drew her up, and kissed her tenderly before sweeping her into his arms and laying her down on the bed.

He smiled as he came down on top of her. "God, I love ye so much."

"I love you, too," she said on a sigh.

Strath rested with one thigh on the outside of hers and the other between her legs, pressing gently to her heated center. He held himself up on his elbows as he leaned forward to kiss and tease her mouth. At the same time, he caressed her breasts, her ribs, and with each passing moment, she grew hotter, her moans more frantic with need.

He splayed his fingers on her bare thigh, moving to stroke the inside, edging closer to her heat. And then he was there, fingers sliding between her folds, over that knot of flesh that had her gasping, hips involuntarily bucking.

"Aye, lass, let me know what ye like." He nibbled at her ear, kissed her mouth, all the while rubbing small, fiery circles over her slick flesh.

Eva could hardly breathe, could barely control her own movements. She jerked, hips rose and fell, thighs opened. Pleasure radiated throughout her limbs. Strath tugged a nipple into his mouth as he slid a finger inside her.

All sense left her. "Oh!" she cried out, her insides pulsing, quickening, reaching for something. She threaded her fingers into his hair, tugging, pushing, wanting the pleasure she knew would come from this.

"Let go, love, let me feel ye climax around my finger," he murmured against her mouth.

She let out her breath only to gasp as he quickened the pace. Not two breaths more, and she was crying out as something inside her shattered, firing off potent waves of pleasure in every direction. Seconds passed where all she could do was feel, riding out the storm of ecstasy. Finally, the waves subsided, and yet she was eager for more.

Strath positioned his knees between her thighs, and Eva wrapped her arms around his waist.

"Lift your legs, love," he whispered against her ear as he teased the sensitive flesh there.

Eva did as he asked, lifting them up around his hips. The thickness of his erection pressed hotly to her center.

Strath reached between their bodies and began to stoke her fire once more. His mouth found hers, and he kissed her with such fierce passion, she felt the stirrings of release once more. And then he was pushing against her, the thick tip of his shaft pressing at her opening.

"This may hurt a little," he murmured against her lips. But he didn't give her a chance to question him.

He pushed against her slickness and surged forward. A painful pinch made her cry out and stiffen, digging fingers into the skin of his back.

Strath stilled, leaned back, and stared down at her. Concern etched his features.

"Does it pain ye much, Princess?"

Eva wiggled beneath him, noting that not only had the pain almost disappeared, but that she *liked* the feel of him inside her, stretching her.

"Not anymore," she said, smiling up at him and trailing her fingers up his back at the same time she lifted her legs a little higher.

The shift had Strath sinking deeper inside her, and Eva moaned. "I think I'm going to like this."

"Aye, love, me, too." Strath slid out slowly, every inch he moved sending ripples of pleasure through her.

When he pushed back inside, his pelvis tucking into hers, she raised her hips, crying out at the sudden, wicked sensation. He took her mouth in a heated kiss as he continued to move slowly in and out of her.

The friction made her dizzy with need, desire. Every movement pushed her closer and closer to that pinnacle point she'd reached before. Now she understood what real desire was, what the bards and minstrels sang about. The deeper meaning beneath their words was revealed to her in Strath's arms. Pleasure was intoxicating, delicious, and what made it more so was that she shared it with a man she loved beyond reason.

He buried his face in the crook of her shoulder, kissing, licking, nibbling on her skin. His pace increased, and Eva found it even harder to breathe. Blood rushed through her ears, and spark after radiating spark fired inside her.

"Strath... Magnus!" she cried.

Her back arched of its own accord, and she locked her ankles around him, writhing as a climax even more powerful than the one before rocked her. A cry of pleasure tore form her throat.

"Oh, Eva, aye, love, let it come," he growled, thrusting faster.

Wave after wave washed over her, drowning her, until she was finally able to catch her breath. But Strath didn't cease his torment. Moments later, he seized her hips as he pounded harder, shuddering and moaning. He collapsed over her, resting his weight on his elbows until both their breaths began to quiet.

"That was stunning," Eva murmured.

"Incredible," Strath replied. He kissed her gently on the lips and stroked her cheek. "Ye're a passionate lover, Princess."

"As are you." She grinned at him, satisfied for having been able to please him as he'd pleased her. "I love you."

"I love ye, too."

Epilogue

Two months later

E va woke to the feeling of softness stroking against her cheek, along with a purring in her ear.

"Strath?" she murmured, not having heard him make that kind of sound before. And what could he possibly be putting on her face?

She reached up, and her hand connected with silky fur and the tiny body of a kitten. Eva's eyes flew open then, and she let out a yelp of delight. "A kitten."

"For my princess." Strath sank down on the bed beside her wearing only breeches.

"Where did he come from?"

"He was just weaned from his mama. A barn cat."

"For me?"

"Aye, love. I remember how much ye loved those kittens in Glasgow."

Eva held the little kitten to her face, and it nipped gently at her nose. She nuzzled him and then laid him on the bed. He batted at her with his paws, letting out little mewling sounds that had to be the cutest thing she'd ever heard.

"I love him," Eva said. "And I love you."

Strath leaned over their wee kitten and kissed her softly. "I would do anything for ye, Eva. Anything."

"I probably can't bring him with us on our journey to see my sister."

"Aye,' but the stable master has already promised to have one of the lads take good care of him while we're away."

"All right."

"Are ye already packed?"

"I am."

Over the last couple of months, they'd had a chance to settle in at Dornoch. Now that it was summer, it was the best time to travel south. A letter had been sent to Jacqueline, and her reply had been received. She was going to meet them at Berwick Upon Tweed, and just to make certain she arrived safely, Strath's uncle Samuel had deployed half a dozen of his English spies to help her. Jacqueline's husband had died of a fever, which had also made her ill, though she was thriving now. Her husband's holding had gone to his nephew, so she had been planning to return to Northwyck where their father's ailing health and lack of ability had caused the holding to fall into disrepair. But Eva had convinced her to return to Scotland with them. Their father could prevail upon his cousin who was set to inherit the holding.

"Is mother here yet?" Eva asked.

"Aye. She's verra pleased ye thought to include her."

"I didn't want to tell my sister in a letter. I thought it best they see each other in person."

"Aye. I think she'll appreciate that."

"'Twill be a long journey, made all the better with your company," he said.

"I couldn't do it without you, Strath. I don't know how I can ever repay you."

"Och, love, ye need never repay me for anything. I love ye. And loving ye means making ye happy."

"I hope I make you happy."

He twirled a lock of her hair around his finger. "I've never been happier."

Eva tickled the belly of her kitten, laughing when it tried to attack her hand.

Happiness filled her heart. She looked over at her husband who lounged back in bed, his tanned skin carved with muscle.

She was home.

More Sutherlands!

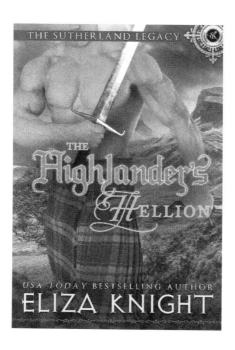

Are you ready for more Sutherlands? Coming Fall 2018!

The Highlander's Hellion

Lady Greer has held the reputation of hellion since the moment she could walk. So it is no wonder, that after being forbidden by her father, the Earl of Sutherland, she steals a boat and rows out into the firth anyway. What was supposed to be a relaxing autumn jaunt irrevocably changes her life when a storm ravages the chill waters. Just when she's certain death is upon her, the sweet caress of land is at her fingertips... but so is a familiar, fearsome Highlander.

Roderick Innes, Laird of Balvenie Castle, did not expect to find a soaked, and venomous, lass upon his shores when he is out scouting his property. When she demands he take her back to her clan, he recognizes her at once as the mischievous lass who taunted him at a festival several years prior. Perhaps he ought to give her a taste of her own medicine.

Certain her father will be raising an army to find her, Greer will do just about anything to get home before she causes war between the Sutherlands and Innes clans. When the handsome warrior says he'd be happy to escort her if she can pass three tests of skill, Greer thinks it might just be too easy. And she's right. What was at first Roderick's taste of revenge on the lass who humiliated him, turns into a merry chase across the Highlands, that leads them both to passion... and maybe even love.

Excerpt from The Highlander's Temptation

Prologue

Spring, 1282
Highlands, Scotland

THEY GALLOPED THROUGH THE EERIE moonlit night. Warriors cloaked by darkness. Blending in with the forest, only the occasional glint of the moon off their weapons made their presence seem out of place.

'Twas chilly for spring, and yet, they rode hard enough the horses were lathered with sweat and foaming at the mouth. But the Montgomery clan wasn't going to be pushed out of yet another meeting of the clans, not when their future depended on it. This meeting would put their clan on the map, make them an asset to their king and country. As it was, years before King Alexander III had lost one son and his wife. He'd not remarried and the fate of the country now relied on one son who didn't feel the need to marry. The prince toyed with his life as though he had a death wish, fighting, drinking, and carrying on without a care in the world. The king's only other chance at a succession was his daughter who'd married but had not yet shown any signs of a bairn filling her womb. If something were to happen to the king, the country would erupt into chaos. Every precaution needed to be taken.

Young Jamie sat tall and proud upon his horse. Even prouder was he, that his da, the fearsome Montgomery laird, had allowed him to accompany the group of a half dozen seasoned warriors—the men who sat on his own clan council—to the meeting. The fact that his father had involved him in matters of state truly made his chest puff five times its size.

After being fostered out the last seven years, Jamie had just returned to his father's home. At age fourteen, he was ready to take on the duties of eldest son, for one day he would be laird. This was the perfect opportunity to show his da all he'd learned. To prove he was worthy.

Laird Montgomery held up his hand and all the riders stopped short. Puffs of steam blew out in miniature clouds from the horses' noses. Jamie's heart slammed against his chest and he looked from side to side to make sure no one could hear it. He was a man after all, and men shouldn't be scared of the dark. No matter how frightening the sounds were.

Carried on the wind were the deep tones of men shouting and the shrill of a woman's screams. Prickles rose on Jamie's arms and legs. They must have happened upon a robbery or an ambush. When he'd set out to attend his father, he'd not counted on a fight. Nay, Jamie merely thought to stand beside his father and demand a place within the Bruce's High Council.

Swallowing hard, he glanced at his father, trying to assess his thoughts, but as usual, the man sat stoic, not a hint of emotion on his face.

The laird glanced at his second in command and jutted his chin in silent communication. The second returned the nod. Jamie's father made a circling motion with his fingers, and several of the men fanned out.

Jamie observed the exchange, his throat near to bursting with questions. What was happening?

Finally, his father motioned Jamie forward. Keeping his emotions at bay, Jamie urged his mount closer. His father bent toward him, indicating for Jamie to do the same, then spoke in a hushed tone.

"We're nearly to Sutherland lands. Just on the outskirts, son. 'Tis an attack, I'm certain. We mean to help."

Jamie swallowed past the lump in his throat and nodded. The meeting was to take place at Dunrobin Castle. Why that particular castle was chosen, Jamie had not been privy to. Though he speculated 'twas because of how far north it was. Well away from Stirling where the king resided.

"Are ye up to it?" his father asked.

Tightening his grip on the reins, Jamie nodded. Fear cascaded along his spine, but he'd never show any weakness in front of his father, especially now that he'd been invited on this very important journey.

"Good. 'Twill give ye a chance to show me what ye've learned."

Again, Jamie nodded, though he disagreed. Saving people wasn't a chance to show off what he'd learned. He could never look at protecting another as an opportunity to prove his skill, only as a chance to make a difference. But he kept that to himself. His da would never understand. If making a difference proved something to his father, then so be it.

An owl screeched from somewhere in the distance as it caught onto its prey, almost in unison with the blood curdling scream of a woman.

His father made a few more hand motions and the rest of their party followed him as they crept forward at a quickened pace on their mounts, avoiding making any noise.

The road ended on a clearing, and some thirty horse-lengths away a band of outlaws circled a trio—a lady, one warrior, and a lad close to his own age.

The outlaws caught sight of their approach, shouting and pointing. His father's men couldn't seem to move quickly enough and Jamie watched in horror as the man, woman and child were hacked down. All three of them on the ground, the outlaws turned on the Montgomery warriors and rushed forward as though they'd not a care in the world.

Jamie shook. He'd never been so scared in his life. His throat had long since closed up and yet his stomach was threatening to purge everything he'd consumed that day. Even though he felt like vomiting, a sense of urgency, and power flooded his veins. Battle-rush, he'd heard it called by the seasoned warriors. And it was surging through his body, making him tingle all over.

The laird and his men raised their swords in the air, roaring out their battle cries. Jamie raised his sword to do the same, but a flash of gold behind a large lichen-covered boulder caught his attention. He eased his knees on his mount's middle.

What was that?

Another flash of gold — was that blonde hair? He'd never seen hair like that before.

Jamie turned to his father, intent to point it out, but his sire was several horse-lengths ahead and ready to engage the outlaws, leaving it up to Jamie to investigate.

After all, if there was another threat lying in wait, was it not up to someone in the group to seek them out? The rest of the warriors were intent on the outlaws which left Jamie to discover the identity of the thief.

He veered his horse to the right, galloping toward the boulder. A wee lass darted out, lifting her skirts and running full force in the opposite direction. Jamie loosened his knees on his horse and slowed. That was not what he'd expected. At all. Jamie anticipated a warrior, not a tiny little girl whose legs were no match for his mount. As he neared, despite his slowed pace, he feared he'd trample the little imp.

He leapt from his horse and chased after her on foot. The lass kept turning around, seeing him chasing her. The look of horror on her face nearly broke his heart. Och, he was no one to fear. But how would she know that? She probably thought he was after her like the outlaws had been after the man, woman and lad.

"'Tis all right!" he called. "I will nay harm ye!"

But she kept on running, and then was suddenly flying through the air, landing flat on her face.

Jamie ran toward her, dropping to his knees as he reached her side and she pushed herself up.

Her back shook with cries he was sure she tried hard to keep silent. He gathered her up onto his knees and she pressed her face to his *leine* shirt, wiping away tears, dirt and snot as she sobbed.

"Momma," she said. "Da!"

"Hush, now," Jamie crooned, unsure of what else he could say. She must have just watched her parents and brother get cut to the ground. Och, what an awful sight for any child to witness. Jamie shivered, at a loss for words.

"Blaney!" she wailed, gripping onto his shirt and yanking. "They hurt!"

Jamie dried her tears with the cuff of his sleeve. "Your family?" he asked.

She nodded, her lower lip trembling, green-blue eyes wide with fear and glistening with tears. His chest swelled with emotion for the little imp and he gripped her tighter.

"Do ye know who the men were?"

"Bad people," she mumbled.

Jamie nodded. "What's your name?"

She chewed her lip as if trying to figure out if she should tell him. "Lorna. What are ye called?"

"Jamie." He flashed her what he hoped wasn't a strained smile. "How old are ye, Lorna?"

"Four." She held up three of her fingers, then second guessed herself and held up four. "I'm four. How old are ye?"

"Fourteen."

"Ye're four, too?" she asked, her mouth dropping wide as she forgot the horror of the last few minutes of her life for a moment.

"Fourteen. 'Tis four plus ten."

"I want to be fourteen, too." She swiped at the mangled mop of blonde hair around her face, making more of a mess than anything else.

"Then we'd best get ye home. Have ye any other family?"

"A whole big one."

"Where?"

"Dunrobin," she said. "My da is laird."

"Laird Sutherland?" Jamie asked, trying to keep the surprise from his face. Did his father understand just how deep and unsettling this attack had been? A laird had been murdered. Was it an ambush? Was there more to it than just a band of outlaws? Were they men trying to stop the secret meeting from being held?

There would be no meeting, if the laird who'd called the meeting was dead.

"I'll take ye home," Jamie said, putting the girl on her feet and standing.

"Will ye carry me?" she said, her lip trembling again. She'd lost a shoe and her yellow gown was stained and torn. "I'm scared."

"Aye. I'll carry ye."

"Are ye my hero?" she asked, batting tear moistened lashes at him.

Jamie rolled his eyes and picked her up. "I'm no hero, lass."

"Hmm... Ye seem like a hero to me."

Jamie didn't answer. He tossed her on his horse and climbed up behind her. A glance behind showed that his father and his men had dispatched of most of the men, and a few others gave chase into the forest. They'd likely meet him at the castle as that had been their destination all along.

Squeezing his mount's sides, Jamie urged the horse into a gallop, intent on getting the girl to the safety of Dunrobin's walls, and then returning to his father.

Spotting Jamie with the lass, the guards threw open the gate. A nursemaid rushed over and grabbed Lorna from him, chiding her for sneaking away.

"What's happened?" A lad his own age approached. "Why did ye have my sister?"

Jamie swallowed, dismounted and held out his arm to the other young man. "I found her behind a boulder." Jamie took a deep breath, then looked the boy in the eye, hating the words he would have to say. "There was an ambush."

"My family?"

Jamie shook his head. He opened his mouth to tell the dreadful news, but the way the boy's face hardened, and eyes glistened, it didn't seem necessary. As it happened, he was given a reprieve from saying more when his father and men came barreling through the gate a moment later.

"Where's the laird?" Jamie's father bellowed.

"If what this lad said is true, then I may be right here," the boy said, straightening his shoulders.

Laird Montgomery's eyes narrowed, jaw tightened with understanding. "Aye, lad, ye are."

He leapt from his horse, his eyes lighting on Jamie "Where've ye been, lad? Ye scared the shite out of us." His father looked pale, shaken. Had he truly scared him so much?

"There was a lass," Jamie said, "at the ambush. I brought her home."

His father snorted. "Always a lass. Mark my words, lad. Think here." His father tapped Jamie's forehead hard with the tip of his finger. "The mind always knows better than the sword."

Jamie frowned and his father walked back toward the young laird. It was the second time that day that he'd not agreed with his father. For if a lass was in need of rescuing, by God, he was going to be her rescuer.

Chapter One

Dunrobin Castle, Scottish Highlands
Early Spring, 1297

"I've arranged a meeting between Chief MacOwen and myself."

Lorna Sutherland lifted her eyes from her noon meal, the stew heavy as a bag of rocks in her belly as she met her older brother, Magnus', gaze.

"Why are ye telling me this?" she asked.

He raised dark brows as though he was surprised at her asking. What was he up to?

"I thought it important for ye to know."

She raised a brow and struggled to swallow the bit of pulverized carrot in her mouth. Her jaw hurt from clenching it, and she thought she might choke. There could only be one reason he felt the need to tell her this and she was certain she didn't want to know the answer. Gingerly, she set down her knife on her trencher and took a rather large gulp of watered wine, hoping it would help open her suddenly seized throat.

A moment later, she cocked her head innocently, and said, "Does not a laird and chief of his clan keep such talk to himself and his trusted council?" The haughty tone that took over could not be helped.

After nineteen summers, this conversation had been a long time coming. It was Aunt Fiona's fault. She'd arrived the week before, returning Heather, the youngest and wildest of the Sutherland siblings, and happened to see Lorna riding like the wind. Disgusted, her aunt marched straight to Magnus and demanded that he marry her off. Tame her, she'd said.

Lorna didn't see the problem with riding and why that meant she had to marry. So what if she liked to ride her horse standing on the saddle? She was good at it. Wasn't it important for a lass to excel in areas that she had skill?

Now granted, Lorna did admit that having her arms up in the air and eyes closed was borderline dangerous, but she'd done it a thousand times without mishap.

Even still, picturing her aunt's look of horror and how it had made Lorna laugh, didn't soften the blow of Magnus listening to their aunt's advice.

Magnus set down the leg of fowl he'd been eating and leaned forward on the table, his elbows pressing into the wood. Lorna found it hard to look him in the eye when he got like that. All serious and laird-like. He was her brother first, and chief second. Or at least, that's how she saw it. Judging from the anger simmering just beneath the surface of his clenched jaw and narrowed eyes, she was about to catch wind.

The room suddenly grew still, as if they were all wondering what he'd say—even the dogs.

He bared his teeth in something that was probably supposed to resemble a smile. A few of the inhabitants picked up superficial conversations again, trying as best they could to pretend they weren't paying attention. Others blatantly stared in curiosity.

"That is the case, save for when it involves deciding *your* future."

Oh, she was going to bait the bear. Lorna drew in a deep breath, crossed her arms over her chest and leaned away from the table. She could hardly look at him as she spoke. "Seems ye've already done just that."

Magnus' lips thinned into a grimace. "I see ye'll fight me on it."

"I dinna wish to marry." Emotion carried on every word. Didn't he realize what he was doing to her? The thought of marrying made her physically ill.

"Ye dinna wish to marry or ye dinna wish to marry MacOwen?"

By now the entire trestle table had quieted once more, and all eyes were riveted on the two of them. However she answered was going to determine the mood set in the room.

Och, she hated it when the lot of nosy bodies couldn't get enough of the family drama. Granted at least fifty percent of the time she was involved in said drama.

Lorna studied her brother, who, despite his grimace, waited patiently for her to answer.

The truth was, she did wish to marry—at some point. Having lost her mother when she was only four years old, she longed to have a child of her own, someone she could nurture and love. But that didn't mean she expected to marry *now*. And especially not the burly MacOwen who was easily twice her age, and had already married once or twice before. When she was a child she'd determined he had a nest of birds residing in his beard—and her thoughts hadn't changed much since.

She cocked her head trying to read Magnus' mind. Was it possible he was joking? He could not possibly believe she would ever agree to marry MacOwen.

Nay, Lorna wished to marry a man she could relate to. A man she could love, who might love her in return.

"I dinna wish to marry a man whose not seen a bath this side of a decade." Lorna spoke with a reasonable tone, not condescending, nor shrill, but just as she would have said the flowers looked lovely that morning. It was her way. Her subtlety often left people second guessing what they'd heard her say.

Magnus' lip twitched and she could tell he was trying to hold in his laughter. She dared not look down the table to see what the rest of her family and clan thought. In the past when she'd checked, gloated really, over their responses it had only made Magnus angrier.

Taming a bear meant not baiting him. And already she was doing just that. She flicked her gaze toward her plate, hoping the glance would appear meek, but in reality she was counting how many legumes were left on her trencher.

"Och, lass, I'm sure MacOwen has bathed at least once in the last year." Magnus' voice rumbled, filled with humor.

Lorna gritted her teeth. Of course Magnus would try and bait her in return. She should have seen that coming.

"And I'm sure there's another willing lass who'll scrape the filth from his back, but ye willna find her here. Not where I'm sitting."

Magnus squinted a moment as if trying to read into her mind. "But ye will agree to marry?"

Lorna crossed her arms over her chest. Lord, was her brother ever stubborn. "Not him."

"Shall we parade the eligible bachelors of the Highlands through the great hall and let ye take your pick?"

Lorna rolled her eyes, imagining just such a scene. It was horrifying, embarrassing. How many would there be in various states of dress and countenance? Some unkempt and others impeccable. Men who were pompous and arrogant or shy or annoying. Nay, thank you. She was about to spit a retort that was likely to burn her Aunt Fiona's ears when the matron broke in.

"My laird, 'haps after the meal I could speak with Lorna about marriage...in a somewhat more private arena?" Aunt Fiona was using that tone she oft used when trying to reason with one of them, that of a matron who knew better. It annoyed the peas out of Lorna and she was about to say just that, when her brother gave a slight wave of his hand, drawing her attention.

Perhaps his way of ceasing whatever words were on her tongue.

Magnus flicked his gaze from Lorna to Fiona. Why did the old bat always have to stick her nose into everything? Speaking to her in private only meant the woman would try to convince Lorna to take the marriage proposition her brother suggested. And that, she absolutely wouldn't do.

"'Tis not necessary, Aunt Fiona," Lorna said, at the exact same time Magnus stated, "Verra well."

Lorna jerked her gaze back to her brother, glaring daggers at him, but he only raised his brows in such an irritating way, a slight curve on his lips, that she was certain if she didn't excuse herself that moment she'd end up dumping her stew on his head. He had agreed on purpose—to annoy her. A horrible grinding sound came from her mouth as she gritted her teeth. Like she'd thought—brother first, chief second.

"Excuse me," she said, standing abruptly, the bench hitting hard on the back of her knees as so many people held it steady in place.

"Sit down," Magnus drawled out. "And finish your supper."

Lorna glared down at him. "I've lost my appetite."

Magnus grunted and smiled. "Och, we all know that's not true."

That only made her madder. So what if she ate just as much as the warriors? The food never seemed to go anywhere. She could eat all day long and still harbor the same lad's body she'd always had. Thick thighs, no hips, flat chest and arms to rival a squire's. If only she'd had the height of a man, then she could well and truly pummel her brother like he deserved.

She sat back down slowly and stared up at Magnus, eyes wide. Was that the reason he'd suggested MacOwen? Would no other man have her?

Nestling her hands in her lap she wrung them until her knuckles turned white.

Magnus clunked down his wooden spoon. "What is it, now?"

"Why did ye choose MacOwen?" she whispered, not wishing the rest of the table to be involved in this particular conversation. Not when she felt so vulnerable.

He shrugged, avoiding her gaze. "The man asked."

"Oh." She chewed her lip, appetite truly gone. 'Twas as she thought. No one would have her.

"Lorna..."

She flicked her gaze back up to her brother. "I but wonder if any other man would have me?"

Magnus' eyes popped and he gazed on her like she'd grown a second head and then that head grew a head. "Why would ye ask that?"

She shrugged.

By now everyone had gone back to talking and eating, knowing there'd be no more juicy gossip and Lorna was grateful for that.

"Lorna, lass, ye're beautiful, talented, spirited. Ye've taken the clan by storm. I've had to challenge more than one of my warriors for staring too long."

"More than one?" She couldn't help but glance down the table wondering which men it had been. They all slobbered like dogs over their chicken.

"None of the bastards deserve ye."

She turned back to Magnus. "And yet, ye picked the MacOwen?" She raised a skeptical brow. Ugh, of all men, he was by far the worst choice for her.

Magnus winked and picked up another scoop full of stew, shoveling into his grinning mouth.

Lorna groaned, shoulders sinking. "Ye told him nay, didna ye? Ye were baiting me."

Magnus laughed around a mouth full of stew. "Ye're too easy. I'd see ye married, but not to a man older than Uncle Artair," he said, referring to their uncle who had to be nearing seventy.

"Ugh." Lorna growled and punched her brother in the arm. "How could ye do that? Ye made every bit of my hunger go away and ye know how much I love Cook's stew."

Magnus laughed. The sound boomed off the rafters and even pulled a smile from Lorna. She loved to hear him laugh, and he didn't do it often enough. When their parents died, he'd only been fourteen, and he'd been forced to take over the whole of the clan—including raising her, and her siblings. Raising her two brothers, Ronan and Blane, and then the youngest of their brood, Heather was a feat in itself, one only

Magnus could have accomplished so well. In fact, the clan had prospered. She couldn't be more proud. If anyone deserved a good match, it was Magnus.

Her heart swelled with pride. "Ye're a good man, Magnus. And an amazing brother."

He reached toward her and gave her a reassuring squeeze on her shoulder. "I'll remember that the next time ye wail at me about nonsense."

Lorna jutted her chin forward. "I do not wail—and nothing I say is nonsense."

"A true Sutherland ye are. I see your appetite has returned."

Lorna hadn't even realized she'd begun eating again. She smiled and wrapped her lips around her spoon. Resisting Cook's stew was futile. The succulent bits of venison and stewed vegetables with hints of thyme and rosemary played blissfully over her tongue.

"My laird." Aunt Fiona's voice pierced the noise of the great hall.

Magnus stiffened slightly, and glanced up. Their aunt was a gem, a tremendous help, but Lorna had heard her brother comment on more than one occasion that the woman was also a grand pain in the arse. Lorna dipped her head to keep from laughing.

"Aye?" he said, focusing his attention on their aunt.

"I'd be happy to have Lorna return home with me upon my departure. Visits with me have helped Heather so much."

Lorna's head shot up, mouth falling open as she glanced from her brother to her aunt. Good God, no! Beside her on the bench, Heather kicked Lorna in the shin and made a slight gesture with her knife as though she were slitting her wrist. Lorna pressed her lips together to keep from laughing.

"I'm sure that's not necessary, Aunt," Lorna said, giving the woman her sweetest smile. At least she'd not told her there was no way in hell she'd step foot outside of this castle for a journey unless it was on some adventure she chose for herself. She'd heard enough horror stories about the etiquette lessons Heather had to endure.

"Magnus?" Fiona urged.

There was a flash of irritation in his eyes. Magnus didn't mind his siblings calling him by his name, but all others were to address him formally. Lorna agreed that should be the case with the clan, but with family, Lorna thought he ought to be more lenient, especially where their aunt was concerned.

Aye, she was a thorn in his arse, but she was also very helpful.

Before her brother could say something he'd regret, Lorna pressed her hand to his forearm and chimed in. "Haps we can plan on me accompanying Heather on her next visit."

That seemed to pacify their aunt. She nodded and returned to her dinner.

Ronan, who sat beside Magnus on the opposite side of the table, leaned close to their brother and smirked as he said something. Probably crude. Lorna rolled her eyes. If Blane was here, he'd have joined in their bawdy drivel. Or maybe even saved her from having to invite herself to stay at their aunt's house.

As it was, Blane was gallivanting about the countryside and the borders dressed as an Englishman selling wool. Sutherland wool. Their prized product. Superior to all others in texture, softness, thickness, and ability to hold dye.

She stirred her stew, frowning. Blane always came home safe and sound, but she still worried. There was a lot of unrest throughout the country, and the blasted English king, Longshanks, was determined to be rid of them all. It would only take one wrong move and her beloved brother would be forever taken away.

Lorna glanced up. She gazed from one sibling to the next. She loved them. All of them. They loved each other more than most, maybe because they'd lost their parents so young and only had each other to rely on. Whatever the case was, they'd a bond not even steel could cut through.

Magnus raised his mug of ale. "A toast!" he boomed.

Every mug lifted into the air, ale sloshing over the sides and cheers filled the room.

"Clan Sutherland!" he bellowed.

And the room erupted in uproarious calls and clinks of mugs. A smile split her face and she was overcome with joy.

She'd be perfectly happy never to leave here. And perfectly ecstatic to never marry MacOwen.

Even still, as she clinked her mug and took a mighty gulp, she couldn't help but wonder if there was a man out there she could love, and one who just might love her in return.

Want to read more? Check out **The Highlander's Temptation** *and the rest of the* **Stolen Bride** *series wherever ebooks are sold...*

About the Author

Eliza Knight is an award-winning and *USA Today* bestselling author of over fifty sizzling historical romance and erotic romance. Under the name E. Knight, she pens rip-your-heart-out historical fiction. While not reading, writing or researching for her latest book, she chases after her three children. In her spare time (if there is such a thing...) she likes daydreaming, wine-tasting, traveling, hiking, staring at the stars, watching movies, shopping and visiting with family and friends. She lives atop a small mountain with her own knight in shining armor, three princesses and two very naughty puppies. Visit Eliza at http://www.elizaknight.com or her historical blog History Undressed: www.historyundressed.com. Sign up for her newsletter to get news about books, events, contests and sneak peaks! http://eepurl.com/CSFFD

facebook.com/elizaknightfiction

twitter.com/elizaknight

instagram.com/elizaknightfiction

bookbub.com/authors/eliza-knight

goodreads.com/elizaknight

Printed in Great Britain
by Amazon